2021248

P9-CQO-032

ALICE FLAGG

The Hermitage (Photo by Sid Rhyne)

NANCY RHYNE

ALICE FLAGG

The Ghost of the Hermitage

A NOVEL

PELICAN PUBLISHING COMPANY
GRETNA 1990

Library of Congress Cataloging-in-Publication Data

Rhyne, Nancy, 1926-
    Alice Flagg : a novel / by Nancy Rhyne.
        p. cm.
    ISBN 0-88289-760-8
    1. Flagg, Alice Belin, 1833–1849—Fiction. 2. South Carolina—
History—Fiction. I. Title.
PS3568.H95A79 1990
813'.54—dc20   89-28782
                                                    CIP

This novel is based on a true story. To protect the identities of
certain people, some names have been changed.

Manufactured in the United States of America
Published by Pelican Publishing Company, Inc.
1101 Monroe Street, Gretna, Louisiana 70053

For
ALICE FLAGG
Born: November 29, 1833
Died: February 2, 1849

A Charleston Idyl

He was running for the station
    when I met him, and he said,
"I'm going to leave the city by the sea."
    When I asked him what the matter was
He only shook his head
    and remarked, "Well, it's not the place for me."

I can put up with the climate
    and mosquitoes very well
With the regulation netting and a fan.
    But I tell you plainly, Brother,
I would rather be elsewhere, than to listen
    to your sweet potato man.

      Sweet potato
      Have um right here
      Only fifteen cents for a peck
      Sweeter than the honey
      Costes little money
      And they ain't have a blemish or a speck.

With a mouth like a tunnel
    in the regions of the coal
And a clapper that is ringing all the day
    With a tender outpouring of his sweet potato soul
And a forty donkey power for to bray.

No the city has its good, and it may be very well
    to endure as many evils as you can
But you must excuse me, Brother, for I'd rather be elsewhere
    than be martyred by the sweet potato man.

And he ran.

S.W.B.
Savannah News
1892

ACKNOWLEDGMENTS

I was fortunate on that spring day when I walked into the Robert Scott Small Library at the College of Charleston and met Oliver B. Smalls, who helped me come to certain conclusions about the educational system in Charleston during the mid–1800s. And that same visit resulted in my meeting Bill Smyth, of the College of Charleston and Mt. Pleasant. During the following weeks I received photocopies and clippings from him that helped immensely in writing the scenes of Madame Talvande's school on Legare Street. It's not every day that authors come upon someone like Bill who is willing to take time from a busy schedule to help track down facts. The people at the South Carolina Historical Society in Charleston also were of inestimable help to me during my visits to their facility on Meeting Street.

My gratitude also goes to my friends who have written scholarly books about the colonial era, books to which I often referred: Clarke A. Willcox's *Musings of a Hermit*; Dr. George C. Rogers, Jr.'s *The History of Georgetown County, South Carolina*; Dr. Charles Joyner's *Down by the Riverside: A South Carolina Slave Community*; and Alberta Morel Lachicotte's *Geogetown Rice Plantations*. There were other books that helped me, such as Elizabeth Allston Pringle's *Chronicles of "Chicora Wood"* and Jim McAllister's *Well, Shut My Mouth, Tales from the South*.

Everyone who enjoys the story of Alice Flagg is indebted to the late Clarke Allen Willcox, who moved to Murrells Inlet with his parents in 1910, after his father bought the Hermitage. After Clarke Willcox grew up and married, he lived with his wife, Lillian Rose, in Marion, South Carolina, but they often visited the Hermitage and they moved there in 1956. For thirty years before his death on June 12, 1989, he invited friends and strangers to visit his home, in the middle of the afternoon on Fridays and Saturdays, to hear his stories and tour the house, which was also the home of the well-known ghost—Alice Flagg.

And to Sid, again, many thanks. One day with my face in an ancient folder as I worked in the solitude of a library, I heard his voice coming from the circulation desk, where he was making an inquiry. "I believe my wife is here somewhere, doing research." I suddenly realized that I had long overstayed my allotted time. Such was the case at many historical societies and libraries and I heard no complaints. What a husband! And to Nina Kooij and Dr. Milburn Calhoun of Pelican Publishing, a "thank you" is not enough. I fell by the wayside several times, but they always got me up and going again.

NANCY RHYNE
MURRELLS INLET, SOUTH CAROLINA

Summer 1985

My husband and I were driving near Pawleys Island when I remembered reading in the paper that a society wedding would be held that day at All Saints Episcopal Church. An executive with a prominent company based in Chicago was to be married in that church, and I envisioned sitting in the parking lot and observing the guests, probably in exclusive gowns. I asked Sid to turn onto S.C. 255, and drive about three miles west of the island to the historic church, and we found a corner of the lot where we were not likely to be observed.

Rather than being attired in gowns, it seemed to me that each woman wore a silk suit, and the suits were of all colors. There were mauve suits, blue suits, and ones of green, pink, lavender, and other hues. Finally, all guests had arrived, and we watched as the groom and his best man entered the small sanctuary. Then the bride came, and as she walked toward the building she held up her veil to prevent it from trailing on the ground. Bridesmaids followed. Because the doors of the building were open, we could hear organ music. Then the ceremony started and all was quiet.

My husband started the car and we were just about to go on our way when suddenly I noticed a girl in a long, white gown standing by the low branches of a dogwood tree, directly back from the church door. She was barefoot, and her eyes were glued on the ceremony taking place in the church.

"Where did that character come from?" Sid asked.

"Heaven only knows," I answered, and just then a thought came to me. *Could that girl be Alice Flagg, the ghost of the Hermitage?* Since her death in 1849 Alice Flagg had been observed not only at her home at Murrells Inlet, several miles from the church, but also in the All Saints churchyard, where it is believed by many that she was buried under the flat marker that says simply, *ALICE*. "Do you think that girl in the white dress could be Alice the ghost?" I asked.

"I don't know that we've ever seen a ghost," my husband answered as we left the scene. "But if we ever did, we just saw Alice Flagg."

SPRING 1848

1

_____

IT WAS A particularly lovely April day when fourteen-year-old Alice Flagg and her body servant Mary One stepped into the "six oared," a vessel propelled by six oarsmen. They settled in, Alice with her music books in her lap, and the boat was pushed from the Wachesaw Plantation landing. In moments it had reached the center of the Waccamaw River. As the river meandered through a heavy forest, the scent of yellow jasmine that grew from one tree to the next filled the air, and the sweet bay trees, honeysuckle, and even the little jug blossom added their dainty essence.

No smile played on Alice's lips as she thought with very little pleasure of the music lesson at Brookgreen Plantation, only a few miles downriver. She didn't find the immense satisfaction in classical music that other plantation girls did, but she relaxed in her seat and allowed the tension to diminish.

"See the dogwoods?" Mary asked.

Alice's eyes turned toward the woods. "The white blooms give an impression rather like white sails in a sea of green."

"Them blossoms'll be gone in a few more days and all of it will be green," Mary observed.

Just then the oarsmen began singing one of the songs that brought hope to their very souls and tranquility to their labors, and they pulled the oars in tempo with the soft harmony. It was, as always, the sweetest of sounds to Alice's ears. The men in livery, uniforms of turquoise satin trimmed in ecru lace, sang the boat songs with their unique rhythm and swing, and they always began from the moment the boat got well underway. Alice's eyes were on the music books in her lap as she listened intently to the words of "Drinkin' Wine, Drinkin' Wine," and then without the slightest break in cadence, another song that began, "In case if I never see you anymore, I'm hopes to meet you on Canaan's happy shore." Each stanza seemed to fill the oarsmen with joy anew.

Alice opened a yellow book and let a finger idly trace the edge of the page as she scanned a portion of a Mozart concerto for piano, some of which she was to play today for Madame Le Conte. She had not really looked at it until now, but if she studied it carefully in her mind, perhaps she could bluff her way through the lesson without being scolded by the music teacher. Although Madame assigned Alice two hours of practice each day, she rarely sat at the piano that long, and when she did, she played her favorite pieces. But as she thought about it, she was appreciative that her brother and mother were generous enough to provide her with lessons, and that the Wards of Brookgreen were bighearted and shared their imported teacher of music. Alice's most recent tutor, who was from Germany, had been excellent in languages, but actually a little lacking in the ability to teach piano playing.

It was required that all daughters of planters learn to play piano as a part of their education. The girls rarely complained, knowing their families were doing their best to prepare them to preside over a grand plantation. Every plantation daughter was groomed from the moment of her birth to become the mistress of a vast estate and the supervisor of a large staff of servants, and top priority went into the preparation.

"Mary, see the sawmill on the bluff?"

"It be the Bucks' sawmill."

"Yes," Alice said, adjusting the music books in her lap, and thinking that it was rare that Mary did not know something about almost any subject she brought up. As she thought about it, Mary One was her very favorite person on the plantation next to her family, even if she did use less-than-gentle persuasion when trying to make her point. Mary could be the calmest person in the world when it came to trifling matters, but if her mind was filled with disturbing thoughts, an unusual power bubbled within her. All of this came to Alice now as she regarded Mary sideways.

With her smooth complexion and dark, short-cropped hair, Mary exuded purity and honesty. Today she wore her usual attire of navy shirtwaist and narrow skirt. Her thin brown hands with long tapering fingers lay in her lap. She was one person Alice could always trust. Just then Alice noticed that Mary was watching something with consternation, her face grave.

"What is it?" Alice asked.

"That man on the bluff. Who he be?"

Alice looked and tried to answer, but could not speak for a moment. Her eyes were taking in the most angelically beautiful man on whom they had ever laid. He was looking at her. His lustrous hair, parted in the middle, had a curl in it, short as it was. She could not see the color of his eyes, but believed they must be blue. His arms she could see, and they were tawny and strong, as he likely worked with long pines, like the ones that had just arrived at the sawmill and were now on the dock. He wore no shirt, and his shoulders and arms were sun-stained in burnt gold.

"He must be a Buck," Alice murmured. "That *is* the Buck family's sawmill."

"I've never seen him," Mary answered.

The cypress boat had now passed the sawmill, and Alice was filled with a sudden heat that made her heart feel aglow. Before she knew it, she was wondering how she appeared to the attractive man. For heaven's sake, she thought, I am almost grown, and have barely given a thought to how I look to any man!

"Mary, do you think I should change my hair?"

A look of surprise spread across Mary's face. "Your black hair be beautiful, parted in the middle and drawn back into a bun. Don't change a lock."

"What about my clothes?" Alice asked, her lizard-green eyes flashing. "You know I have never given much attention to them."

"You not be one who stands before mirrors," Mary pointed out. "But your mother and brother be going to Charleston soon, and you get what you like."

"That's it! I shall have the most exclusive dressmaker in Charleston make some dresses just for me."

"But why the fuss? Why right now?" Mary asked fiercely, her face tense.

Alice's eyes flickered with a hint of deviousness. "Look at me!

Really look at me, Mary." Her eyes blazed chartreuse lights. "I do not look like a woman a man could love."

"It be that sawmill man," Mary said as her opaque eyes regarded Alice. "Don't tell me you be taking notice of a man out of your own kind."

Alice blinked and sat up with an abruptness that was almost violent. Just seconds ago she had felt so drawn to the handsome lumberman. Something about his presence had quickened her senses and she had suddenly come alive. She pictured the lumberman, standing on the bluff and looking down at her. The thought upset the very harmony of her body, and she trembled.

But as Mary had pointed out, he was not her kind. A sawmill worker would be considered far beneath any member of a planter family. Such a man would never be the master of a great plantation, and his wife would not be the mistress of a large estate. In her society, this question of the classes was so deep it defied philosophy. It was something of the universe. No woman she had ever known had challenged the code and become attracted to a man lesser than a planter. It was the architecture of the classes: a planter's son married a planter's daughter, cousins married cousins.

Alice felt foolish now for even giving a thought to the lumberman. Whether he was good-looking or no, she had been brought up to ignore his kind and would continue to do so. She settled back in the boat, put him out of her mind, and thought once again of the music lesson ahead.

2

THE WOMEN ALIGHTED from the vessel and soon came to the "rice-field steps," as they were called, and the gardens on the river side of the mansion. As they had come by boat, they were not afforded the opportunity of arriving by the avenue of famous, 200-year-old oaks draped with moss.

An impressive home had never been at the top of Joshua John Ward's priorities, although among his several plantations were some homes comparable to the architectural treasures of Charleston. Ward could have moved to Prospect Hill, a copy of Clifton, which was a house of such beauty it had been distinguished in the diary of General George Washington. But Ward put other things ahead of a distinguished dwelling, such as his family, his church, and his rice, which was said to be the finest ever grown. Brookgreen house was a simple frame structure, with a hipped, cypress-shingle roof and two chimneys.

Sitting in the drawing room, which featured striking wallpaper of a plantation scene with the white-pillared mansion in the forefront and the river in the background, Alice and Mary could hear the tinkling of a piano coming from the ballroom. From where Alice sat on a brocade chair she could see Madame standing at a window, gazing out. But Alice knew that Madame's thoughts were only on the music she was hearing, which was being played by one of the Brookgreen Plantation daughters, either Penelope or Georgeanna.

The music stopped and the only sound was that of the metro-nome, the mechanism ticking as the pendulum moved. It was beating the exact time of the piece just played.

"Play the last measure again," Madame Le Conte said, not turn-ing her head from the window. After several notes, she said, "You missed the F sharp. Go back." The excerpt was done again and it obviously met with Madame's requirement. She turned and went to the piano and moved the pendulum, stopping the ticking in-strument. "Practice the last two lines several times each day. Work on timing, even if you have to count aloud: *one and two and three and four and.* The metronome will help you. During the next lesson I will start you on a little Clementi sonata."

Penelope left the room and Alice went in quickly, not taking time to chat with her friend. All Penelope really wanted to talk about was Allard, Alice's brother. She was always asking "Allard this" and "Allard that," and Alice knew that someday they would marry. Such a marriage would be perfect, for the joining of two prosperous South Carolina plantations such as Wachesaw and Brookgreen would receive great attention.

The walls of the ballroom were mostly ceiling-to-floor windows where one could get glimpses of the boxwood gardens and live oak avenue, which ended at brick posts topped with decorative pineapples, symbol of hospitality. The piano sat against a cypress-paneled wall, near a carved mantel, and along the window-walls stood a table and chairs and benches—many filled with music books. No carpet was on the floor, each board being from a single pine tree.

Madame took Alice's music books, opened one to a piece that was mostly scales, and asked her to play.

Alice sat down at the square piano made by Steinway & Sons, and arranged her long skirts. She played the first line, giving special attention to the placement of her fingers, moving her thumb under her middle finger in order to complete the scale.

"Very good," Madame said from the window. "Go on."

As Alice continued the piece she could picture Madame, stand-ing at the panes but not seeing the view. Alice finished the piece.

"Have you practiced your music this week?" Madame asked, turning to face Alice.

"No," Alice admitted. "I just . . ." Then she thought of Mary, and how the servant girl had taught her always to try her best at a task. "I haven't practiced, but on the way here today, I resolved to give my music lessons more attention. You shall see improvement next time."

"Let us hope you speak the truth," Madame said.

Madame Le Conte came to the piano and turned the music book to the Mozart piece Alice had scanned in the boat. Madame said, "Let me hear what you can do with this one. Keep in mind that Mozart is showing his skill in combining melodies that he had learned from studying the music of Johann Sebastian Bach."

Alice played choppily, unsure of herself, and Madame asked her to move away and let her play a page or two for demonstration. Madame moved her delicate frame gracefully onto the piano bench and carefully placed her fingers on the keys. Alice thought that Madame Le Conte was quite beautiful. Her rich brown hair was piled high in a pompadour, and her white, round face was smooth and free of blemishes. Her hands were white and soft, unlike the hands of most dedicated musicians, who had long, thin fingers. But as Madame began to play in the fluid, translucent texture of her own piano style, the music offered new possibilities. When the piece was finished, she closed the book, asked Alice to practice further on the work, and they went back to the scales.

Madame turned on the metronome and insisted that Alice play to the tempo she had set. Soon the lesson had ended. Alice collected her books and left the ballroom.

Penelope had been waiting in the drawing room. "Oh, Alice, what's the news of Allard?"

"Allard runs a plantation and practices medicine as well," Alice said, thinking that Penelope had heard her poor piano performance. "He is a busy man," she added.

"Will you tell him I send greetings?"

"Of course."

"And, Alice, one more thing. Will you tell Arthur that Georgeanna sends her greetings as well?"

"Arthur is still in Charleston finishing medical school, but he will be home this month as it is time to plant the rice. I am sure he will see Georgeanna when he returns."

Mary One walked ahead of Alice as they left. They passed through the hallway that was noted for its wallpaper, since it was more like an original painting than wallpaper. Alice sometimes stopped to gaze at the fruit motif, but hurried past today.

Although she liked the Ward girls, she was exasperated at them for thinking of nothing but her brothers. *There wasn't another thought in their silly heads!* And Alice found this concern difficult to understand, since she herself had not seen any man who made her head turn. *Or had she?* The thought startled her and she shook it out of her head.

Back in the boat, Mary said, "Now, Miss Alice, don't you cast no glance toward that sawmill man if he be standing on that bluff."

"Mary," Alice shot back, "this vessel will pass the sawmill faster than hot water makes tea. I couldn't do any harm in so short a time. Stop fretting. The Flaggs are my family after all, and I would do nothing to hurt them. I know precisely what my life is supposed to be like, and although from time to time I am confused, I am going forward in the way I am expected to go."

Just then the boat rounded the bend and Alice saw him. The pine trees had been removed from the dock, and the lumberman was standing where the trees had been stacked. The boat would go close enough to the dock for her to see the color of his eyes and satisfy her curiosity. After all, there was no harm in looking!

"Stop it, Miss Alice. Stop it this minute. Don't you look at that man, and don't you let no thoughts about him rattle your brain. If you do, bad times are ahead, and you don't want that."

Alice was mildly annoyed that Mary was creating such a fuss over her innocent interest, but allowed her gaze to dwell a few moments more on this picture of masculine perfection. He was unusually handsome, and looked so cheerful. Alice felt that inexplicable pull again, and before she had time to examine it, the lumberman smiled the most brilliant smile and Alice smiled back without thinking.

3

THE SUN THAT had sparkled the surface of the river was now retreating and the black water, stained by rich cypress roots growing underneath, looked inhospitable under overhanging foliage. Alice left the vessel and walked ahead of Mary as she climbed the steep hill. Wachesaw Plantation was secluded, and the immense plantation manor house sitting on the bluff and facing the Waccamaw was occupied only by her uncle, the Reverend James L. Belin, the man who had given the plantation to Alice's brother Allard. The Reverend was born in All Saints Parish in 1788, and was from one of the first families to settle on the Waccamaw Neck. Clearly, the Reverend did not feel up to serving a pastorate and overseeing the production of rice on a large plantation, and he chose to fill the pulpit at the local Methodist church.

But Alice and her mother and brothers found the atmosphere of the Hermitage, the house on the seashore portion of the property, relaxed and friendly. There were miles of views from most windows, and after the three o'clock meal, the most formal one of the day, seagulls swooped down for any leftover bread carried outside by the cooks. The smell of salt spray filled the rooms, and nothing was more thrilling than riding a horse on the seabeach, although Alice hadn't gone early enough to watch the sun miraculously rise from the barely discernable line that divided the ocean from the sky.

Nature's paintbrush splashed the landscape with color during all seasons. In winter there were camellias, and spring brought violets, jasmine, lilacs, and apple blossoms. Summer offered soft, white magnolia and gardenia blooms. Gardenia was Alice's favorite flower, as well as that of her mother.

But this was April, which had come in full on the blooming, and Alice's spirits were suddenly buoyed as though lifted by the spring air. She stopped on the crest of the hill and looked about. Her late father's words came back to her then, as they did from time to time, and she could almost hear his voice speaking to her of the Indians.

The river was named Waccamaw after the tribe who lived there before the white men came and took the land away, and the manor house had been built directly upon an old burial ground. The Waccamaws were listed as the most numerous in the 1715 Indian census, having six villages with 610 inhabitants. In 1720 they made war on the settlers, and at least 60 Indians were captured and sent into West Indian slavery. Besides the Waccamaws, there were the Wachesaws, Pee Dees, Santees, and Seewees.

When disease spread, Indians were sometimes buried in a common grave. Alice's father had unearthed such a grave of nearly twenty Waccamaw Indian skeletons, all buried in a circular zone, their heads laid in the innermost part of the ring. Eye sockets had been filled with Indian trading beads of brightest red. Some burial urns had also been excavated, and they held beads as well as bones. It was a plantation law that no person touch a skeleton or bead, as the owners of Wachesaw Plantation had always believed that such remnants of illness might harbor dormant disease that could magically come to life and cause a new epidemic.

Each spring when the vegetable gardens were plowed, arrowheads were tossed up, and Alice had a collection of them in a hatbox in her armoire. Indian relics were treasured as there were few objects to be had of that long ago period. Some years before, after an especially violent hurricane, a carved tomahawk was found in the debris on the seabeach. The notches were believed to indicate the warrior's achievements.

It was funny, Alice was thinking, how the Belins and Flaggs treasured their Indian legacy, and how the stories had been indelibly etched on their minds. Sometimes when a hoot owl gave his dismal call, Alice believed she could see Indian braves on white horses, dashing about the forest. And when a deer herd came to the clearing near the Hermitage on moonlit nights, she occasionally pictured a warrior's profile leaning against a pillar on the veranda. Wachesaw would always be "Indianed," and what was left of that ancient time would never be lost.

"Come on, Miss Alice," Mary was saying, breaking into the spell. "Get into the carriage."

Alice stepped into the vehicle waiting to take her and Mary to the Hermitage, nearly four miles away.

That night, staring toward the sea from a window in her bedroom, Alice again thought of the Indians who had once inhabited that land and used the waters. Their name was on both. The land had thrived under their loving touch, and the rains had come to the rhythms of their dance. Their eyes were as keen as the osprey who watches over all from her nest in the tallest tree on the bluff.

Wachesaw Plantation was a mosaic of the mysteries of the ages. Strong, generations-old oaks stood like giants, guarding the land from the haunts of the sea. *The sea.* Stories of buccaneers were every bit as dramatic as tales of the Indians. The pageantry of the past swept in on winds from the shafts of clouds and flaming sunsets. It was all beauty and sadness.

The major crop here was rice, and up to 50 million pounds were produced in the county. Every rice planter produced more than 100,000 pounds a year, and on the eastern shore of the Waccamaw River was a line of huge adjacent plantations: Woodbourne, Wachesaw, Richmond Hill, Laurel Hill, Springfield, Brookgreen, The Oaks, and Turkey Hill. Others were farther downriver.

There had been some dispute over the meaning of *Wachesaw.* While some believed the Indian name meant "happy hunting ground," others claimed that the correct translation was "place of the great weeping." The plantation and the Hermitage contained 937 acres.

Since the tides were needed to drain and flood the crop, rice planting was confined to the fields adjacent to the river. Harrowing began in March, followed by plowing and trenching, the trenches being about a foot apart. The seed was sown by hand in April, and the "sprout flow" remained on the seed from three to six days. After the sprouts were allowed to grow in the sunshine, another flow was put on for several days. Then the land was dried for working with a Jack hoe. There were other various flows and periods of culture before the harvest, which began early in September.

The reapers were women who moved into the fields after the last flow was withdrawn. They cut the grain with rice hooks, and left the plants lying on the stubble for a day of drying, after which rice plants were tied in sheaves and transported to the threshing yards. After the rice was cleaned, it was sent to a factor in Charleston, who sold it for a commission. Rice brought a high price and made it possible for the planters to live charmed lives. Alice took in a little longer the spectacular view from her bedroom window that night—meditating on the planter's life she was fortunate enough to enjoy—and finally turned in.

The Hermitage was not an old house in the sense that plantation manor houses were, nor was it as formal and elegant. The patina that comes from passing years was missing. Yet Alice loved the place.

Most seashore houses, like the Hermitage, were planned by their owners with the assistance of joiners and housewrights, but without professionally trained architects. In most cases, the owners supplied an idea for the building's plan, giving the builder a sketch as a model, and always the design took advantage of the prevailing breezes and ocean views. Almost all the rooms at the Hermitage had an ocean exposure, including the drawing room which, in tones of gold, red, and blue, was a cozy place. The heavy furniture, including a walnut secretary and pianoforte, gave the room a handsome appearance.

One day when Alice was feeling particularly appreciative of her surroundings at the Hermitage, she decided to talk of it with her mother, who was sitting in the drawing room, embroidering a dresser scarf.

"Mother, do you believe the rice planters have reached their peak of status?"

Mrs. Flagg put aside her sewing and thought about the question. Finally she said, "Now that you have brought it up, I cannot believe there will come a time when this close-knit group of planters will ascend to further prestige. You remember that two of them signed the Declaration that gave us our freedom from England."

"They may be prestigious and wealthy, but that is not the part of the existence that really appeals to me," Alice ventured to admit.

A little annoyed, Mrs. Flagg picked up her embroidery. Not looking at her daughter, she asked, "What *does* appeal to you?"

"Oh," Alice began dreamily, "living in a big, airy house where I can view the salt marsh and ocean, hear the bellow of male alligators between midnight and dawn, ride my horse on the seabeach, listen to the old tales told by the servants. . . ."

Mrs. Flagg put her sewing on a table, got up, and came to sit on the sofa by her daughter. "When you are older you will understand the structure and responsibilities of the planter aristocracy. One who is born to it, lives it to the fullest, all of it."

"I do live life to the fullest, Mother."

"And that gives me the greatest satisfaction," Mrs. Flagg said softly. "You inherited the spirit and energy of your ancestors, and I have no doubt that the world could be yours, or any part of it that you desire."

Getting up, she went to a window and gazed at the vast salt marshes threaded with ribbons of tidal water, moving faster now, rippling toward full flood. She desperately hoped that her daughter was getting properly prepared to become mistress of a plantation. This would be the perfect time for them to have a talk, and Mrs. Flagg's intuition told her that she must bring Alice to a stronger awareness of her envied position as the daughter of Wachesaw. Not turning away from the Low Country landscape that stretched before her, she began.

"If you look at the globe you will notice that the northern half of the coast of South Carolina is in the shape of an arc," Mrs. Flagg said.

"Like a new moon," Alice answered, not realizing she was giving her mother the longed-for assurance that she was listening to every word.

"Like a new moon. It is in that moon's arc that the most productive rice lands in the world lie, and to those who live there and own the fertile rice lands comes an inflexible obligation."

"But I thought rice plantations also extended along the rivers to the Atlantic, from the Cape Fear River in North Carolina to the Savannah River," Alice said.

"You are right. They do. But as I said, it is in the moon's arc that the most *productive* of the rice lands lie. Of course wonderful plantations sprawl along the Cooper and Ashley rivers near Charleston, and the Broad and May rivers near Beaufort, but *our*

rice is the best, as judged by the expositions in Europe, and of
course we produce more of it. For some reason, the soil here is
mellower and just perfect for rice. Besides that, we have the proper pitch of the tide, and salt does not invade our river water."

Alice again felt lucky to have been born in the very curve of the
South Carolina Low Country. She thought about the rich rice
fields, and the process of the harvest. "I have always wondered
just how those women, the ones who cut the rice, learned that little
trick of maneuvering the sickle and cutting three rows at a time."

"That trick, as you call it, has come down to them through the
generations, the same as their spirituals, and their storytelling. It
is a part of their lives on the plantation."

"We are lucky to have the Ones," Alice said, thinking of Mary
and her family.

"We are very fortunate to have all that we have," Mrs. Flagg
said, now turning and easing herself into a chair by the window.

"Just how did these particular planters get this particular land?"
Alice asked, genuinely interested in her heritage.

Mrs. Flagg was so moved by her daughter's interest that she
wanted to reach out and touch her, but she resisted the urge. "In
the late seventeenth century," she began, "the English lords proprietors offered attractive terms to bring settlers to the territory.
There were three categories of grants then: seigniories, which
would go to the lords proprietors; baronies, which would be
granted to members of nobility; and plantations and farms, which
went to commoners who could provide slaves to produce materials
for export."

"How did one get a grant of land?"

"A person went before the royal governor and council to request a grant, and if the request was approved a warrant was
issued to have the land surveyed. After the plat was recorded, the
grantee took an oath pledging allegiance to the crown. It was all
very judicial and proper."

Alice was intrigued to hear about the grant procedure. She
asked how much land they usually received.

Her mother replied, "Heads of families received 150 acres, as
well as smaller tracts for each member of the household, and you
must remember that slaves were counted as members of families
for purposes of land grants."

"That means the more slaves, the more land," Alice said, looking in the direction of the sea. The smell of marshes was coming in the window, an acrid essence of the marsh mud, cord grass, salt water, and animal life that filled the air when the land eagerly accepted the flood of the tides. Alice went to the window and looked at the palmettoes lining the creek, and her nostrils quivered with the spices of her unique home. It was a heavenly place to live, and as she thought about it now, there was no other that would attract her as much.

"I am glad you are looking back, Alice," her mother said, breaking into her thoughts. "You can only look ahead by knowing what went on before you were here."

"How did the Belins come to settle here?"

"The colonists came mainly from three sources: Englishmen seeking new opportunities, Scots in search of mercantile establishment, and French Huguenots looking for land and religious freedom."

"Did the Belins come over from England with the Allstons?" Alice asked.

"I think not, as they were French Huguenots," her mother answered. "I believe the first Belin inherited Wachesaw from an Allston. You see, at one time, the Allstons owned nearly every plantation on this finger of land between the Waccamaw River and the seabeach."

Walking across the carpet, Alice said, "The Allstons were the wealthiest of all the planters."

"Probably true," her mother agreed. "I am always especially pleased when you include the Alston women in your circle of friends. You know, of course, that their grandfather was the one who dropped one of the *l*s from his name." She paused. "'King Billy,' they called him. Clifton was the grandest of all the plantations of that generation. George Washington visited that plantation and wrote of it in his diary."

Alice, now tired, flexed her muscles. "And all of that simply means that he could do anything he wanted to, including removing a letter from his name."

Mrs. Flagg wasn't sure whether or not she detected a hint of sarcasm, but she decided to overlook it if it was there. Sweeping into the Alston story, she began, "Of course dropping one *l* distinguished him from the William Allston who founded Brookgreen. The one-*l* William's second wife was Mary Brewton, youngest daughter of Rebecca Motte of Revolution fame, but we won't go into that old story. That marriage brought the Miles Brewton house on King Street in Charleston to the Alston family holdings, and their life-style was the kind that I want you to consider, Alice, if you hold one up for study. Theirs is the existence that all other planter families strive for."

"They spent their winters on their plantations, their summers on the sea islands, and from the St. Cecilia ball until Lent at their Charleston house," Alice said, her voice showing a little disapproval at the extravagance.

"True," her mother answered, not allowing Alice's attitude to fluster her. She went on to say how every day that Mary Alston was in Charleston, her carriage pulled by four beautiful bay horses was at the door to take her shopping on King Street. William raced his favorite thoroughbreds in the Jockey Club races there, his horses winning the cup year after year. There were legends about those animals—Gallatin, Shark, Comet, Black Maria, and many others, including Anvilina, bred by Lord Clermont from the Prince of Wales' famous horse, Anvil.

Mrs. Flagg reminded Alice how very large the Miles Brewton house was, touching from King to Legare (pronounced la-*gree*) Street. The entrance was through heavy iron gates, and steps led to a stone portico with massive white columns. Inside, rooms flanked a stone hall, and a broad stairway climbed to the drawing room on the second story, a beautifully proportioned room with a high arched ceiling and handsome chandelier. Other lovely features were the mirrors, portraits, marble mantels, and white doves in fresco on the ceiling. "William imported his wine by the pipe," Mrs. Flagg informed her daughter, "and he had a family dinner every Saturday when all of his sons and daughters and their children were expected to attend. And like all planters, William was a member of the St. Cecilia Society and attended its balls."

Alice got up and stretched, indicating she was weary of so much conversation. Mrs. Flagg decided to bring up one more matter before stopping.

"The reason I am pointing all of this out to you is that some of the Alston descendants are unmarried men, and they would make very appropriate husbands for a young woman of your position. You should select the one of your choice and allow him to notice your interest."

Alice went back to the window. A slight breeze was swaying the gray moss hanging in beards from the trees. Her mother was waiting for some response, and in the stillness she could hear birds singing. After a moment she turned to Mrs. Flagg.

"Of course I shall marry into a prominent planter family. This is where my roots are, in the arc of the moon." She kissed her mother lightly on the cheek, and just before she left the room Mrs. Flagg told her that Arthur was expected home tomorrow. The news put a pleasant smile on Alice's face. Arthur was her favorite brother.

4

THE DAY BEFORE her next music lesson Alice practiced for two hours, her metronome ticking away and the music floating out from the ceiling-to-floor open windows. At first she worked on the scales, and then she turned to the Mozart piece. As Madame had cautioned, she kept in mind that the author had demonstrated the skill he had learned from Bach. One measure was especially difficult, and she went over it again and again, finally playing it perfectly. When she had practiced until her back ached and her fingers cramped, she stacked the music books on a chair and went upstairs to select the dress she would wear to her lesson.

In her room, a large tester bed was flanked by two many-paned windows that afforded views of the marsh and distant sea. On the opposite wall was a mantel of no decoration. An armoire stood by the door leading to a dressing room alcove in which a small dormer window gave a perfect view of the seabeach, and a mirror in a walnut frame hung above a washstand where handpainted bowls and pitchers from England held water for Alice's use. Although the Hermitage had been built in keeping with the simple design of most seabeach houses, Mrs. Flagg decorated it with her taste for fancy accessories, and Alice's bed had a lace canopy and the curtains were of the finest Brussels embroidery.

Mary One was standing at Alice's armoire when she came in.

"Mary, what do you think I should wear to the music lesson tomorrow?"

Mary looked around, a questioning expression on her face. "You never be concerned about that before."

"I know," Alice said, brushing off the remark. "But I just thought I would wear the pink and white dress, and the straw hat with the large green satin ribbon."

"Miss Alice, you not be going to Brookgreen for a dance, you be going for a music lesson."

Alice sighed and tried to turn her thoughts away from her clothes. All this recent talk about meeting men and becoming a plantation mistress was making her itch to improve her appearance, but she realized she was being silly to bother about all that today.

"Anything will do. It is only a music lesson, but I did practice my pieces," Alice said as she went over and looked out a window, deliberately closing her mind to her clothes. After a moment she left the window and flopped on the bed, where she fell into a deep sleep.

When she awoke half an hour later, Mary was gone, and Alice was suddenly wide awake and fresh, and giggling slightly to herself. Why shouldn't she start making a special effort about her attire and begin enjoying the privileges of her position? She leapt from the bed, went to the armoire, and pulled out her pink and white dress and straw hat. It was a perfect combination to wear on a nice spring day.

The next day, as she and Mary got into the carriage for the ride to the Wachesaw dock, Mary's penetrating look grated on Alice's nerves and her mouth went into a pout. Soon they were in the boat and when they reached midstream, the oarsmen's song was "Roll, Jordan, Roll." Alice sat very still, her music books in her lap.

Alice stared into the distance as she thought about the music lesson, and she pictured the notes in her mind with her fingers actually playing them. At first she did not notice the sight of the sawmill and the lumberman standing on the bluff, his back to the river. She caught her breath.

Alice shuffled her feet nervously. "Don't you lift a finger to that sawmill man," Mary cautioned, "or you'll be sorry."

Alice lowered her head so that she couldn't see anything but the bottom of the boat, but soon raised her head just enough to get a glimpse of the lumberman. Here she was, all dressed in finery designed to attract the attention of a man—any man but this one.

Only the circle of rice planters was open to her, but she had never seen there the appeal this man possessed. His skin had been bronzed by sunshine, and his strong muscles testified to his raw energy. His beauty was even more striking to Alice today than before.

The boat continued to glide down the river, leaving the sawmill behind. Alice began thinking back to her conversation with her mother regarding the Alston men. She tried to picture herself married to one of them, and found the idea a little daunting.

"Mary," Alice said haltingly, "how did you meet Michael?"

Mary didn't move a muscle as she began her narrative. "I be a little girl and Michael be a little boy, and when we get big, Michael be the plantation carpenter and I be the weaver, and we marry and have our twins, Margaret and Michael."

As Mary talked, an aura of total admiration enveloped Alice. Mary was all integrity, courage, and compassion. She was utterly selfless in so many ways, and Alice truly loved her. "I so seldom thank you, Mary, for all that you do for me," Alice said thoughtfully. "You never appear rushed or distracted, even though you have a husband and twins at home."

"Ritta, my aunty, she take care of the twins at the Children's House. All us mothers keep our babies there while we work," Mary answered.

"You are so young, Mary. You must have fallen in love with Michael the first time you laid eyes on him."

Mary shrugged her shoulders. "I don't know about no love, Miss Alice. It just seem the right thing to do. I be the weaver, Michael be the carpenter, and we marry."

"You didn't actually *love* him?" Alice asked.

"Oh yes, I love him. But I don't remember acting like you act when you see that sawmill man."

"Hush, Mary, I am being serious. You *did* marry the man of your choice. No other person told you whom to marry."

"No. I don't guess they did that."

"I do not think anyone should be told whom to marry," Alice said, her eyes flashing. "Everyone should have some say-so in such an important matter."

"I don't know nothing about such as that, Miss Alice, but I do know that you be supposed to marry a rice planter and that's all there is to it."

Alice turned her head away and again tried to picture herself as the wife of an Alston, with all the advantages and burdens that entailed. She felt overwhelmed by the image, and wanted to think about something else. She asked Mary if she had ever heard any stories about unusual marriages.

"Our stories be about animals, and plat-eyes, and such as that," Mary explained.

"Then I shall tell you a story about a marriage," Alice said.

"Where you hear such a story?"

"The Alston women always have marvelous tales that came from Charleston," she responded. "Those twins are full of glorious stories."

"Tell me one of them stories," Mary said.

"As I think about it now, I don't believe you and I have ever told stories, and I have always believed that is a most enjoyable pastime." Alice turned slightly to face Mary. "There was once a wealthy and eligible bachelor who lived in a fine Charleston mansion. He was so prissy that he sent all of his linens and handkerchiefs to France, where they were embroidered with his entire name, George Edwards."

"That sure enough be prissy," Mary agreed.

"Many Charleston women desired to become the wife of George Edwards, but none seemed to suit him, for he was just as particular in the choosing of a wife as he was in other matters."

"Did he ever marry?" Mary asked.

"Oh yes. And this is how it happened. One night a couple gave a large dinner and dance in honor of their daughter, Elizabeth, and George Edwards was invited. Elizabeth, like the other single women at the party, thought that George Edwards would make the most divine husband. Each single woman was trying to attract his attention. Just before the elaborate supper was to be served at midnight, George and Elizabeth were dancing. The music stopped and a servant carrying a tray of glasses filled with champagne walked over to them. Each of them accepted a glass, and then they stepped out onto the balcony, but just then, Elizabeth tilted her glass and champagne spilled on the bodice of her lace gown."

"What happened?"

"George removed a handkerchief from his pocket and began to wipe up the spill when Elizabeth noticed the artistic embroidery and asked to see the handkerchief."

"Did he let her hold it?"

"He handed her the handkerchief and she held it before her eyes, saying 'Oh, what a perfectly lovely name.' But George was thinking that she meant the embroidery was lovely and he suddenly wanted to make her the gift of the handkerchief. So he told her, 'If you like it you may have it.'"

"He be talking about the handkerchief and she be thinking he talking about his name?"

"Precisely. And she quickly called her father and said that George Edwards had offered her his name and she would like to be married immediately, and her father right that very minute announced the news to the guests. As each one congratulated George Edwards, he was too shaken to deny the proposal."

"Do you think Elizabeth knew what she had done?" Mary asked.

"I am not sure. Do you?"

"Yes. She musta did it on purpose in order to marry George Edwards," Mary replied.

"All the people in Charleston whispered the same thing! They said it was pure chicanery."

"Miss Alice," Mary said seriously, "don't you get no such ideas about doing anything such as that. No woman of Wachesaw be tricky."

"But sometimes a woman has to be convincing when she loves a man."

"If that woman has to convince a man, he not be worthy of being convinced!" Mary snapped. She thought about the story a little longer. "And did Elizabeth and George Edwards live happily?" Mary asked.

"No. They did not live together after their marriage but in separate houses," Alice said. "He did not love her. That is what happens to someone who marries a person that does not love her. It is tragic!"

"That story be told to you by the Alston twins?"

"Yes."

"They live at Rose Hill Plantation?" Mary queried.

"Yes. Their father is William Algernon Alston."

"I saw him when he came to see Marse Allard," Mary said.

"He attended Princeton," Alice responded before she realized that Mary did not know what Princeton was.

The oarsmen were now stopping at the Brookgreen dock, and Alice lifted her skirts and music books. It was perfectly wonderful that she had taken the time to practice her music, she thought, still filled with a desire to improve herself. Her mind had wavered back and forth on other subjects, but she had been steadfast about *that!*

5

"You are much improved," Madame Le Conte commented from the window. When Alice completed the piece, Madame came to the piano and turned off the metronome, then went to the table. "I am going to start you on something more advanced."

Undisguised curiosity flickered onto Alice's face. "What is the piece?"

Madame was consulting a large stack of books on the table. "Something by Beethoven would reveal new possibilities," she said, mostly to herself. "But you are not ready for his Moonlight Sonata; that will come later. Let me look for another composer."

"I shall work diligently, Madame," Alice promised. "To play well is my new goal."

Madame chose a music book and walked to the piano. "To set a goal for yourself is a form of achievement in itself," Madame replied. "So many people do not set goals, and of course they never improve their situations. Those people are as trivial as their goals would be, if they had any."

Alice pondered that statement for a moment, studying this woman whom she admired so much but who remained a bit of a mystery to her. "Madame, you know about goals? And aspirations?"

"Of course my dear. How do you think I came here from France? Because my family desired it? Of course not! They were against it, but it was one of my goals. A goal comes from the heart."

"Would you be willing to let me share with you my thoughts about my future?" Alice asked, her gaze not straying from Madame Le Conte. "I feel that I have so many questions that no one will accept from a girl of my position. It is very difficult."

Madame's face broke into a delighted smile. "Of course, Alice. I would love to advise you. But not today. Others are waiting for me, and we must get on with the lesson."

"Next time I come?" Alice asked. "In four days?"

"You sound quite concerned about your future," Madame said kindly. She leaned forward and squeezed Alice's arm affectionately, in a reassuring way. "In four days," she answered.

Alice could hardly believe her good fortune. She had not realized until now how sorely she needed a sympathetic confidante, who could listen to her growing fears about marrying a powerful planter and directing a large estate. And yes, someone with a cool head who could advise her about her strange attraction to this handsome lumberman. "Are you quite certain?" Alice asked.

"Yes, I am *absolutely* certain," Madame answered. She turned her attention quickly to the music book she held. "There is a Polish composer in France. His name is Frederic Chopin, and I have recently received his Polonaise in A."

"May I learn it?" Alice squealed, filled with desire to please Madame.

The teacher spread the music on the piano music stand. "Try to learn the first three lines for your next lesson." She leaned over Alice and wrote some words on the page, but Alice could not see what she was writing. "You must pay attention to the timing," Madame said as she wrote. Then she asked Alice to move to a chair and listen as she played the piece.

Madame played the first page of the dramatic score, and Alice watched the white fingers fly about the keys. The music was so inspiring that Alice seemed to be emotionally lifted until standing on tiptoe. She was still in a daze when Madame closed the book and handed it to her, again cautioning her to concentrate on the timing of the piece.

As Alice left the room, she looked to see what Madame had written on the music. In the margin, in a spidery handwriting, was "Allegro 1/16." And above each note was the time allotted for that particular musical symbol: "1–2–3–4–5–6." One beat for each of the six notes.

Alice closed the book, and, as always, Penelope was waiting for her, her eyes sparkling with sudden vitality. Penelope moved a few steps forward with the usual Ward grace, and laid her long, cool fingers on Alice's hand. Alice noted that her English-rose complexion was perfectly flawless, and her caramel hair was silky and luxuriant. It fell to Penelope's shoulders like a rippling surf, and the widened eyes and tumbling hair gave her a look of girlish innocence.

Alice was suddenly embarrassed about the personal conversation she had begun with Madame, and her heart dropped into her stomach. "Did you hear us talking, Madame and I?"

"No. I just came into the room," Penelope answered.

Alice fervently hoped that Penelope was telling the truth. She would die a thousand deaths if Penelope had heard her asking Madame to advise her on her goals. It was simply unheard of for a planter's daughter to be concerned about her future.

"I have been thinking today how warm the spring is becoming. What do you plan to do this summer?" Penelope asked.

Alice considered the question and knew it was likely she would remain at the Hermitage. While other planter families had to be removed from their plantations during the humid months to avoid contracting malaria fever, which came from the low-lying rice fields where mosquitoes bred, Alice and her mother and brothers could remain in their home, for it was on the seashore rather than on the river, as plantation manor houses were. "I suppose I shall stay at the Hermitage. Will you go to the Broad River in North Carolina, as usual?"

Penelope nodded enthusiastically, and Alice asked her what sort of things they did when they were in the mountains.

"Father takes his account books, and some of the records from All Saints Church. He catches up on all of the records of births, deaths, and marriages that must be recorded in the church registry. There is a piano for practice, and many books are taken from the library, some for pleasure and others for learning."

"It is rather dreary here during the summer," Alice remarked, "as everyone goes away, although some only go so far as the seashore."

"True," Penelope answered, keeping up with Alice as they trooped toward the entrance of the house. "The Alstons always go to their home on Debordieu Beach, then Greenville, and the two-l

Allstons of Matanzas Plantation go to Pawleys, where most of the other planter families congregate. And there are a few who take the Grand Tour of Europe."

"Won't you be planning a tour?" Alice asked, stopping at the front door.

"No. Father is becoming interested in politics, and he doesn't want to leave the country. But I really don't wish to go to Europe and leave my friends. By the way, how is Allard?"

Penelope's interest was not lost on Alice, but she did not let on. "He is working hard at rice planting now, and Arthur is home. There are four of us at the Hermitage rather than three."

"Give Allard my best," Penelope said. "Will you be back in four days?" Not awaiting a reply, she added, "Madame will soon leave for her home in France and remain there until after the first frost of next fall."

"For some cracky reason I am suddenly enjoying my music lessons," Alice said, but she was thinking that it was the custom for all tutors to go back to their European homes from spring until late fall, and if anything happened to prevent her talk with Madame Le Conte about her goals, she would be very disappointed.

Madame would be able to offer Alice a unique perspective on her expected role as plantation mistress. She was not of the planter aristocracy and she had far-reaching views—European thinking—and Alice needed to talk with her in depth, she thought. Not too long ago, Madame was Alice's age and must have worried about failing, but she had succeeded. This woman had the confidence to pursue her own dreams; Alice was only now wondering what her own dreams were and if she were allowed to have them.

But Madame would not fail her, and she knew it. Alice could hardly wait for four days to pass. As she thought about it now, Alice glanced back toward the ballroom, and she could hear the faint tinkling of the piano. Madame was in the midst of a music lesson, probably instructing Georgeanna.

"You are becoming quite proficient at the piano," Penelope was saying, calling Alice back out of her thoughts. "You shall be famous someday."

Alice felt less certain of her own talent, and was unable to meet Penelope's fixed stare. "I do not really aspire to become famous.

Anyway, I do not have the name for it. Who ever heard of anyone famous with such a name?" Alice flopped her hat on her head and tied the wide bow over an ear.

"You *make* the name, goosey! No one ever heard of anyone's name until they became famous, and their name acquired a sort of ring to it. I think Alice Flagg would be a fine famous name."

Alice looked near the drawing room for Mary and motioned for her to hurry along. "I don't think my name will ever be famous," she continued. "Not in the sense of the great pianists and opera singers." Penelope followed Alice and Mary out of the house.

"Who can know? You may be a prima donna someday," Penelope called out as Alice and Mary waved good-bye and flew downhill toward the dock.

As the two women descended into the rice-field steps, Alice was thinking about the landscape architect who had designed them, and she believed his name was Wasdin. That old stairway leading from the formal boxwood gardens down to the rice fields and the sandy lane that rambled to the boat landing had always been cherished, and the Wards never failed to mention that a newspaper article about Wasdin was sealed under the brick. Someday, maybe hundreds of years later, someone perhaps would restore the steps, find the article, and learn of the origin of the entrance to the rice fields. The arrangement was typical of almost everything about the coastal plantations—set a little above the rest of the world. Just before she stepped into the vessel, Alice turned her eyes up to the stables and three artesian wells. Joshua John Ward provided the best of everything for the members of his family!

Alice perched on the bench in the boat, and Mary, in her navy blue skirt and shirtwaist, slipped in beside her. As the boat left the Brookgreen dock, Alice smoothed the pink and white dress. Her head was swimming and she felt weak. Within minutes she would again pass the Buck sawmill, and it was likely she would see the lumberman. She placed her elbows on her knees, put her chin in her hands, and peeked from under the wide brim of the straw hat. Her steady gaze aimed straight ahead as she wondered why she had never noticed the young man when the Flaggs passed by on their way to All Saints Church each Sunday morning. For years they had gone to church by boat, and she had never seen anyone near the sawmill. Finally she decided that the people who labored at the sawmill must not work on Sundays.

When the boat rounded the bend, Alice, her elbows still on her knees, noticed the lumberman standing on the dock. Her eyes were fixed on him, and her mouth was slightly open as excitement brought a flush to her pale face. Minutes sped into seconds, then the seconds vanished, and there he was, almost close enough to reach out and touch. Alice realized she was not wrong in her assessment of him. There *was* something very special about the lumberman. It showed in his kind face. The wind had now ruffled his black hair into a mass of dancing curls, and he had a carefree air about him. Just before the vessel passed by, he bowed his head and said, "Miss Alice Flagg."

"You know my name?" she called out.

He nodded.

"Do I know you?" she persisted.

"Not yet."

When the boat pulled up to the Wachesaw dock, Alice saw Allard, sitting tall and straight on his stallion, Sylvan. Allard's bronzed face was ringed with neatly curling brown hair, and his clear, blank green eyes were surveying the land. Alice shivered slightly. How cold and remote Allard was, how like a shark as he circled the plantation in order that all of it be under his control. He missed nothing, *nothing*.

Alice peered at Allard. All during the boat ride following her intriguing exchange with the lumberman, she had been considering this idea that they would become acquainted. Now, as she looked at her strong-willed brother, she was rudely reminded that she would never be allowed any kind of friendship with someone of whom Allard disapproved, and he would never approve of a person he would judge to be a loutish commoner. *Never*. Such a notion was preposterous.

6

No ONE HAD ever accused Dr. Allard Flagg of being friendly, or even cordial, for that matter. But he was known as being debonair, and neighborly to the planters—even sociable when among his peers. To his family he was civil, but never warm. Alice believed there would be no such thing as getting close to that brother, and she wondered what Penelope saw in him, other than the opportunity to become mistress of Wachesaw.

Holding onto her hat, Alice stepped from the boat and turned to take in the view that Allard was eyeing from his saddle. Although more than a hundred women were in the fields planting rice, no head or face could be seen, as all were bending from the waist while sowing the seed. The vast fields were now freshly turned soil, but within weeks they would be a sea of green plants, gently blowing in the breeze.

As she considered all of it, Alice could begin to understand why Allard was so obsessed with his plantation. He had been fortunate to acquire such a large and valuable estate when so young, and perhaps his uncle had seen in him the very qualities that Alice found distasteful, characteristics the uncle likely desired in the one who would oversee Wachesaw Plantation. If Allard thought about anything other than Wachesaw, Alice could not name it. Of course, as a doctor, he treated all of the plantation people who became ill, but any real softness or abiding affection shown by him was for his estate. For the last several months Alice had tried to fathom just what militant forces were below the surface of Allard's skin. Her only conclusion was that he was both ruler and prisoner of his station in life.

In his mind, he had probably already chosen Penelope Ward as its mistress, and he would advise her of the decision only when it was time to take a wife. She would be perfect, for as a daughter of Brookgreen, she would bring to Wachesaw that perfect combination of hostess, teacher, mistress, mate, and mother. All of her life she had moved quietly about a mansion, watching thin, sure hands polish bowls, trays, and pitchers fashioned by England's finest silversmiths. She had learned early how one presided over dances in a ballroom, or barbecues and oyster roasts under the trees. She could add her expertise to anything from caring for the sick to entertaining a president, and the time would come when she would birth wonderful babies.

Alice couldn't remember when Allard was not a grown man. When she was a small child, he already rode his horse with grace, spoke with authority, and felt compelled to protect the things he loved most.

Arthur, on the other hand, was quite different. It had been said that no two children were alike, and that was certainly true of the Flagg offspring. Arthur was by nature a mild man. If Allard was a descendant of thunderstorms, then Arthur was a son of birdsong, and the drifts of sand that sometimes looked like snow banked against sea oats. He was lovable, spiritual, angelic. And he had not inherited Wachesaw.

Her brothers represented the finest of their lineage, but Alice did not see herself as a great belle. Perhaps Madame would be able to guide her along the best course—for her family's happiness and her own. She could hardly wait for their woman-to-woman talk.

If Alice had been male, she would have been the least likely to be awarded a tract of land. She always seemed to be walking the middle plateau, never aiming for a different situation yet not always satisfied with her present one. But now, as she was beginning to feel turmoil over the roles expected of her, she realized that she was probably the only one of her mother's children who *could* accept change. Allard was the crusader, Arthur was to the manor born, but Alice yearned for a chance to follow her spirit and heart wherever they would lead her, whether that was within the confines of planter society or not. As she thought fondly of the lumberman, whose friendship was socially forbidden to her, she could almost picture her future as a gloomy hallway, with many, many other wonderful doors closed to her.

As Alice was pondering the joys and burdens of the Flagg name, Mary waited at the open door of the carriage. Alice smoothed her skirts and, without uttering a word to her brother, stepped inside; the driver swiftly transported her and Mary towards the Hermitage.

That evening at the usual informal dinner, Allard sat at the head of the table, and Mrs. Flagg at the other end. Alice and Arthur sat opposite each other. The soft plum-violet sheen of the draperies set off the wallpaper, which was in the motif of roses ranging in color from the palest pink to fuchsia. The white mantel was English, and the painting over it as well as the mirror over the sideboard were originally in a Charleston house. English china had been used for place settings, and the focal point of the table was a handsome silver candelabra and a mirrored plateau. As usual, the last meal of the day was simple, mostly leftovers from the three-o'clock dinner.

"How are the music lessons coming along?" Mrs. Flagg asked her daughter.

"Better than I expected," Alice answered honestly. "I really love Madame Le Conte, and she has such splendid music, straight from France. I am starting work on Chopin's Polonaise in A."

"I trust you are giving your attention to the lessons," Allard said, as he finished a glass of milk and set it aside. "You must never cease to prepare yourself for your future."

"I am doing so, Allard. Of course I won't study physic and become a physician like my brothers, but I shall find something that interests me."

"Simply find a wealthy planter who interests you and we will all sigh a breath of relief," Allard quipped.

"Pay no mind to Allard, Alice," Arthur said, coming to her defense. "You are far too young to be interested in any planter."

"Some girls mature early, and proceed to select a man so they will be ready for marriage when they reach fifteen," Mrs. Flagg said.

"We do not need so many weddings in this family," Alice countered. "It is clear there will be two. Penelope just hangs onto every

word of Allard, and now Georgeanna is showing interest in
Arthur."

Allard placed his fork and knife on his plate. "We could fare
worse."

"Oh, let us forget all this nonsense." Alice arose. "One never
knows what the future will bring." To change the subject, she
asked, "How do you think we shall spend this summer?"

"What do you mean?" her mother asked.

"Will we stay here as usual? Penelope said the Wards will again
be going to the Broad River in North Carolina."

Mrs. Flagg set down her silverware and a thoughtful look
spread over her face. "You know, I have been thinking of that. We
may not be as immune to malaria fever as we think. Maybe we
should look over that section of the North Carolina mountains."

"It would be cool there all summer," Arthur reflected. "And
you all know that August, even on the seashore, all but singes our
hair. There isn't a breeze in August."

"And the mosquitoes from the rice fields make their way over
here during that month," Allard added. "It is not known what
brings on the fevers, but the men in science will surely find out
soon. Some say it is the moss, but as for me, I agree with the
theory that a certain strain of mosquito which breeds in the stag-
nant water is to blame."

"We cannot deny that many have died from the fever," Mrs.
Flagg said, a look of sadness now on her face. "Many a friend of
mine has lost a child to it."

In the silence that followed, Alice reiterated her question, but
her mother responded that she would need to consider it further.
Alice did not wish to go away from the Hermitage, but she knew it
would not be very eventful there. If they moved to another location during the humid months, the days would go by faster.

"Mother," Allard said as a sudden thought struck him, "if you
do desire to speak with Joanna Ward about the mountains of
North Carolina, I shall be going to Brookgreen tomorrow to see
Joshua John about some rice seed. Would you like to accompany
me?"

Mrs. Flagg touched her lips with an embroidered napkin. "I
believe I would," she replied. "There are several things I would
like to discuss with Joanna Ward."

"We will leave about eight."

Mrs. Flagg looked up at her daughter. "Alice, would you like to come with us?"

Alice quickly evaluated the situation. It would be a disaster if the lumberman attempted to speak to her in a friendly manner with Allard in the boat. No, it could be very awkward. And besides, she could ride her chestnut mare, Egypt, on the seabeach and gather her thoughts for her chat with Madame Le Conte. "Thank you, but I will decline the invitation this time," Alice said.

"Well we would love to have you, and Penelope and Georgeanna are always glad for your company," her mother said in an anticipatory tone.

"I see them almost every time I take a music lesson," Alice replied. "I will stay here tomorrow."

The next day at eight the Flagg carriage, bearing the family's coat of arms, left Wachesaw for Brookgreen, as it was finally decided to go by coach rather than by boat. With the house quiet except for the moving about of the servants, Alice took the opportunity to practice the piece by Chopin, counting to the time that Madame had noted on the sheet. After that she asked a groom to saddle her mare, Egypt, for a ride to the seabeach. She wanted absolute privacy as she contemplated what she would say to Madame. It could be the most important dialogue of her entire life.

Alice, having dressed herself in a casual frock with a slim skirt, mounted her horse while the groom held the reins. Sitting side-saddle, she cantered off toward the seabeach. The noise of the hoofs increased until she was beyond that last ridge of dunes, and the breathless moment was at hand when she, the horse, and the sea were one, together. The hard-packed sand had been her turf since the time of Dabster, her first pony, and riding on the sea-beach was an exhilarating experience she still treasured. On this day Alice pushed the mare to her peak of performance, and she rode in peace, as this place was usually deserted.

At last she slowed, and actually rehearsed the discussion aloud—in her own voice and that of Madame's. When the conversation was over, Alice had been victorious. All of the questions that had pestered her had been answered. Her future was going to be bright and beautiful, and her heart pounded against her chest as she thought about it. Oh! She wondered what in the world she would do without Madame Le Conte, a woman who had come into her life at the very moment she needed her most. The sea would never be sunless again, and she would shake the impression she sometimes gave of an oppressed little foal. She had Madame Le Conte and everything was wonderful.

Alice had changed into a filmy dress of lavender, with a violets motif, and the cooks had prepared crab casserole and spoon bread for supper, when Allard and his mother arrived home. Arthur came in at the same time.

When they were seated at the table, Allard said grace, as usual thanking God for the blessings of owning Wachesaw Plantation, and asking that the entire house and family be further blessed and free of evil. He ended the petition by thanking God for the food before them, and said that the strength derived from it would be used in divine service.

The meal was well underway, and it was almost as an afterthought that Mrs. Flagg said, "Oh, Alice, all of the Ward women are distressed, and they asked me to tell you that Madame Le Conte had to return to her home in France due to the severe illness of a sister. But they expect her back in late fall, and your lessons will be taken up where they were left off."

Alice was thinking that no one at that table had any conception of how sharply the words had pierced her mind.

"And another thing," her mother added, "William Algernon Alston was there, and he invited you to spend several days with his girls at Debordieu, just prior to their leaving for Greenville. I had already decided that I did not wish to leave the Hermitage at this time for the North Carolina mountains, and a few days at Debordieu Island will surely make the summer less dreary for you."

SUMMER 1848

7

WILLIAM ALGERNON ALSTON was the third son of the first marriage of William ("King Billy") Alston, and since the death of William Algernon's brothers, Governor Joseph Alston and Colonel John Ashe Alston, he naturally came by his father's reputation: being considered the most ambitious and prosperous of the Waccamaw River planters. In 1806 he married Mary Allston Young, the sister of artist Washington Allston and the widow of Thomas Young. She inherited Young's plantation, Youngville. William Algernon went on to acquire other plantations, including Marietta, Friendfield, Strawberry Hill, and he was casting an eye toward the acquisition of Calais and Michaux. His lands were producing nearly two million pounds of rice each year. Although Alice hadn't expected to enjoy a minute of the summer that year, she admitted to herself that it was an honor to be invited to become almost a member of the Alston family.

Although William Algernon had four sons and five daughters, the list of children still under his roof was short. There were the twins, Anna Louise and Charlotte Maria, son Joseph, and stepdaughter Maria Young. William Ashe, a son, had died six years earlier, after returning from a tour of Europe and marrying a Louisiana sugar heiress. Another son, John Ashe, had married Fanny Fraser, and Mary had wed Dr. Seaman Deas, a planter on the North Santee River.

As Alice had put all consideration of her future aside for the summer until Madame Le Conte returned, she planned to make every effort to be convivial with the twins. Her mother had pointed out that any girl on the Waccamaw Neck would have been overjoyed to be chosen as a companion of the Alston women. Although Alice was a few years younger than the twins, when she arrived at the Debordieu cottage they received her as though she were a very dear friend.

Her first afternoon there, Alice sat with the twins on the porch of the cottage. The view was quite different from Wachesaw, where a large marsh area lay between the house and seabeach. At the beach house on Debordieu Island, there were no competitive forces with the huge expanse of sea and sky, and Alice felt as though all of heaven was looking down at her.

As she beheld the breathtaking view, she thought of the many beautiful things she had seen inside the manor house, before they left for Debordieu—especially the extraordinary portraits and other works of art. "Your father seems to have a great love of art and music," Alice said to Charlotte.

"Our paintings mean a great deal to our family," Charlotte answered. "Did we show you the new acquisitions?"

"No," Alice answered. "Tell me about them."

"You do know Thomas Sully," Charlotte said.

"You mean the famous portraitist of Charleston?"

"That is the one."

"Well I do not know him, and I *do*. Everyone has heard of the famous Mr. Sully."

"Some of our portraits hang in the ballroom, where Mary and Seaman were married."

"Do you have portraits of everyone?" Alice asked.

"Yes. And Mr. Sully has bought some paintings for us, including a Rembrandt," Charlotte explained, "but as you know, my grandfather had a great collection in his Charleston home, and we also have a part of that."

William Algernon strolled through the door onto the porch, stopped for a moment to listen, smiled, and walked on toward the beach. It was obvious that he felt his children's lives had been enhanced by the presence of some world-famous paintings.

Alice's long black hair was loosely hanging about her shoulders, and with a toss of her head she threw it back. "Is your father foremost a politician?"

"No," Anna said sharply. "He is a scholar and an agriculturist."

"And does he come to Debordieu frequently?"

"Oh of course," Charlotte answered. "He comes here all the time, as he has a saltworks on the island and spends time here during all parts of the year. With the seawater here, Father's saltworks can produce up to fifty bushels a day."

A faint echo of her mother's voice came back to Alice, and she said, "The Alstons, both the one-*l* and the two-*l* ones, have always been the most, uh, prosperous of the planters. You are the ones the others look up to. Do you live like the rest of us? In other words, do you, say, have a big meal in the middle of the day and only a light meal at night, as we at Wachesaw do?"

"Oh my yes," Charlotte answered. "At night we have milk, potatoes, and sassafras tea, and that is about all."

"The same with us," Alice said, feeling a certain warmness drawing her to her friends. Alice was much intrigued by them and in her mind she was seeking the appropriate word to describe Charlotte and Anna. Dignity! That was it. They were not ordinary people, as much as they tried to pass themselves off as such. They were ladies. The way they spoke reflected this. There was no Southern melodious merging of vowels, and no dialect or local slang.

"Tell us about your brother Allard," Anna said.

Oh Lord, Alice was thinking. Allard *was* the perfect age for the twins, but he would never glance at a woman other than Penelope Ward. "If you have to have a brother, he would suffice," Alice heard herself say.

There was a little pause, and Alice interjected a question to change the subject. "Have you had the Grand Tour of Europe?"

"Not yet," Anna answered.

Not yet. Where had Alice heard those words that now shook her to the bottom of her feet? Yes, the lumberman had answered "not yet" after Alice asked if he knew her. Those were the last words she had heard him say, and she could hear his voice now. The shaken Alice turned her head to face the thick foliage blowing nearby in the breeze. Her breath caught as she dwelled on the memory of this man, the only man who ever invaded her thoughts although he was forbidden to her. But gradually her composure returned, and she heard Anna's words.

" . . . and when Father takes us to the Continent he plans to enter his Carolina rice in the Paris Exposition that year."

"My mother explained to me that you live a charmed life, and she was right," Alice responded.

"Only the same as other families," Anna replied casually. "The Wards of Brookgreen are *really* the prosperous ones. Sometimes I think that Father doesn't try to stay ahead of anyone, but simply tries to keep Joshua John Ward from passing him!"

"The planter families are members of the St. Cecilia Society, the South Carolina Jockey Club, the South Carolina Historical Society of Charleston, . . ." Charlotte was saying.

"And the Winyah Indigo Society of Georgetown," Alice added, "and the Hot and Hot Fish Club, and several agricultural associations. . . ."

"Do I detect just a tinge of sarcasm, Alice?" Anna asked, her eyes narrowing.

Alice was suddenly put on the spot. How would she answer the question? she wondered. She had not meant to use a mocking tone, but now saw that this reflected her opinion. Even though she was dealing with the Alstons on matters very close to their hearts, she decided to speak freely. "This society is perfectly lovely for all of you, and I too have always enjoyed the privileges of my station. But of late, I have been thinking on the life that is prearranged for a planter's daughter. Do you never shudder at the thought of all those tedious events and races and balls you must organize or attend?"

"Alice Flagg!" Charlotte sputtered.

"Oh, Alice, just you wait," Anna chimed in. "Before the summer has ended, you shall be the happiest person in the world for the plantation life, and you will thank God for his mercies that you were born into it."

"How do you mean?" Alice queried.

"You will be fifteen in the fall, and that is such a milestone. By then you will be ready to welcome all the blessings of your position."

"I expect you are right," Alice said to appease her friends.

8

"Oh, the delights of this island," Charlotte sang out in the pitch of darkness the next morning.

"*Must* we get up now?" Anna asked sleepily.

"Of course," her twin sister answered. "Father has set the example, and we must keep up our usual routine from before sunrise until three o'clock."

Alice was wondering what in the world they did from before sunrise until the three o'clock dinner. The Alstons might be among the richest in the land, but they had some odd habits. She soon became aware of a hurricane wind outside, and put her hands over her ears to shut out the roar. "Are we having a storm?"

"Holy waistcoats!" Charlotte said, laughing. It was clear that Alice had surprised her with the question, since Charlotte rarely used slang. "The tide is not even high."

"That roar is the tide?" Alice asked. "It sounds like the end of the world."

"Your house sits back from the seabeach," Charlotte explained. "But there are only a few lines of dunes between this room and the ocean, and sometimes it sounds as if the sea is rushing in."

Accepting the explanation, Alice then asked why they were rising so early.

Anna said, yawning, "We have to get up with the chickens. Father's goals are accomplished by a tremendous day's work, and he must get started early," Anna explained, her words going mostly into the pillow under a part of her face. "And he expects the very same of us."

Goals. That is what Alice and Madame Le Conte were going to discuss, but the conversation had never taken place. Now Alice would somehow have to get herself through months and months of worries about what her future held, until she could talk with Madame Le Conte in late fall. Numerous, horrible thoughts were running through Alice's head, and she was glad when a servant came to the door of the Room for Females, which had several roughhewn beds lined up against the oceanside wall. Although plantation manor houses were magnificent, and the Charleston homes elegant, beach houses were plain, and it would have been almost sacrilegious to decorate them in any way. "Any of you ladies interested in an early ride on the seabeach?" the servant asked.

The Alston women told the servant, whose name was Cinda, that they were indeed interested, and although Anna was still a little reluctant to leave her bed, she was soon standing at a window, looking out into the darkness and stretching her arms.

"Good. Horses being saddled," Cinda said, who reminded Alice a little of Mary One. "After that, breakfast be on the table. Phoebe be frying chicken now."

"Oooh," Alice swooned. "Fried chicken for breakfast?"

"All that you care to eat," Cinda answered. "There be plenty and Phoebe likes to fry before breakfast all the chicken she plans to use for the day."

Charlotte and Anna wiggled out of their nightgowns, and went to the washstand to bathe with sponges. A painted pitcher, placed in a large bowl, held the clean water, and linen towels were folded nearby. In a few moments they had on colorful dresses, slightly shorter than their ruffled pantalets of the same cloth.

"Can someone close the board?" Alice asked, shivering. It was clear she was not accustomed to a brisk sea breeze blowing into the room.

Charlotte got down on hands and knees, and slipped the board in place, shutting out the wind. In order to bring additional fresh air into the house, sometimes a wide board near the floor was slipped out of its slots so wind could rush in from the ocean. Alice bathed and shimmied into a narrow-skirted dress of green, with ecru jabot. She pulled a silk cloche the color of jonquils over her thick, dark hair to keep it from blowing in the wind. The women left the room in a flurry of excitement, and held to the rails as they made their way down a flight of wooden steps.

By the time the grooms held the horses for the girls to climb up on, light was spreading across the sand that had been washed by the night's tides and redecorated as if a wealthy man had come and generously tossed spiral shells, cockles, olives, and coquinas at random. A line of brown pelicans moved just above the water, their beaks ready to snatch a meal from a wave. The early hour wasn't necessarily as bad as Alice had at first perceived, she thought. She hadn't wanted to crawl from the feather mattress, but now, as she sat on a black horse and surveyed the rinsed-down strand, so pristine, she realized early risers enjoyed some rewards. Just at that moment, she saw the first of the sun, and although she had expected it, the fiery smudge startled her. Everyone was quiet as they watched the panorama, and Alice thought that the sun came up much faster than she had expected. The day that had its beginning in pure darkness had now fully broken.

Charlotte maneuvered her horse in front and called back, "Follow me!"

Anna and Alice galloped behind as they rode a mile or so south on the seabeach. Charlotte's horse slowed down only enough to make a wide turn, and the others followed, heading back to the Alston beach house that was sometimes called "The Castle," a sobriquet chosen to accent the cottage's simplicity. There were many dramatic stories about that house, and Alice turned her full attention to it.

It was of clapboard that had once been whitewashed, but was now mostly gray wood. The roof was high-pitched, and a brick chimney extended from the roof. A porch stretched across the ocean side as well as the inland side of the structure. Several outbuildings made up the compound, one for the kitchen, and another for servants. When they rode to the stepping block to dismount, Cinda was standing on the porch.

"Is breakfast ready?" Charlotte called.

"It be on the table," Cinda called back.

After the horses had been taken away, the women walked up the flight of steps from the sand yard to the wide porch. Alice strolled between Charlotte and Anna, who each put an arm around her shoulders. Alice was liking the Alstons more and more, and she felt now an unutterable gladness to have a few days away from Wachesaw Plantation.

"As we are now in our twenties," Charlotte started to say as they crossed the porch, "Father does not impose any strict rules on us regarding our activities, but Anna and I still hold onto some of our old habits. After breakfast we shall probably begin our usual tasks."

"Like what?" Alice asked.

"We devote ourselves to reading, writing, and practicing our music each day, just as we did when we had a tutor, and after the three o'clock dinner, we do anything of our choice, usually walking on the seabeach."

"What exactly do you have scheduled for today?" Alice queried.

Charlotte stopped at the front door and removed her arm from Alice's shoulders. Anna did the same. "We shall write a page in our journal about our arrival here, and we shall read from a classic for half an hour. We believe our taste has been formed by our morning readings. Today I have chosen Motley's *Rise of the Dutch Republic*. And of course we shall practice the piano."

"And after we prove that we are not going to run wild this week," Anna said in a frivolous tone, "we shall partake of dinner and take a dip in the ocean or read a novel. I have selected some I believe we will relish!"

As they went inside for breakfast with the rest of the family, each of them looked forward to this rigorous schedule they had given themselves, and Alice realized that in such a household her spirits would surely rise to normal. She had superb health and energy, and the Alstons were treating her as one of their family, even to the point of including her in their daily educational activities. They were doing their best to see that she had an enjoyable time at Debordieu.

If Alice didn't delight in every moment here it would not be the Alstons' fault—only the troubling thoughts that swept over her from time to time would be to blame. For no one could completely remove the apprehensions she still felt for the coming fall and the initiation into womanhood that would soon occur. Thank heavens no one had yet prodded her about which planters she especially fancied, for the only image that was dancing in her mind was the lumberman. His name would never be mentioned, for Alice herself did not know it. But as she considered the days that stretched ahead, she reminded herself to abandon all thought of a man who would surely be denied her, and concentrate on enjoying her sojourn on the island. All in all, the days ahead would be as happy as was possible.

Mr. and Mrs. Alston, Joseph, and Maria Young were just sitting down when Alice and the twins came into the dining room. Alice moved forward, then paused behind her chair until Charlotte and Anna reached the table. It was definitely the light, she decided, fascinated as always by the luminous sky over the seabeach. The light dominated the room, and Alice thought that no artist had ever captured light on canvas in quite the same manner as the heavens radiated it. The clean, cool sky was forever associated in her mind with the shining seabeach she had grown up with.

Sitting down briskly between the twins, Alice looked around at the room. The sun and mists had faded everything to a delicate beauty, and the room looked as though it had not changed in a hundred years. Old furniture, old wood, old linens—everything bespoke and smelled of the sea.

As they settled down at the table, Charlotte whispered to Alice that after they went to bed that night she would tell the stories of that creepy house where at least one death had occurred and a hurricane nearly washed away the dwelling with Charlotte and Anna inside!

9

THE FLOORBOARD HAD been removed, and a stiff breeze was coming in from the ocean. Alice pulled a light quilt over her legs and thought how welcome a night of peaceful rest would be after such a strenuous day. She was not accustomed to a day with every minute used in activity. The Alstons were exhausting!

"Alice," Charlotte said in a half-whisper.

"Yes?"

"Would you like to hear the stories now?"

"All right," Alice answered, summoning her best behavior for these women who had been considerate of her in every way.

"We can talk without fear of disturbing others," Anna said, pulling her shoulders up and propping herself on her elbows. "The sea breeze will drown out any noise we make."

"We were babies, but I remember it as if it were yesterday," Charlotte began. "Both Anna and I had nannies, and they took very good care of us."

"Did you have a nanny, Alice?" Anna asked, interrupting the narrative.

"Mercy yes. Doesn't every baby?" Without awaiting a reply, Alice added, "I am thinking how it would have been for your mother, to have twins and a nanny for each of you."

"Our family spent all summer here at Debordieu back then, and sometimes I wish we did now," Charlotte went on, ignoring the break made by her sister and Alice. "Going to Greenville is just too much bother."

"But it wasn't only our family," Anna explained, flopping her head down on a pillow. "All of Grandfather's family came here for the summer. This house was packed and jammed."

"How long did they stay?" Alice asked.

Charlotte thought about the question, then answered, "Until after the rice season. When we returned to the plantation, the rice had been harvested, taken to Charleston, and sold."

"And many people who stayed on the plantation died during the summer months," Anna added. "Every fall when we returned home the first question always was 'Who died?'"

"It is the very same today," Charlotte said, her voice taking on a sympathetic drone. "When someone has the 'country fever,' bandages and a basin are quickly brought for the bloodletting, and calomel is sure to follow. And if by some good fortune the fever runs out of the system, the patient has to swallow tumblers full of Peruvian bark."

"And by the skin of his teeth the patient has escaped a summer funeral," Anna added.

"Oh, it's too awful to contemplate," Alice said. "Go on with the stories of Debordieu. By the way, how did this place get that name?"

"It is so called in honor of an old Frenchman who was the first known person to live here," Charlotte explained.

"Go on, Charlotte. Tell the stories," Anna urged. "My eyelids are closing."

"Well, I shall proceed," Charlotte assured her. "But first I should point out that Grandfather lived at Fairfield Plantation after Clifton burned, except for the winters, which he spent at the Miles Brewton house in Charleston. He was known for his attention to sturdiness in his residences. Even this beach house is built on an underground frame of heavy timber that keeps it safe from wind and wave. Not all beach houses on Debordieu were constructed with a careful eye toward security and fortification."

"Get on with the story about the storm of 1822," Anna said on a yawn.

"As I said, we were here, with our nannies, and our cousin who was only eight months old was here, also with his nanny, and there were others."

"If you are going to tell the story, then tell it," Anna declared, lifting her head.

"And if you wish to go to sleep in your soft nest, twin, go on," Charlotte retorted. "But stop that whining and complaining." Without further delay, she went into the story. "The people who lived nearby were named Meyers, and we could see their house from this one. They were lovely people and we adored them. That October, 1822, the evening was beautiful, and the moon was shining. We looked over and saw the Meyers family in their house with their lamps on. All was fine. But during the night the most destructive, violent storm in the history of South Carolina struck without warning."

"You did not expect it?" Alice asked.

"Not a word had come from the Charleston docks about a cyclone at sea, and we noticed no other clues that would have given us warning. Of course the sea birds may have gone inland without our observing them. But my nanny woke me, and I can remember her holding me to a high window and telling me to look at the Meyers house, which was floating to sea. And the lamps were still on, and the Meyerses were floating out to their deaths."

"Floating out?" Alice repeated.

"Yes. You know that during a hurricane a surge comes in, and the waves are on top of the surge, and that is what does the destruction."

Alice did not have time to answer before Anna mumbled, "Wind does not destroy beach houses, as a rule. It is that storm surge."

"Well the surge came in, and when it went back out it took the Meyers house with it, and Anna and I witnessed it," Charlotte said.

"Oh how awful," Alice said. "I trust this won't be a bad year for cyclones."

"We can withstand any storm if it does not come on the one important day of the year," Charlotte stated.

"And what day is that?" Like Anna, Alice was so sleepy she could hardly hold open her eyes, but she didn't let on.

"The day after the rice has been tied in sheaves and stacked in the stableyard, before it has been cleaned and sent to Charleston. There have been instances of a hurricane washing away a whole year's work if it comes on that day. But as I was telling you, this one came in October, after the rice had been sold."

"Tell Alice about the sun." Anna's voice came from her pillow.

"Oh. The next day the sun came out prettier than ever before. After that violent cyclone. And it was almost like heaping insult on injury, for there in the sun was the destruction, too terrible to even mention."

"Now go into the story about the boy's death," Anna sort of croaked, "and let us go to sleep."

"Joseph Alston, my father's brother who was governor of South Carolina, married Theodosia Burr, the only daughter of Aaron Burr," Charlotte began quickly.

"The man who killed Alexander Hamilton in a duel?" Alice asked.

"The one and the same," Charlotte went on. "Well Theo never really liked South Carolina, although Joseph provided her with everything that John Jacob Astor gave *his* wife. They lived with my grandfather at Clifton, and everybody knows that Clifton was the finest manor house ever built."

"But it burned," Anna said wistfully.

"And Joseph had a fine home on Meeting Street in Charleston, and they went down for the balls and the Jockey races, and all of that. They were the darlings of the Low Country, but Theo was frail, and she was not accustomed to the humidity, and many other things."

"Do not start in with the old superstitions," Anna said, now alert. "I do not wish to hear again about the treatment some of the nurses gave her."

"They did everything possible to keep up her health, but the only thing that restored her was the birth of her son, Aaron Burr Alston—'Gampy,' they called him. But even then Theodosia could not remain strong. And when her health failed, *really* failed, Grandfather insisted that Joseph and Theo and our cousin Gampy come here, to this house, for a time of relaxation. It was while they were here that Gampy fell ill with the fever and died. Theo just went into a fit of hysteria, and her condition worsened. Joseph was then governor, and he could think of nothing to do except to send Theo to New York to visit her father. He outfitted a sailing vessel, *The Patriot,* and off Theo went, carrying with her a portrait of her and trunks of her silk and lace gowns. But *The*

Patriot was never heard from again. And Uncle Joseph died shortly thereafter. It was a terrible blow to our family. Three deaths,
pop, pop, pop, just like that. It nearly killed Grandfather but he
lived until ten years ago."

"And the child actually died here in this house?" Alice asked.

"Likely in this very room," Charlotte added.

"Oh aren't you the one for drama," Anna said. "This room had
nothing to do with it!"

"And how do *you* know? It *could* have been this room."

"Theo was so beautiful, according to Grandfather," Anna said
reflectively. "Her gowns and jewels came from Paris, and could
she dance! It has been said that there was never a lovelier young
woman than Theo, when she dipped and twirled in a waltz. Others would move back and form a ring around the room to watch."

"Oh do let us not go to sleep on such a sad note," Alice said. "I
shall dream all night of the storm and the deaths."

"Do you actually remember what you dream, Alice?" Charlotte
asked.

"Of course I do! I think dreams are sort of like special mes-
sages, at least sometimes, and I try to remember them."

"Then we shall talk of something else before we sleep," Charlotte said. "We will talk of school."

"School!" Anna wailed. "Then *I* shall have nightmares. I never
liked school, and you did not either, Charlotte."

"School was not so awful," Charlotte answered. "Father built us
a little two-room schoolhouse in a sunny spot. Each room had a
fireplace, and our tutor kept splendid fires burning in the winter,
as there was always a large supply of oak wood. We went at nine
and remained until two, and during those hours cake and tea
came in on a big silver waiter carried by the butler." Charlotte
slowly reconstructed the scene in her mind, as it had been several
years since the twins had attended any school.

"Alice, do you have a tutor?" Anna asked.

"I have had several, but none right at this moment. However I
have had the most marvelous music teacher at Brookgreen,
Madame Le Conte. She had to return to her home in France
suddenly, but will resume my lessons this autumn."

Now Alice was again thinking wistfully of Madame. Outside the
windows and beyond the dunes the waves were approaching the
high tide line, and so were her days sweeping on towards another

time. Life was fickle! One had to grab for the things one sought, and if one missed the catch, the years passed.

Could it be that she might never see Madame again—or the lumberman, for that matter? And if she never saw them again, never again glimpsed the free lives that they enjoyed, would God reward her in some way? She listened to the running tide, whooshing in, running back, whooshing in further, running back again. Somewhere near the Waccamaw River, only miles from Debordieu, the lumberman lay sleeping. And on the seas were schooners carrying away Carolina pine, cypress, and oak, carefully dressed by him. Was she, like these schooners laden with wood, moving away from the lumberman and all the other simple joys these shores held? As she reflected, Alice noticed that Charlotte and Anna had now fallen into rhythmic breathing and were deep in repose. But Alice, with her thoughts awhirl, was not even drowsy.

Morning came, and the day began with a ride on the seabeach, followed by breakfast. The women were by no means idle, as they wrote in journals, read from the classics, practiced piano, and after dinner took a glorious dip in the surf. In the evening they again rode horses on the seabeach, stopping at a remote place to sit on a dune and identify as many different species of birds as they could. Later, they made notes in their journals about their bird watching. It was one of the best accounts of the week, they believed.

When the days of living on the island ended, Alice felt as though she had been given a dose of restorative medicine. She had come to learn that the life of the rice planters was certainly an envied one. Who else in the land could live the enchanting lives of the Alstons? And how the women had flavored each moment with their individual gusto! They had learned the secrets to accepting life as it came to a person, and they were not above giving thanks to God for his blessings.

Sometimes Alice thought back on her time at home with her mother and brothers, especially Allard. Had she misjudged them? Had she been blind to all that was available to her? Had she inherited the same characteristics as Allard, whom everybody knew to be unchangeable, obdurate? She hoped not. But from now on she would keep the life-style of the Alstons at the forefront of her thinking, and she would use them as a model for her own happiness.

Perhaps it was divine providence that had taken away Madame Le Conte, for Alice was now feeling generally contented with this life of luxury at Debordieu. She was going to have to sort out her feelings; she wanted to do it soon. She realized that rice harvest time would come almost before she knew it, and she would likely be urged to go to Charleston with Allard when he took his best, long-grain rice to market. And Charleston society life was surely the grandest of all.

FALL 1848

10

ALLARD FLAGG SAT bolt upright in the vessel being propelled by six liveried oarsmen, and he felt a little pompous after receiving such a high price for his rice. The fall trip to Charleston was usually favorable as the rice from Wachesaw brought a sky-high price in England, and his factor always held out for the best price going, but this time his capital had grown even more. Swelled with a feeling of complete satisfaction, he now forgave his mother who had insisted on going to the sale and taking Alice with her.

Alice had actually looked forward to accompanying her brother and mother to Charleston, and she had even gone so far as to visit the most exclusive dressmaker and order several dresses fitted over a hooped petticoat, the latest rage in England. But the one in which she'd shown the most interest was a creation of white that flowed gently as she moved about the dressmaker's room, glancing at herself in several mirrors as she dance-stepped around. It was so like the gowns she had seen in *Vanity Fair*, a periodical sold in New York hotels, and other places. The white satin dress had a white lace overskirt, with a skirt flounce and also a flounce below the high neck. Narrow strips of black lace accented them. Alice had been glad that there was only one ruffle on the skirt, for a hoop was underneath and it would fit her small frame more suitably than a skirt of two or three flounces.

As Alice pranced around the dressmaker's in this dress, she was actually remembering Madame Le Conte's appearance in lovely

gowns that moved gracefully around her ankles as she walked
from the piano to the window and back to her student. The picture of that orderly, gallant woman would be with her always, and
she longed to talk with her and study every movement of her
proud gait, so like a thoroughbred horse she was, and learn of her
background, her family, her goals, and how she had achieved
them. The days were passing quickly, bringing ever closer the day
that Madame would again be teaching piano in the Brookgreen
Plantation ballroom.

"My dear," Mrs. Flagg asked her daughter as the vessel glided
on, "are you picturing yourself as you waltz around in your white
dress at the St. Cecilia ball this winter?"

"Oh Mother!" Alice's green eyes flashed. "You know I love the
Hermitage so much that I *never* want to leave. There's something
about Charleston I detest, but, yes, I suppose as always I'll go to
the St. Cecilia ball."

Mrs. Flagg fanned her face with a hand and took several deep
breaths. *How long was it going to take Alice to grow up?* Surely she
should appreciate what a great social opportunity the ball afforded to young marriageable women. Alice could certainly have
the planter of her choice if she only spent a little effort. This ball
would introduce Alice to many suitable men. Their interest would
be great, considering Alice was not only the most poised and
elegant of young women, but was also from one of the choicest of
rice plantations. Everyone knew that the Flaggs of Wachesaw were
millionaires.

Alice stole a glance at Allard, wondering what he was thinking.
His thoughts were surely on the fortune he had made from the
recent yield of rice, and Alice was pleased she had agreed to
accompany him on this trip. Just then he said in a brittle voice,
"I'm going to stop at the Buck sawmill."

Alice's hand automatically went to her face. Did Allard mean
that sawmill—where the handsome lumberman worked? She had
not seen him all summer. "Oh, oh," she uttered.

"Be calm, my dear," her mother soothed. "Your brother can
make the stop now and save himself a visit to the sawmill later."

Alice looked quickly to see which dress she had on, and she was
pleased with her choice. Her traveling suit of tapered skirt, shirtwaist, and tailored jacket gave her a look of maturity as well as
understated elegance. She was also relieved that the oarsmen had

met the family in Georgetown so they wouldn't have to complete the journey on that clumsy rice boat. She was in the very same vessel, operated by the same oarsmen, in which the lumberman had previously seen her. "Why is Allard stopping here?" she asked.

Allard did not give his mother time to answer the question. "Because I need some lumber for a chapel I intend to build for our people."

Alice thought about the servants she dearly loved, such as Mary One. It was time they had a chapel where they could worship in their own manner, and sing the old songs they had composed. Her eyes went to the oarsmen, dressed as usual in their turquoise satin suits. One was humming "Honey in the Rock." "I think it's fine, Allard," she said. "Do you plan an elaborate church?"

"Not so elaborate, but graceful," Dr. Flagg answered. "I should like lancet windows and a high-pitched roof with some filigree, perhaps." Just then he indicated to the oarsmen to turn the boat toward the shore. When it pulled to a stop at the dock, he assisted his mother from the vessel and walked her to shore, where she stood under a tree affording shade.

Alice held up her skirts and put a hand on her hat to keep it from blowing off as she stepped ashore. When she looked up, there ready to assist her was the lumberman, and he was more handsome than she remembered.

"The sun's a-coming down," he said. "There's a shed you can rest in."

"Oh, no," she answered, a little shaken. "I'll stand over there. By Mother."

"I am Quitman Buck, but my family and friends call me Whit," he said, as he and Alice alternately stared at each other, neither of them acknowledging that they had ever seen the other.

Alice went to her mother and stood demurely, her eyes on the wood dock, but gradually her green eyes lifted and moved in the direction of the young lumberman. Her heart beat a little frenziedly as she squinted at him, trying to examine his face. His blue eyes were large and soft, and seemed wise, but somewhere behind them there lurked an irrepressible merriment and frolic. The large, sturdy body was still moving as rhythmically as it had when he tied up the boat, but now he was carefully stacking logs that had arrived at the sawmill by a flatboat, riding at anchor.

Alice made an effort to divert her attention, but she was quite unable to do so. Whit was six feet three inches if he was a foot, and he was now looking at her. The smile which was spreading over his face brought dimples to his cheeks, and his face had taken on an amazing vitality.

Suddenly he called to a helper, "These logs are ready for the debarker." Now the young giant had turned back toward her and was actually walking in her direction. Although some of his genial good humor was transferring itself to her, Alice reminded herself that she must not let her mother note her interest in Whit. It seemed the hardest thing in the world not to return his open smile.

"Miss Alice Flagg," he greeted her, bowing his head slightly but with a rakish grin. Alice realized that for the first time in her life she had met someone who loved life and lived it to the fullest without the obligatory regimentation of the rice planters. How refreshing! She was completely intrigued and mystified by him.

She did not know if he intended to strike up a conversation, and with her mother right beside her, she felt awkward. Surely Mrs. Flagg would be able to tell that her daughter and this lumberman had encountered each other before.

"How did you know?" Mrs. Flagg asked, jutting out her delicate chin a little.

"I have seen her . . . more than once."

Alice's eyes glowed, and all of the fatigue and monotony of the return trip from Charleston miraculously evaporated, like smoke in the wind.

Mrs. Flagg's tone took on a sharper edge. "We are quite familiar with the Buck sawmills, young man, and you are to be commended for the success you have achieved here in the South Carolina Low Country. However, the virgin pines and cypress and oak trees are God's work, and the Bucks just happened to arrive from Maine at an appropriate time to mill the lumber."

"Mother!" Alice was astounded by her mother's lack of tact.

"We Bucks are hard workers, Mrs. Flagg," Whit explained. "And we *are* making our fortune here in South Carolina from the pines and cypress and oaks. But we are decent, God-fearing people." He paused, thinking that for all his directness and honesty, Mrs. Flagg would be difficult to impress. Whit lowered his voice. "I know I have not been tutored by instructors from England,

France, and Germany, as Miss Alice has, and I am not a member of Charleston's St. Cecilia Society, but there is little about any Buck that you should be ashamed of, and I would like your permission to call on Miss Alice at Wachesaw."

Mrs. Flagg swallowed deeply and cleared her throat several times as she tried to think of a response that would be less cutting than the words forming in her mind. There was a small silence, and just then Allard walked over and announced that he had completed his business dealings and was ready to depart. He motioned to his oarsmen to take their places in the boat. Mrs. Flagg took Alice's arm and turned her in the direction of the vessel, and within minutes they were on their way as if nothing had happened.

That night Mrs. Flagg went to Alice's room and found her daughter standing at a window, gazing at the North Star and the Big Dipper above the silhouetted moss-draped oak trees. "I know where your thoughts are, Alice," Mrs. Flagg said. "They are on that man whom you observed in the most flagrant way today at the Buck sawmill."

Alice turned. "As a matter of fact, Mother, I *was* thinking of Whit Buck."

"I was horribly embarrassed this afternoon," Mrs. Flagg said. "You looked at that man so . . . so outrageously."

"Don't you mean *adoringly*, Mother?"

Mrs. Flagg was taken aback by her daughter's directness, and she fixed Alice with a hard stare. "He is a common lumberman, Alice, and you must save yourself for a rice planter. You know that."

"I only know, Mother, that you and Allard want me to become a grand lady, and a rich one, as the wife of a planter."

Mrs. Flagg sat down on the bed, her eyes reflective. "You are a precious child, a lovely daughter, but misguided at the moment. You talk as though we wish to condemn you to some empty existence. But you shall certainly come back to your senses and see that I and your brother want only the best for you as we guide you to save yourself for a rice planter worthy of the daughter of Wachesaw Plantation."

Mrs. Flagg scrutinized her daughter, thinking that Alice was indeed an original, but she would not rest until she had straightened out her daughter's quirks of heart and mind. She would use whatever method was necessary to restore Alice to her former mellowness. This disrespect for the Southern aristocracy was simply a phase, and it would pass. By next month Alice would be an adult, seasoned and mature enough for marriage. And she and Allard had no intention of allowing her to make the unparalleled mistake of becoming interested in a common lumberman.

Soon Mrs. Flagg decided to drop the subject for the time, rather than incite her daughter further through scolding. After her mother withdrew, Alice continued gazing out her window.

She remembered the manatee that had come ashore once on the seabeach. The unusual animal with two flippers in front and a spoon-shaped tail was a curiosity, and the plantation workers called it a "merman." They believed in mermaids, and from that day on declared that a merman lived in the ocean near Wachesaw.

When Alice's father saw the manatee he said they had to get it back into the water, as it was out of its element on the sand. With the help of Allard and Arthur, he carried the animal in his arms as they stepped into the high tide and moved toward deeper water. Alice had touched the tail, and she'd never forgotten the feel. In a way it was like leather and yet the same as stone, or marble. But she had only a fleeting touch, as she was cautioned to go back, away from the water. She had walked to the top of a dune and watched as the animal was turned loose, and for a moment it seemed unbalanced and unsure of itself.

Alice had closed her eyes and prayed for the manatee to go on its way, and when she opened her eyes, it was still floundering. She prayed again. And then, before her eyes, it sped off, and she heard her father's voice saying the animal was on its way back to its home on the Gulf Coast.

Alice had turned her head so her father and brothers would not poke fun at her for crying. But the tears were joyful ones, for she was delighted to see the animal slide through the blue-green waters, making its way to its desired destination.

As if a sort of transformation were taking place, Alice now thought of her sense of place. If her future looked brutal and frightening, what was there to keep her from dipping a toe into new waters? Or was she now so strongly held by that powerful and compelling family into which she had been born that she would always be a part of it, and do its bidding as naturally as breathing? Could she venture onto her own course, as the manatee had done, and begin a courtship with the forbidden lumberman who now had completely taken over her heart?

If she chose to try to extricate herself from her social "obligations," she would be entering unknown territory, for she knew of no other plantation daughter who had chosen such a pathway. Would the departure be worth it? She did not know, but she smiled to herself.

Alice turned her thoughts to the members of her family. How they were ruled by the social restraints of their position! Unlike them, Alice vowed, she would one day blow her trumpet toward the sky, for life as she saw it was too short to waste, and she would follow the natural path which her heart dictated. She would be the one who would venture beyond the breakers into a placid place where others dared not come.

All of it really did hang on Madame Le Conte's advice now, and whatever Madame did to leave her family behind, Alice would do the same. Such a pathway had been cleared by Madame, and all Alice had to do was to find it. She would not go to another country as Madame had done, nor even another county, but she would move to a different plateau, and there she would live her own existence, and the muscular lumberman would surely play a part of the drama.

Alice would wander away from her family's fold and claim the new land as her own. There would be no tumultuous returning of the prodigal daughter. And it all would happen with the aid of Madame Le Conte.

The next day, after spending a restless night in her bed, Alice requested that Egypt be saddled for a ride on the seabeach. It was not long before she and the sleek animal were on their way. For the first hour of the ride, Alice thought some more of the consequences of her new emotions for Whit.

If she made a move to withdraw from the expectations of the planter aristocracy, her mother would refer to her as being "not quite right," and "a little unbalanced." Allard would look on her as being a burden, a smear on the Flagg name. Arthur, he would love her she supposed, but would probably go along quietly with the censure of the others. It would be desolate, that place she would carve for herself, without a family to sustain her.

And yet . . . when she thought of Madame Le Conte the music of Mozart, Bach, and Chopin filled her ears. The meter of Egypt's hoofs now took the tempo of the notes played by the soft, white hands of Madame as they flew over the keys, and Alice ascended to another level of pleasure, as though the horse had the wings of Pegasus.

For the next hour Alice's only thoughts were of Whit, but finally it was time to turn back. Rushing home with utmost speed and exertion always brought a liveliness to Alice's heart, and she usually sat tall and straight, the sound of the surf at her back. But today, it was different. The indecision that had torn her nearly to pieces still plagued her. Her family wasn't confined only to the Flaggs, but it extended throughout the South Carolina Low Country. The planters were like a family, and as she thought about it, Alice realized that every member of the gentry knew her grandfather's name. If she broke with her family in favor of the lumberman, she would be breaking from everyone she knew and everything they stood for.

That old proverb from the fourteenth century came back to her: *Rather to bow than break is profitable; humility is a thing commendable.* Or had Chaucer been correct when he said nothing ventured, nothing gained? Madame would know, and Alice would just wait until she had the opportunity to discuss the matter with that worldly woman.

Several days later, Alice was sitting on the white-pillared porch, gazing at the almost imperceptible ridge where the ocean and sky met, when she heard hoofs. She arose, lifted her green skirts, and flew down the steps to see who was approaching the Hermitage. To her utter surprise, there was Whit Buck, prancing a spirited stallion to a stop.

"Whit! Can it *really* be you?"

"It is I, Miss Alice, and not a ghost. I . . . I wanted to see you, and if I had arranged it in advance, there might have been some unpleasant consequences, considering the impression your family has of me." Whit slid off his black stallion.

"I have been thinking of you as well, I confess, but as you probably know," Alice said, her eyes glancing around to see if anyone was in sight, "my brother and my mother would not think our meeting like this is respectable."

"I have considered that, but under the circumstances still feel that we should talk. Where can we go?"

Alice looked around again, wringing her hands with apprehension. If Dr. Flagg happened to come home from the rice fields at this moment, he would surely harm Whit Buck. "I must be losing my senses due to being at the height of confusion, but help me on your horse and let us go to the seabeach."

Whit led his stallion to a stepping-stone, where he quickly jumped up on the animal, and reaching down he pulled Alice up in front of him. In a flash they were off, the wind blowing against their flushed faces. Alice knew that her action was quite irrational, but she didn't care. At this moment she was feeling the strength of Whit Buck on whom she was leaning, and it was more delightful than anything she had ever known. It came to her that she would lie, cheat, steal—do anything she would have to do to foster the friendship of this man, this man whom she couldn't deny that she *loved*.

After racing through rows of high dunes where thick sea oats waved in the breeze, they came to the sandy beach. Whit looked around and finally saw a scrub pine where he could tie his horse, Bootblack. "Do you think it will be safe to walk on the sand? I would dislike for your brother to spot us and make your life miserable. In such an event, mine would be even more miserable."

"Allard rarely comes here," Alice answered. "He has a 'fish boy' who takes a small boat out to sea each day to catch the fish for our table. But he has completed that task for this day."

They strolled along slowly, each intensely aware that this was their first moment alone together. "I have been anxious to learn all about you. Tell me about your life," Whit said.

"There is little to tell. I am a planter's daughter, and my brother and my mother expect me to become the mistress of a plantation soon, although I find myself balking more every day."

"Why do you detest the plan?"

"I don't truly know. I am simply not like the rest of them—the Flaggs and the other planter families. Allard will surely marry Penelope Ward of Brookgreen Plantation, and the wedding will be a glorious occasion. Arthur will more than likely marry Georgeanna, of the same family."

"To unite Wachesaw and Brookgreen will be a national event," Whit said, a little sarcastically.

"Oh, I cannot bear the thought of all that extravagance, sometimes. I am realizing that my satisfaction comes from simpler things. I wish my family would allow me to enjoy those things."

Whit nodded mutely and picked up a seashell. He gazed at it for a second, then threw it as far as he could into the ocean. A mournful expression had spread across his face. "Have you thought of confronting your family about your feelings?" Without waiting for an answer, Whit added, "Surely they can bend to your wishes."

"Allard and Mother are concerned only with wealth and position," Alice answered. "They do not seem to consider that sometimes happiness lies beyond those factors."

Whit took out his pocket watch and looked at the time. It was almost three o'clock, and he knew that three o'clock was the time that dinner was served in plantation manor houses. He looked at Alice. What a face! So full of excitement, expectation, and yes, even happiness. "And you consider happiness a necessary ingredient to life?"

"I do. Oh, I do. I believe happiness is the most important ingredient. But I do not know what is in store for me if I pursue it rather than follow my family's desires."

Whit nodded, admiring the brave determination of this girl. But as he tried to picture her escaping the expectations of a plantation daughter, the vision soon faded into the air. He could not see how she would ever in her life change her fate. He shook his head, vaguely irritated with himself for not having a solution to the problem.

"Please do wipe that frown off your handsome face," Alice chided.

The gloom didn't leave Whit as he memorized Alice's face in order to bring her quickly to mind when he was at the sawmill. She had the Flagg nobility, but there was also a purity and innocence in her countenance. The look etched itself in his memory and he would take it with him when he left. For that moment their eyes had met and locked and neither of them seemed able to look away, but finally Alice dropped her head. "Will I see you again?"

"Seeing you again is the most urgent matter to me," he answered. "May I meet you here tomorrow?"

"Of course. But do not come to the house; come straight to the seabeach. I shall be here."

"Do you want me to take you home?"

"No," Alice answered. "You must ride away quickly, and I will stroll home, as though I have been alone with my thoughts."

11

ALTHOUGH A NOR'EASTER had passed over during the night, the sun was shining brightly, sparkling the choppy water. As Alice strode the seabeach, her manner brisk and her face composed, she was vastly relieved when she detected the sound of a horse's hoofs. Whit *was* coming. It hadn't been a dream.

She watched him as he tied Bootblack and ran to her, his face and arms slightly sunburned. Alice shook her head. As strange as it seemed to her, this was the kind of man she had envisioned for herself in her childish fantasies. Tall, broad-shouldered, straight, his black hair gleaming and his blue eyes vivid against the tanned skin, she could hardly believe they had found each other. When he came closer, Whit bowed from the waist in a grand gesture, and said, "Would the belle of Wachesaw care for a stroll on the seabeach?"

"I was afraid you would not come," she admitted. "I was beginning to believe it was a dream."

"It is very real," he answered. "Why, there is a snakeskin hanging on a limb of the pine tree."

"Is it hanging belly-side-up?"

"How did you know?" Whit asked. "Did you see it or are you a student of the transmundane?"

"Oh you are impossible," Alice teased. "To answer your question, some of the old people believe that if one comes upon a snakeskin and hangs it belly-side-up on a limb, rain will follow."

"*Very* absorbing, as we had rain last night."

"Yes. I have come to believe that many of the old superstitions have a germ of truth in them. I remember once when I came upon Michael One, Mary's husband, when he was hanging a snakeskin on a limb. He said, 'We be short on rain. Hang snakeskin belly-side-up, rain come.'"

"And did rain follow?" Whit asked.

"A drenching downpour. But it was no surprise. As I said, the old superstitions have a germ of truth, and that is a way of life with many of the people who live on the plantation."

"That man was doing what came naturally," Whit said with a gentle smile.

"Yes. Isn't it shameful that all of us cannot do what comes naturally?" Alice asked, and then was sorry she had brought up a subject so gloomy for the bright day. She was relieved when Whit let it pass.

"Does your brother own other properties?" he asked eventually.

"Yes. He is the master of Oak Lawn, on Sandy Island."

"Does he spend much time there?"

"No. He employs an overseer, and goes there only to supervise the planting and harvesting of rice."

"The Flaggs of Wachesaw are in an elite class," Whit said. "Their rules are strict."

His words, spoken without rancor, pierced Alice's brain and touched her so deeply she felt a stab of pain somewhere near her heart. Whit Buck had every reason to hate the practices of the planters, and even despise the Flaggs, as her mother had tried to hurt him the other day. But he bore no hostility. Here was a man who loved the sea, the land, and the sky, and he was as free of pretense as the gulls that ascended and dived above their heads. That face, solid and peaceful, reflected everything good. It was a clear image of love and happiness with no whisper of desire for power and wealth. But in her house the concern for status suggested itself everywhere, and she was suddenly uneasy.

Observing Alice's embarrassment, Whit said softly, "Would you like to tell me something of your family? If you do, I'm a-listening."

She hesitated.

"You don't have to be sheepish," Whit said, in an effort to put things in perspective. "It is life. Those fortunate enough to own great tracts of land that border tidal rivers can become million-aires from rice production. However, some of us must make a livelihood from the pines by producing pitch, tar, turpentine, and dressing and selling lumber."

Alice's eyes were clouded briefly by a haunting sorrow. "It is true that I am from the aristocracy, but I do not subscribe to all of their beliefs. However, I must tell you that I am very proud of our plantation as my ancestors worked like tigers to clear those rice fields and make them produce in good seasons and bad."

"You would be less of a person if you were not proud of your plantation," Whit interjected, while walking at a steady pace.

"This is the way it started," Alice said reflectively. "Dr. Henry Collins Flagg of Rhode Island had served in this region as a surgeon in General Nathanael Greene's army, and at the end of the Revolutionary War he married the widow who owned Brookgreen plantation. The marriage proved to be a happy one, and Henry and Rachel had a son who became a physician and later had nine children, and I am one of the nine, but only three of us survived to maturity. However, the way Allard came to own Wachesaw was through a gift from my uncle, the Reverend James L. Belin—he still lives in the big manor house on the river."

"Who was your mother before she married your father?"

"She was Margaret Elizabeth Belin, and my father was Dr. Ebenezer Flagg."

"When did your father die?"

"Ten years ago, in 1838."

Whit took Alice's hand, and his grip was firm. "It is a distinguished family, and I want you to know that I understand their motives in desiring that you marry within the planter community."

Alice's heart dropped at the mention of such a marriage, but nevertheless she kept her face calm and made an attempt to appear untroubled. "You know it is not truly my desire."

Whit stopped walking and his blue eyes searched Alice's green ones thoughtfully. He scrutinized this young woman who was being so solicitous of him, helping him along more generously than she would ever know. "I have a gift for you," he said.

Whit took from his pocket a simple, silver ring. He made no effort to place it on Alice's finger, as it was given as a token of his affection for her, and he desired that she have something to hold, to look at, to remind her of him.

Alice's eyes darted to the silver ring. She beheld it with uncon-
cealed curiosity. It wasn't grand like many of the rings she had
seen, but it had a certain appeal.

Alice instinctively knew that Whit was giving her a gift, and not
an engagement ring. What else would this man give her for a gift
except a piece of jewelry? she asked herself. He knew nothing of
the flowers and white gloves young men gave women who were
about to attend a ball. There was no way he would know about
things like that, and the act of giving her a gift of a ring was likely
one of the most poignant examples of the differences between the
aristocracy and the lumber dealers. She took the ring and held it
in her hand, realizing that by accepting this gift she was sanction-
ing his way of life, accepting it as approval.

Although the ring was unembossed and almost a pretense of
the other rings she had seen, it was a declaration of Whit's regard
for her. But as much as she had desired such a pronouncement,
there was deep within her a warning that if she was receptive to
this tender advance by Whit, she was forever changing her standard, her life. She looked up at him, and Whit's face was all but
bursting with devotion for her. Endearment, even passion, came
from every pore. Although he wasn't saying a word, his intentions
were earsplitting: *Please accept my gift. I love you.*

As Alice thought about it, she realized that she had wanted this
man from the first time she saw him. Night after night her eyes
had stared into the darkness as she pictured him standing on the
dock or bluff at the sawmill. Trying to reconcile her attraction to a
lumberman with the expectations of her station had been pure
agony. She had thought that the only route was through Madame
Le Conte, and now it was happening so quickly and so easily, and
without the help of any other person.

And yet . . . there was something about all of it that wasn't as she
had pictured. From the bottom of her heart she loved Whit, there
was no question about that now, but as he handed her the gift, he
was in a way saying, *Make my way, your way.* Until this moment she
had not fully recognized how complicated the situation was.

Oh how arrogant he must think I am, Alice was thinking. She
must appear to be like Allard, with a heart of iron. But she wasn't
like Allard in any way, and she never wanted to be like him, or any
of the planter race. They were materially ambitious. She had no
desire to be one of "the quality," the "superior people."

The answer had finally come to her from the depths of her heart. She desired *his* way. How could she have been so blind as to resist acceptance of the ring for even a second? she wondered. With a stab of surprise Alice was aware that Whit intended to marry her at some later time. "I accept your gift with deepest gratitude," she said in a most gentle voice. "But I must tell you that I cannot display it. As you must know, my family would not approve."

Whit placed his fingers over her lips. "Say no more about your family. I understand perfectly."

"But I shall put a velvet ribbon through it and wear it around my neck, concealed by my clothing," she said, picturing the path ahead of her as leading only to the time when she would become Whit's wife. "This ring shall rest over my heart."

12

THE NEXT MORNING Alice awakened early, realizing as she slipped into consciousness that she was frowning. *What problem was weighing on her mind?* And then it came to her. Her brother and her mother surely hated Whit Buck, and she could not speak to them of her love for the lumberman.

Suddenly she remembered the ring and her hand went automatically to her heart. As if by some miracle, with her hand over the ring, life was now bright and shining and splendid, and she would see that it was always so. She made a declaration to herself: no person—not her mother, not Allard, or anyone else—would take away the happiness she had found in Whit.

It did not matter a snap to her that he was not exactly a pillar of the community or the backbone of an Old South plantation, but what did rattle her brain was how she would refrain from speaking his name. Of course she could talk to Mary One about anything, and Mary would be the person in whom she would confide, but perhaps now and then she could speak in a casual way of the lumber business and feel the warmth that flooded her body at the thought of Whit Buck. As she pulled herself out of bed and dressed in a long gray skirt and white ruffled blouse, Alice was thinking that Whit was everything she'd ever dreamed of in a man.

"Allard, has the lumber you ordered from the sawmill arrived?" she asked bravely as she ate breakfast with Allard and her mother. Arthur had remained at the Hermitage, having completed his

Charleston coursework, but was away from the house at the moment.

Allard took the time to spread orange marmalade on a thick slice of bread before answering, and his sister observed his inflexible mouth. A dull flush came to her face as she thought that he may be suspicious of her interest in the subject, and she added quickly, "I only wondered how the progress on the slave chapel is coming along."

Allard drank deeply of the dark coffee in his porcelain cup. "It is unusual for you to take an interest in plantation matters, but the answer is yes. The cypress lumber has arrived and work on the building should start immediately."

Wondering what to say next, Alice observed her brother. He was small-boned for a man, but there was no question that he had a cool and refined mind, which was quite brilliant. He could also ride and shoot like the gentleman he was, and he owned so many guns that he gave them names and won so many tournaments at the Georgetown Rifle Club that he had declared he would decline future invitations to participate in the competition. As she thought about it, he appeared rather the peacock today in his smart bottle-green coat and highly polished boots. "But as we have such exceptional cypress trees on the plantation, why did you order the lumber from the sawmill?"

"The rice crop is in for this year, but that does not mean that the work is done. My workers are clearing a forty-acre field for next year's crop, and I do not want them to lose time with the work. With all the talk on the Charleston docks of a hurricane at sea, I would not like them scattered about in the woods, cutting cypress trees when the lumber can be obtained from Buck's sawmill."

"You always work out everything to the fullest," Mrs. Flagg said to her son. "It is such a blessing to me that my living children have taken the time to cultivate their minds and are endowed with the gentility and courtesy expected of them."

Alice threw her mother a scathing look, feeling compelled to defend herself. "Don't you mean your living *sons*, Mother?"

Mrs. Flagg inclined her head toward her daughter. "I am proud of *all* my children."

Alice had tightened her mouth unconsciously, and a small knot of anger twisted her face. "I am afraid my qualities are not what you expected in your only surviving daughter."

"Don't carry on so expansively, Alice," Allard snapped.

"Now that is the pot calling the kettle black if ever I heard it," Alice answered, making no attempt to calm herself. She turned to her mother and asked, "Has Allard always been so . . . so jarring?"

Mrs. Flagg considered Alice's question seriously for a moment. "Yes, I think he has. Arthur is the quiet one, but Allard has always been outspoken."

"Well I am glad you admit that another of your children is not perfect," Alice said, shaking her head.

"Alice," her mother soothed, "Allard is right. Don't carry on so. We are all proud of you. I am especially pleased that you are now giving more attention to your wardrobe, ordering those lovely dresses in Charleston."

Just at that moment Mary One cleared her throat, and the others turned and saw her standing in the doorway, holding a piece of cloth she had weaved.

"That material is lovely, Mary," Mrs. Flagg said, her face still a little tense from the heated discussion.

Alice's eyes regarded Mary blindly as she wondered how much of the conversation Mary had heard. She appeared not to have heard anything, but one could never tell. Mary's face was stern in its fixity of purpose as she brought the cloth closer for Mrs. Flagg to examine.

"You have done an excellent job," Mrs. Flagg said. "Take it to the seamstresses and have them make a lap robe for me."

"I should like a lap robe made of that too," Alice said, rising from the table. "Do you think you could make some cloth for me?"

"Child, you knows I'll do anything for you," Mary answered.

"That is the God's truth," Allard cut in. "You have taken care of Alice and jumped at her every whim since the day she was born."

"Allard!" Mrs. Flagg objected at her son's ungracious tone, then glanced at Mary. "Some silks and dresses will be arriving from Charleston, as well as some China teas and other objects. When the barrels arrive, would you attend to Alice's dresses?"

It didn't escape Alice that her mother wished to remind her of all the fancy items the daughter of Wachesaw was able to enjoy.

"You know, Mary," Allard said, "you people are going to have your own chapel soon."

"You mean . . . place where to pray? Have prayer meetings? Shouts?"

"Precisely. You can have all the shouts you desire when the building is completed, and the carpenters should be starting it right away, perhaps today even."

"Marse Allard," Mary answered, "what be the name of that church?"

"I don't care. Name it what you like."

"Pearly Gates?"

"Pearly Gates sounds fine to me. It is *your* church."

"Will Parson Glennie come?" Mary wanted to know.

"Dr. Glennie has told me he will hold services in the little church at least once each month, and he intends to instruct the children."

Mary turned to go, and Alice thought she heard Mary say something about her twins learning the "Postle's Crease." Perhaps she had been a little abrupt with her brother as she thought about it. He was doing a rather thoughtful thing in providing a church for the slaves. With their very own building, they would have a place to worship in their very own way. And she intended to attend services with them, if they would allow it. Nothing was more pleasing to Alice's ears than the songs and prayers offered by the slaves.

"Allard," his mother asked, "how did you come up with the idea of building a slave chapel?"

"It was not my idea, but Dr. Glennie's."

"Dr. Glennie is the most lovable minister ever to come to All Saints Church," Alice added.

"Dr. Glennie has asked all planters to construct chapels for their people," Allard explained. "Although it is a long way, and probably an arduous journey on horseback, he plans to hold services at each chapel at least once a month, and he will teach others how to officiate when he cannot come."

"Allard," Alice said softly, "you are to be commended for building the church. It will make the most profound difference in their lives."

"Well," he responded casually, "this confluence is over. I am getting on with my plans."

"What do you plan to do today?" his mother asked.

"Have you forgotten that this is Friday?"

"Of course. You will be having dinner at the Hot and Hot Fish Club."

A sudden quiver rocked Alice as she remembered mocking that

club at Debordieu over the summer. Elaborate meals were served there by liveried servants. Waccamaw planters would come to bowl and play billiards in the comfortable clubhouse each Friday from June to mid-October. That club was nothing more than a social gathering from all that she had been able to ascertain. There was a universe of more important things to be done. For one thing, he could supervise the building of the slave chapel. "How does going to the Hot and Hot Fish Club each Friday enhance your ability to run this plantation?" she heard herself say.

Allard answered swiftly. "We planters are hardworking men who run huge estates, and we *do* require periods of relaxation, if you can understand that."

Reflecting on Allard's role as master of the household, Alice said, "It *does* take some time to relax from the burdens of your life, Allard. Of course you *do* have help with all that you do. Your body servant, Hector, brings coffee to your bed in the mornings, presses your clothes, shines your boots, saddles your horse, and attends to your hounds, not to mention making your mint juleps in the summer and hot toddies in the winter. Anyone can see that you need some periods of relaxation."

Allard's voice rose in anger. "You are being childish and impertinent. To go so far as to suggest that it is a waste of time to belong to the Hot and Hot Fish Club shows just how much you know about the responsibilities of the head of this household."

"Allard," his mother pleaded, "do not distress yourself so. Alice does not understand."

"She is disgusting!" As he strutted from the room, Allard's face was ashen with anger.

After his departure, Mrs. Flagg regarded her daughter with coldness. "I think you should ask your brother's forgiveness."

Alice stared at her mother. "You are mistaken, Mother. Allard should ask my forgiveness."

Mrs. Flagg walked to the other side of the room and observed Alice's reflection in a mirror hanging above the sideboard. "If the three of us are going to live in this house, you should make more of an effort to be gracious. I cannot understand what has gotten into you of late."

Even Alice was aware that her outbursts that morning had been unusual, but she knew they sprang from frustrations about her situation with Whit. She felt the urge to declare that if she was not allowed to profess her love for Whit Buck there would never be any peace in the house again. But she restrained herself, and answered, "I am simply discovering that I am not like the rest of you."

She left the dining room quickly, not allowing her mother the opportunity to respond. As she reached the stairway landing, the clock was chiming eight, and she was suddenly flooded with a sense of relief. Hadn't she promised herself that very morning that she would not allow Allard or her mother or anybody else to take away the happiness she had found in Whit? Of course she had. And she would stick to her vow.

As she pictured Allard leaving the house in a huff, it came to her that she was now free to walk the seabeach without worry of detection. Perhaps Whit would show up and they could have a stroll on the sand and a talk. Alice picked up one side of her skirts and swept up the remaining stairs to her bedroom, where she would wait until she was sure that Allard was far away from the house.

13

THE NEW SENSE of direction in Alice's life was settling into place, and walking the seabeach became a regular routine, although she didn't always see Whit on her strolls. She grew used to waking to the crimson light of a Southern dawn and to watching the sunrise from the two windows of her room that faced the ocean. She settled into the habit of taking an early stroll about the grounds, slowly working her way to the seabeach.

Whit fashioned his routine to match Alice's when he could, but there were many days when his services at the sawmill didn't permit his taking any time away. On those days he didn't laugh quite so cheerfully and was a little stern as he supervised the unloading of logs arriving on the flatboats. Although he was away from Alice physically, emotionally he was with her, never forgetting the vision of her walking the seabeach, her hair pulled up and back and knotted into what resembled the tail of a black trotter.

As the fast-paced days of autumn slid one into another, the air turned cooler. One could literally feel the heat slipping away. One day at the usual three o'clock dinner, Allard announced that the Wards of Brookgreen would be having their annual oyster roast the following Saturday, and the Flaggs would leave for Brookgreen immediately after breakfast.

Alice's first thought was that she detested going to the Wards' oyster roasts, if for no other reason than that her mother pounded into her head every detail of how she must behave when visiting Brookgreen. When Mrs. Flagg said, "Alice," a crease puckered Alice's smooth brow and she thought dismally, oh dear, here it comes.

But Mrs. Flagg did not give her usual dissertation on this occasion. Instead, she said, "Alice, you and Mary must select one of the dresses that fits over a wide hoop, and if you turn your toes in slightly and walk with each foot immediately in front of the other, your skirt will sway just enough to attract the attentions of some of the young rice planters."

"Mother!"

"Alice, please," Mrs. Flagg said. "I am so glad the dresses have arrived from Charleston and I am anxious to see you display one at the roast." She turned to Allard. "Dear, do you know who the guests will be?"

He shrugged. "I presume the usual planter families that attend the oyster roasts. Including the Heriots, Petigrus, LaBruces, Vaux, as well as the Izards, Poinsetts, and the Reads."

Alice had the most overwhelming impulse to leave the room and escape the boring discussion, but she exercised restraint, not wishing to start another family quarrel. There had been so many of those lately that she decided to be generous enough to appear to look forward to the oyster roast. "I don't mind admitting that I enjoy the music of the slave band, and the food at Brookgreen is heavenly," she said, but Allard was looking at her askance, as though he didn't trust her.

"Please remember, Alice, that I plan to ask Penelope to marry me," Allard said. "You would not embarrass me at Brookgreen, I hope."

"I shan't embarrass you, Allard," Alice replied dryly. "I am of the gentility, or the *quality* as you sometimes say, and I intend to represent the Flaggs of Wachesaw in that manner."

Before Allard had an opportunity to respond, Mrs. Flagg said, "Alice, we would trust that you will behave beautifully. It is just that we have had some ugly scenes of late."

"You can be sure I will be the picture of civility, Mother." What Alice really wanted to say was that if she would be allowed to ask Whit Buck to accompany her to the oyster roast they would see the most divine young woman, one who represented the very foundation of the planter families, but she wished to avoid further disagreements with her mother and Allard. The fights were taking a toll on her and she preferred to keep her energy as high as possible for her meetings with Whit. She couldn't allow her mother and brother to completely destroy her will. One day, in some way, she would convince them that although he was not a millionaire planter, he was a man of quality and gentility, and she would never in her life love another enough for marriage.

For the trip to Brookgreen, Allard chose the most elaborate of their carriages, the one that bore the Flagg family coat of arms. It was pulled by four matching bay horses. Arthur had gone on ahead, riding his favorite horse.

Thomas, the coachman, sat on the box and held the reins as they rumbled toward their destination. Allard was elegant in gray, while Mrs. Flagg wore a silk gown in the shade of summer peaches. Alice's silk dress, over the huge hoop skirt, was hand-embroidered in shades of blue, lavender, and ashes of roses. Tiny tassels of silk thread, sewn on her bodice, bounced as they rode along. Alice stared abstractedly from the brass-framed window of the black coach.

Allard and his mother talked jovially as they traveled past Richmond Hill and Laurel Hill plantations, and soon their carriage was turning into the Brookgreen Plantation avenue of oaks. The trees were hundreds of years old, massive in size, and so draped in Spanish moss that the embellishment appeared to be fish nets thrown over the giant trees. "This is one day that will not be boring," Allard predicted. Alice, her skirts bunched up on her lap and touching her chin, wholeheartedly agreed.

Servants in uniforms of green plush with red facings and trimmed in silver were standing on the steps, waiting to assist the guests. Just before Alice left the coach she noticed James Michau, a bachelor planter, and her heart fell. Obviously he was waiting to greet the Flaggs, and after that she would likely be stuck with him for the remainder of the day.

Alice pressed her hands firmly against the sides of her skirts in order to pass through the carriage door as surreptitiously as possible, but there was no way to quiet the rustle of her garments. Allard followed her and assisted his mother out. When Allard spotted Arthur and Georgeanna Ward coming down the steps, he smiled engagingly.

"And how is Mister Doctor Flagg?" Arthur asked with mock aloofness as he shook Allard's hand.

Before Allard answered, Penelope Ward came flying from the house. Holding up her magenta skirts, she ran down the steps and took Allard's arm.

Smiling down at her, Allard answered his brother. "I am better now."

The Ward women came to Alice and fluttered around her, both talking at the same time about how marvelous Alice looked.

"Thank you," Alice said, and she complimented them in turn. "I have missed seeing you when I come for my lessons. Do you know when Madame Le Conte will be returning?"

Before they had an opportunity to answer, James Michau stepped near and said in a high, singsong voice, "Miss Alice, I have been waiting for you."

The last person in the world that Alice wanted to be paired with at the roast was James Michau of Kinloch Plantation. No woman in her right mind would cast a sideways glance at that fop who called himself a rice planter. He wasn't so bad to look at, but his eyes never opened more than halfway, and that high-pitched voice had never been known to say anything worthwhile.

But when Alice saw her mother gazing at the two of them, and she suddenly remembered her promise to her mother and Allard not to cause problems, it came to her that perhaps, after all, James would be someone with whom she could spend the day. If she tired of his voice and modulated him right out of her mind, he would not be bright enough to notice. Besides that, if she stuck by him the other bachelor planters would keep their distance.

"Why, how nice to see you, James," Alice drawled. "What shall we do first?"

A blush spread across his face. "Miss Alice, I believe the ladies have gathered in the mansion, and the gentlemen are down by the river where the oysters are roasting on hot coals in the ground."

"Then I shall go inside," she answered as she lifted her skirts, "but, James, I am planning to sit by you at the table."

"It would be an honor, Miss Alice."

Alice made her way to the house, noting that the Ward women must have slipped away and gone there too during her conversation. She proceeded to the drawing room, which was nearly filled with visitors. Georgeanna glided across the carpet toward her, her face radiant. "Alice Flagg," Georgeanna said in a rush. "Arthur told me that Allard told him—of course that is a roundabout rumor if ever there was one, but it is true I'm sure—that on your trip you bought everything Charleston has to offer."

"Oh, what Allard told Arthur, and Arthur told you, is not quite the truth," Alice answered.

"I am sure you are just being modest," Georgeanna continued. "From the rumor, and certainly from this dress before me, I can ascertain that your purchases are celestial."

Penelope joined them. "You are talking about Alice's new wardrobe."

"It is only a rumor," Alice said. "I needed a few things and mother helped me make some decisions, but my dresses cannot compare with those of the Ward women."

"That is not true, and you know it," Penelope said, her face glowing. She inclined her head toward Alice and whispered, "You are just what I have always desired in a sister-in-law."

"Has Allard proposed?" Alice asked.

"Yes. But we are not announcing it yet."

Alice, who was truly pleased with Allard's choice of a wife, grabbed Penelope's hands. "It's lovely, Penelope. I just wish I were getting married too."

"Well, you will be fifteen next month, and you can be married. Didn't I just see you talking with James Michau?"

Alice looked at her future sister-in-law and smiled. "I do not think there is a Michau in my future."

"You could do worse," Penelope answered. "Father mentioned that Kinloch Plantation will produce over three hundred thousand pounds of rice next year. And as they say, that ain't hay."

"I am with Alice," Georgeanna said soberly. "James Michau is not nearly the man she deserves."

All of this talk was to Alice's annoyance, but she didn't let on. "Oh, James is a likely companion for this day. I have promised to sit with him at the oyster roast, but as for anything further, I would not know about that."

She hoped that her distaste for the whole subject wasn't too noticeable. Alice's eyes swept over to the window. "Speaking of oysters, are they being steamed yet?" She walked to a ceiling-to-floor, many-paned window and lifted a lace curtain. In the distance she saw a congregation of men, all planter aristocracy. As she looked them over, she knew there still wasn't one who stirred her in the manner of Whit Buck. And there wasn't one who lacked self-importance. "That is an elite bunch down there," she commented.

Penelope and Georgeanna joined Alice at the window. In the distance, linen cloths were being spread on long tables, and chairs were being carried down the hill. When the oysters were finished steaming on beds of wet seaweed over red-hot coals, other food would be brought from the kitchen, a building away from the main house.

"They *are* elite," Penelope said.

Alice was thinking that Penelope and Georgeanna had missed the true meaning of her remark, and she was suddenly glad. She tried to erase her actual feelings by saying, "As cream rises to the top of milk, the planters have risen to the top of the men in South Carolina."

Georgeanna nodded. "They are not like other men," she said. "They are intelligent and successful. And we will each marry one!"

"As a matter of fact, you will be marrying Arthur Flagg, and I know it," Penelope told her sister.

"How do you know?" Georgeanna asked on an unsuppressed giggle.

"I shan't tell."

"Oh please, Penelope," Georgeanna begged. "Has Allard said anything?"

"I cannot say."

All of this talk was now too much for Alice. "Why don't we walk down the hill and see what is taking place? It cannot be long before dinner."

The Tuckers were arriving from Litchfield Plantation by boat, and there was a flurry of excitement as they were helped to the dock. Alice was relieved that the attention went to the Tuckers for she was suddenly rocked from the bottom of her feet as she remembered Whit helping her to a similar dock. He had changed her life.

Alice watched the planter families around the dock and felt sad that they would never allow themselves to become friendly with an "outsider." They were so desirous of keeping their land grants in the family that they sometimes married cousins, and their cordiality was rarely extended to anyone beyond the planter circle. How superior they felt. And if Whit Buck had come today and was among them, they would surely be condescending, when he was just as good as any of them. His family may not own anything like Brookgreen, but they had effected a sort of dynasty in Low Country sawmills. Why, as she thought about it, they had three within five miles of this dock! And Whit was head and shoulders above any of the planters in freshness and initiative. This so-called planter gentility was poppycock.

But Alice couldn't dwell on it, for she had promised Allard and her mother that she would present a proper "daughter of Wachesaw" to the people attending the oyster roast. And if she was half the person that Whit was, she'd live up to her word.

James Michau caught sight of her and hurried over. "Miss Alice," he said hesitantly, "they are putting some of the food on the tables."

"Well, James, that means that you and I should find a good place to sit."

"Yes, miss, it certainly does at that."

James just stood there, making no move toward the tables, and his lack of determination annoyed Alice. "Well James, find us two chairs."

"Yes, miss."

When they were seated, Mrs. Flagg came over to her daughter and put a hand on her shoulder. "Alice, I am so pleased that you and James are enjoying yourselves."

"Yes, Mother."

As Mrs. Flagg moved away, Penelope rushed over. "Alice, please save room for Allard and me. There are so many things for us to talk about."

Alice answered, "Of course, Penelope." She moved two chairs away and mouthed to James, "I am saving these places." It was her good fortune to be able to move away from him temporarily at someone else's suggestion.

He smiled from ear to ear.

The servants were now placing trays of sliced duck, turkey, and ham on the tables. That was followed by rice, boiled potatoes, dressed cabbage, and fried tomatoes. At the end of each long table, a place reserved for desserts, the cooks were arranging mincemeat pie, LaFayette cake, raspberry charlotte, and sweet potato pone. Just then Joshua John Ward and his wife Joanna took seats. Allard and Penelope arrived at the table and Alice moved beside James to let them sit down.

"Well, behold the Flaggs," said Joshua John, the grandee of the rice planters. "The Flaggs have been connected with Brookgreen since Dr. Henry Collins Flagg married the widow Rachel."

"That is quite true," Allard answered with more noblesse oblige than Alice had ever witnessed in him. Behold, indeed! Allard was in awe of Joshua John Ward! "How was your rice crop this year?" Allard asked the big planter.

"Exceptional, but I am thinking on next year. It is my belief that I will harvest over four million pounds."

"Your rice is outstanding," Allard said eagerly. "I appreciate how very generous you were to share your seed rice with the Flaggs. It certainly has improved our product."

Joshua John forked a piece of turkey to his plate. "It was ten years ago that my overseer, Mr. James C. Thompson, a very judicious planter, accidentally discovered in the barnyard during the threshing season a part of an ear of rice, the peculiarity of which induced him to show it to me. We planted the seed from that ear and the next spring it yielded forty-nine bushels. The following year we planted twenty-one acres and the yield was over a thousand bushels. If I had not shared it with you I think the Almighty would have washed away my fields with a hurricane."

"It certainly helped all of us," Alice chimed in. "My father died the year that your long-grain rice was discovered by your overseer, and though it could not aid Father, my mother and Allard and Arthur have all benefitted from your generosity."

"Your concern for your family's crop is commendable, my dear," Joshua John said, glancing at her curiously. "Especially for a young girl. Just how old are you now?"

"I shall be fifteen soon."

"Then you shall be marrying before too long. Has a rice planter deserving of your qualities been selected?"

"Father!" Penelope objected at the directness of his question.

"Oh he is just talking," Georgeanna, sitting next to Arthur, said. "Do not pay any attention to him, Alice."

"I would be interested in hearing the answer to the question," James said.

Alice was on the spot. What could she say? she wondered. She stole a glance at Allard, and his face had gone white—for this topic had many times prompted her to make some unpleasant statements about the bachelor planters. She looked down the table and also saw her mother's tightening face extend toward her. All was quiet. It seemed that everyone had heard the question and was awaiting an answer. Alice looked down at her hands and cleared her throat.

"As a matter of fact," Alice replied, "there has."

"And you have not told us?" Penelope chirped.

"Alice Flagg," Georgeanna squealed. "How can you keep a secret like that?"

"Why, Miss Alice," was all that James could squeak.

Allard dropped his fork. Mrs. Flagg looked as though she had turned to stone.

Alice herself wondered why she had blurted out such an answer. But even more she wondered why Joshua John Ward had asked such a thing. She was sitting here with James, and such a question had to make him uncomfortable. And in all truth, Joshua John made Alice uncomfortable. Was he as tough a man as she had heard? It was said that he made his slave women work a half-acre of rice each day, and that once they bent over to work a row, he didn't allow them to rise up until they had reached the end of that row. Alice swallowed, attempting to subdue the feeling of revulsion that swamped her. How disgusting he was. If he had dared challenge her, then he deserved to get an answer.

"And who is the lucky planter?" Joshua John asked, his eyes for the first time really looking at Alice and taking an interest in her.

"This is not the time to make an announcement," she answered, quickly glancing at Penelope and Georgeanna. "I think some other women should have the privilege of making such an announcement before I do." And then to assuage her mother, she added, "I will tell you this much. He is a Low Countryman. And that is all I am going to say."

Allard was noticeably confused, having had no notion that a man had interested his sister, but Mrs. Flagg was visibly relaxed. Mercifully, just at that moment the Brookgreen musicians appeared to entertain the guests. Divine, Summer, and Daniel Horry, three slave brothers, struck up the band to the tune of "Honey in the Rock."

14

SERVANTS WERE NOW bringing huge pans of steamed oysters to the tables, and each guest was assigned a servant who opened the oysters with a sharp knife. The guests' eyes widened in anticipation as they were handed the opened oysters, and much slurping and little conversation was heard for over an hour. Finally, all of the seafood had been consumed, and desserts were being served.

"Too good to be true! Too good to be true!" Joshua John gushed, licking his lips. "We here in the Low Country are blessed." In an expansive gesture in the direction of the forest, he added, "We have turkeys from the woods, ducks from the ponds, and oysters from the marshes. What more could any man ask?"

"Amen," a slave intoned.

"And my faithful slaves are my greatest asset other than my dear wife, Joanna, and our children," Joshua John went on. "My family is loyal to me in every possible way. My love for them is inestimable. Not one of my children has disappointed me in the slightest." Joshua John's voice was now more gentle than usual. "My children must have every advantage, and that reminds me . . . finding a new music teacher for my daughters is foremost in my thoughts, as Madame Le Conte will not return to Brookgreen. She desires to remain in France."

Alice's face colored, and she gave Joshua John a curious look. "What do you mean?"

"Simply, my dear, that the music teacher will not be returning to

Brookgreen, and it is imperative that I find a new one, and very soon at that. My daughters must not come up lacking in that art."

Alice was shocked to her very toes, and she stared at Joshua John, trying to grasp his words. For a moment she was disbelieving, but then with a sinking heart she knew that he had spoken the truth. He was an honest man. Alice reached for her glass with a shaking hand but did not remove it from the table. Whatever she did, she must not allow anyone to notice how upset she was, and in an effort to disguise her deep hurt, she told herself that she had already set her goals and made her decisions and did not really need Madame Le Conte after all. Suppressing a slight shudder, she looked across the table and gave her attention to Joshua John, who was still recounting his blessings.

"God has given me more than I deserve, with the rise and fall of the tide in every twenty-four-hour period, making it possible for me to make a fortune from my rice fields." He paused and everyone else remained quiet. Finally, he ended his speech with, "I am so blessed."

Joshua John's words, spoken so earnestly, pierced Allard's heart like a lancet, and he sprang to his feet. "You are blessed, Joshua John, as are we all. You have been given many gifts. But, as the Scriptures say, 'For unto whomsoever much is given, of him shall be much required.'" Allard's eyes crinkled with amusement. "Joshua John, I require something from you."

Joshua John was a trifle startled. "And what might that be?"

"I would like the hand of Miss Penelope in marriage, sir."

"Allard," Penelope began, but didn't finish the statement.

"Penelope," Allard said to her, "I had not planned to ask for your hand today, but this is the most appropriate moment I shall ever have."

"Well done, Allard," Arthur said. Georgeanna was gazing eagerly at Arthur. How she wished he were asking her father for *her* hand.

Everybody was perfectly quiet. Even no sound came from the musicians, who had quizzical looks on their faces as they held their musical instruments.

Joshua John stood. "Allard, I have kept my ear to the ground these last months, and if I displayed surprise at your request it would be a mockery. I have expected you to ask for Penelope's hand. You are a grand lad, and to join the Wards of Brookgreen with the Flaggs of Wachesaw would be a distinction."

Penelope jumped up and held onto Allard's arm. "We shall have the most glorious wedding this plantation has ever seen, and you are all invited." Astonishment mingled with joy spread throughout the group of guests.

Arthur looked at Georgeanna, and in her eyes he saw something so pleading, so completely unguarded, that he turned to her father and said as he stood up, "Sir, I would like to ask for the hand of Georgeanna."

"Are you sure, or are you just attempting to keep pace with your brother?"

"Oh, I am sure, sir. I have never been more sure of anything in my entire life."

"Indeed," Joshua John replied. "If there is anything better than joining the Wards with the Flaggs, it is to have a double union. Both of you, Allard and Arthur, shall be welcomed into this family and treated as though you had been born to it."

The guests got up from the tables and Allard, Penelope, Arthur, and Georgeanna mingled with them, all showing great happiness over the good news. Alice rose too, but her mind was on Whit. He would never be permitted to ask for her hand at such a gathering of planters!

Mrs. Flagg, who had been twittering with other ladies as she watched her sons and their future mates, now noticed Alice. She came to her daughter, took her arm, and guided her aside. "Aren't you happy, dear?"

"I am so happy for Penelope and Georgeanna, Mother. I really am. They shall be more like sisters to me than sisters-in-law. They will be the sisters that I have never had."

Mrs. Flagg responded but Alice wasn't listening. In spite of her happiness for the Ward girls, she was suddenly filled with a nameless terror from which she wanted to flee. "Don't you think we should be leaving, Mother?"

"It *is* getting late. I will tell Allard to have a groom bring the carriage."

Penelope, Georgeanna, and Arthur stood by the carriage as Allard, his mother, and Alice were climbing in. "Alice, I am going to throw my bouquet to you," Penelope said, "and you will be the next bride in the family."

"And if Penelope's does not work," Georgeanna added, "I shall throw mine. Two bouquets are bound to work."

"And you shall be my bridesmaid, and what joy we will have

when the dresses are being made here at Brookgreen," Penelope said. "But my wedding dress will be fashioned by the most exclusive dressmaker in Charleston."

"Yours cannot outdo mine," Georgeanna countered, laughing.

Alice was now in the carriage and had pulled her hooped skirts in and bunched them in her lap. She was trying desperately to think of something cheerful to say to her future sisters-in-law. Having been reared in the Southern tradition of carrying her burden and still retaining her charm, she was not about to let Penelope and Georgeanna detect her sadness.

But as her hand went to her chest and she felt the ring over her fluttering heart, she did not know how long she would be able to conceal her true feelings, which were a mixture of happiness for the Wards and disappointment at her own situation. The road ahead looked gutted and crooked. It would be difficult, but she intended to travel it.

When all goodbyes had been said, and the carriage was rolling under the oaks in the avenue, Alice detected the voices of some of the slaves, coming from the trees. She asked Allard to stop the coach. He knocked on the window and motioned for Thomas to pull over to the side.

The voices of a slave choir floated on the moist air and Alice listened intently to the words.

> Oh march down to Jordan, HALLELOO!
> Oh march down to Jordan, HALLELOO!
> Halleloo! Halleloo!
> God told Naaman to go to Jordan, HALLELOO!
> God told Naaman to go to Jordan, HALLELOO!
> Halleloo! Halleloo!
> As you march down to Jordan, HALLELOO!
> As you march down to Jordan, HALLELOO!
> Halleloo! Halleloo!
> I laugh when I gone down, HALLELOO!
> I laugh when I gone down, HALLELOO!
> Halleloo! Halleloo!

"They are the most splendid hymnists the world will ever know," Alice said, "and their words have deep meanings. Let us go, Allard. I am ready to start my march down to Jordan."

The trip back to the Hermitage was uneventful. Fortunately, what with Allard's and Arthur's exciting announcements at the oyster roast, everyone had apparently forgotten about Alice's strange "news." Allard especially did not think to press her for information on her mystery man.

That night, Allard sat at the large, walnut secretary in the drawing room and worked on his accounts.

"What are you laboring over?" Alice asked, as she came into the room.

Allard put the pen aside, rubbed his eyes, and flexed his shoulders. It had been a long day, although an extremely happy one for him. "I am endeavoring to inventory our assets."

"How do we stand?"

He picked up the paper on which he had been writing. "Very well, but if compared to the standard of the Wards, we are not their equal."

"No one else is either," Alice answered, "and we should not aspire to match them. Do you have any idea what we are worth at the moment?"

"The cash value of this plantation is $50,000. And our Charleston house is valued at $11,000. We own nine slaves."

"Oh? I am curious how all that measures against the Wards."

"Joshua John's plantations have a cash value of over half a million, and he owns over a thousand slaves."

"Why are you working on these records tonight, Allard?"

Allard stood up and walked across the room to a window, erect and composed. It was dark outside, and the only sound was of waves lapping on the shore of the inlet as the tide rose to full flood. "I am thinking of what we have and what we must do to preserve it. I must anticipate any future expenditures or acquisitions, and handle them intelligently. Arthur and I are getting married and before too long there will be another generation of Flaggs."

15

Two WEEKS LATER, as she was walking the seabeach, Alice thought back to the day that Whit had given her the ring. Until the day she died she would remember that moment. What a short time had passed between their meeting at the sawmill and her acceptance of the gift from him. Of course the words "engagement" and "proposal" had not been mentioned, but in her heart of hearts she felt as betrothed to him as the Ward women were to her brothers. He loved her, and she could see it in his eyes when he gave her the ring. There would never be any blank spots in her memory about their meetings, for she had mentally recorded every word, expression, feeling.

With the ocean groaning and whishing before her, Alice pictured herself as a bride and, eventually, a mother. The standards for the day were for a woman to bear children until she was well into her thirties. She considered some of the women she knew to be in their thirties, and as she thought about it, the sparkle had gone from their eyes. Most of them had borne several children and buried some of them. With so many deadly fevers around, it was rare that a mother raised all of her children to maturity.

Thinking on her own mother, Alice recognized her as being undaunted, even at times of death in the family—a trait that had been instilled in her as a very young woman to be sure. It had not seemed too much for her mother to preside over a table with many guests, immediately after the funeral of a member of her

109

family. And it was never considered to be a sacrifice for her mother to take gardenias to the Belin Cemetery sites of her buried
children and husband on special occasions, even during violent
storms. Alice only hoped that in November, when she would reach
the age of fifteen, she would suddenly be infused with a like
manner, efficient and controlled enough to face the daily
emergencies that would arise in her life. More than all Alice
hoped for the ability to look at both sides of a matter before
making a resolution.

On the matter of marriage, however, she simply could not think
with a cool head. She still felt no attraction to spending her days as
the mistress of a spacious plantation manor house, and of a
Charleston town house that rivaled the town houses of London,
responsible for the well-being of dozens of servants, going into
the vapors when threatened by the successful achievements of
other plantation mistresses, and studying the designs of the latest
fashions from Paris, silver from England, and crystal from Ire-
land. What she did desire was a husband of her own choosing, her
own home and children, and enough funds to live comfortably.
Beyond that, any assets would simply be vulnerable to the perils of
taxes, hurricanes, and other menaces of destruction.

Alice closed her eyes, and realized a certain tumult was mounting under the waves. A sudden chill had come to the air, and just
as she turned toward home she saw Whit on his stallion, riding
between two dunes onto the seabeach. Alice breathed deeply, filling her lungs with the pure air, and ran to her beloved.

"Whit! I have not seen you in simply ages."

His hair was blowing in the breeze that was now getting up. "I
have been wanting to see you, Miss Alice, but I have been away, in
Charleston."

"Charleston?"

"Yes, miss. And you will never guess what I bought while there."

"Tell me quickly."

"A carriage!"

"A carriage?"

"Yes. A carriage of my very own, by Jove. I had to go to
Charleston to deliver some virgin pine for the floor of a house on
East Bay Street. I saw the most splendid carriage, and it is mine!"

Alice was smiling, and giving Whit a soft, loving look. How
unutterably dear he was sitting up there on Bootblack, his eyes

twinkling with excitement. She put out a hand and he slid off his horse and drew her to him. "I love you."

Alice didn't answer, but she was thinking how very much she loved this man, everything about him, from the strength of his arms to the merriment in his eyes, to the proud way he had of defending his family and their station in life, and especially to the sudden magic that had come to him by owning his very own carriage.

"I shall never own a knight's estate," he said, "or a baron's castle with coachmen and servants. I am a common man, and sometimes hard measure is dealt out to the common people. Not knowing what your fate will be, do you think you could give me your word that you will marry me?"

Thinking about Whit's words, Alice listened now to the deep moaning of the sea, and she pulled away and glanced at the heaving waves. "People are carried away on that expanse of water," she said, thoughtfully. "Carried across the world before the wind. That is what marriage to you will be like. Free!"

"And you believe that you can be truly happy on what I can provide for you?"

"Don't be silly! Of course I shall be happy with what you provide," Alice asserted fiercely. "I love you and you love me. For us to be married is a natural outcome of our love, and I shall be happier than I have been in my entire life."

For a moment Whit gaped at Alice, his shoulders tensely set. "Alice, I believe you," he said suddenly. "And I am going to do something that may not be the easiest thing in the world for either of us, but it has to be done."

"What is that?"

"I also acquired some new clothes in Charleston. On Sunday afternoon, I shall call on you at the Hermitage, and I shall be properly attired, riding in my new carriage. I shall go to the door and ask for you, and we shall enjoy a ride on the country lanes."

Alice was suddenly gripped with fear at the prospect of exposing their relationship. Her panic was heightened by the ominous black clouds gathering overhead. Her eyes consulted the sea, and it was plain that a storm was imminent. The ocean was the same color as the sky. "I do not know," she said. "I think we had better discuss it at a later time. I must go home immediately."

"This is not the time for us to argue," Whit began, "but I refuse to leave until you give me your word that you will be waiting when I call at your house on Sunday."

Alice had been anticipating such a situation, fearing it, for weeks. She knew Allard would cause a huge scene, and her mother would side with him against Alice. Whit might not feel strong enough to face up to them and hold his own. He might leave and never come back. Alice clasped her hands behind her neck and she felt haggard and tired. "I do not think you should come on Sunday."

Whit's eyes took in this girl whom he singularly loved. All of his dreams and hopes were centered on her. His biggest thrill had been to select a shiny, new carriage with which to impress her, a carriage in which she would be happy to ride. He had not expected her to respond to his invitation with such trepidation. "Are you so afraid of your brother?"

In a flash Alice's mind went back over the vows she had made to herself regarding Allard and her mother. Although they were an inflexible enemy when it came to men of Whit's station, she had determined that they would not ruin her life. She would accept Whit's invitation. "I would love to ride with you on Sunday. We do not return from divine services until after three o'clock."

Rain had now begun to fall, and Whit climbed up on his stallion. "I don't think I shall sleep a wink until Sunday, when you will be sitting with me in my carriage."

On Bootblack, Whit flew across the beach and disappeared in the dunes. Alice raced in the opposite direction, toward the Hermitage. The young woman who had looked so lovely just moments ago, in a yellow dress that had ruffles beginning at the small of her back and extending to the hem and around the entire skirt, a dress that emphasized her willowy figure and symmetry of movement, was now cold and wet. She had allowed her hair to fall about her shoulders, and now it hung in wet strings that clung to her neck.

Her breath came in gasps as she hurried on; she knew that she must get home and to her room without being observed by Allard. By some devious method, he would wring out of her where she had been and why she was away from the house, in the same manner that she would wring water from her dress when she dropped it to the floor and stepped out of it. Since the oyster roast, Allard had been unsuccessful in extracting details from Alice about any man in her life—and Mrs. Flagg had no intention of informing him—but he had become extra watchful of late.

Alice ran on mechanically, as though in a daze. Fortunately, when she reached home, Allard was away and her mother was off in the kitchen building. Alice ran up the steps and into her room, where she threw herself on the tester bed, perfectly exhausted. Just at that moment, Mary One came into the room.

"Miss Alice, you be wet to the bone and you gonna take your death of cold. Get out of them clothes."

"Oh, Mary, please help me. I was walking on the seabeach and got caught in the downpour."

Mary ran to a trunk and removed a quilt. "Chile, you just step out of that frock and them pantalets and wrap yourself in this quilt. And then I'll go and get some hot tea."

"No, Mary. Don't disturb Mother, or Allard when he returns. I will be fine."

"Now, chile, I'm not accepting any of that talk. I'll fetch a whole pitcher of tea for you. No woman of Wachesaw Plantation gets cold and wet and is left to catch a chill. Not when I'm here."

Alice undressed, taking care to hide her ring from Mary's sight. She now had the quilt wrapped around her thin, white body and high around her neck, but she was shivering violently, and the tea sounded wonderful. "What would I do without you, Mary?"

"I hope you don't ever have to," Mary replied, as she left the room.

As she warmed, Alice stopped shivering, and she went to a window and looked toward the marsh and beach beyond it. A cold rain was still falling, and she knew that somewhere Whit was on his horse, also getting soaked. She fervently hoped that he didn't become ill.

For the first time she realized just how much she looked forward to seeing him on Sunday, and riding proudly beside him in his new carriage. What a terrible thing it would be to disappoint him, when he had gone to so much trouble and expense to buy the carriage and the new clothes. But more than that she wanted to ride with this man who was now truly her fiancé. And no one, no person alive, would prevent her doing so.

Alice was still at the window when Mary returned. She was carrying a silver tray on which a porcelain teapot sat, along with a cup and saucer. "Now, Miss Alice, you get in that bed and cover up, and drink this tea."

With no further coaxing, Alice turned and went to the tester bed. After stepping up to the high bed, she lay on the feather mattress, which was soft and deep. Mary filled the cup with steaming tea, and Alice held it to her lips, but before she took a sip she asked, "Of my dresses, which is the prettiest for taking a carriage ride?"

"Why you ask that question now when you be sick?"

"I don't know," Alice said. "I simply thought if a gentleman asked me to ride with him, I would need to know which dress to select."

"You get your mind off that. Drink that tea and take a nap!"

16

Sunlight was spreading across the marsh when Alice awoke with a start on Sunday morning. Her first thought was of the carriage ride with Whit, after church services. *Church!* She'd have to hurry, for judging by the light she was waking later than usual. Dinner, which would be eaten at All Saints Church, was surely by this time packed in baskets that would be taken to the boat, where the liveried oarsmen were probably already waiting.

But something seemed different on this morning. For one thing, more noise than usual was floating up the stairs from the drawing room. Alice threw her legs over the edge of the bed, lifted a side of her nightgown, and ran to the top of the stairs. "Is anything wrong?" she called out.

Mrs. Flagg came to the bottom of the stairway and Alice could see that she was fully dressed and even had her hat on. "Were you going to church and leaving me here?" Alice questioned.

"Of course we wouldn't do that," her mother answered. "But do hurry and get dressed, and while you are getting ready I shall send up a tray of breakfast."

"What has happened?"

Mrs. Flagg smiled up at her daughter. "It is nothing to be alarmed about. Everything is well taken care of."

"But what is it?"

"Katrina had her baby this morning, and it was born with a caul over its face."

"Oh, dear God in heaven," Alice wailed. Katrina, one of their seamstresses, was even younger than Alice, but Alice had always believed that she was wise beyond her years and admired her. "Is the baby all right?"

"Yes. I have been to Katrina's cabin, and she is well. She had a little boy."

"Where is Allard? Is he there?"

Mrs. Flagg sighed and stared off abstractedly. "Not now. But he did not leave Katrina until mother and child were resting."

"Did he remove the caul?"

"Yes, very quickly of course," Mrs. Flagg explained. "But as you know, Alice, there have been several births at Wachesaw when a baby came into the world with a caul, and there is no need for alarm if a physician is present. Or even a good granny woman."

Alice relaxed her hand and let her nightgown's hem drop. "That boy will always have second sight," she said.

"Indeed he will," Mrs. Flagg answered.

Alice ran back to her room, poured water into a bowl from a porcelain pitcher, and began to splash it on her face. Just then Mary One rushed in.

"Miss Alice, Katrina done had her baby with a caul over his face. That boy sure have second sight."

"That is so, Mary. He will be an asset to this plantation."

Mary took a fresh pair of pantalets from a drawer and handed them to Alice, then Mary started making up the bed. "Katrina's boy be named Solomon."

Alice began to dress, but not before she dropped her ring down her back behind her loose hair when Mary was not looking. Wiggling into her pantalets, she said, "Oh, what a perfect name for that boy." She was thinking of the biblical Solomon, a king of Israel and an extraordinarily wise man. Katrina had realized that she had birthed a child who would one day be especially wise. It had been proven many times on Southern plantations that when a child was born with a portion of the embryonic membrane covering the face, that child would see things others could not, and prophesy events that would come true.

One of Mrs. Flagg's sisters had been born with a caul over her face, and she was the one the others went to for information. She could foresee hurricanes before their landfall, and if a member of the family, although many miles away, became sick, she could sense the illness. She had also seen ghosts. And now there was a little boy on the plantation who would be able to do all of those things, and Alice felt a deep sense of love for him although she hadn't yet seen him. But she would have no time today for a visit with Katrina.

Mary removed a blue dress from the armoire, shook out any wrinkles, and was spreading it on the bed as a servant brought a tray into the room.

"Oh no, Mary!" Alice reached for a ham biscuit. "I do not think that dress becomes me."

"Why that blue just brings out that thick dark hair, Miss Alice." Mary suddenly looked at Alice askance. "You don't want to wear this dress?"

Alice sipped coffee from a cup then shook her head, drawing her lips together in a pout of indecision. She pushed the tray aside and waited until the servant had left the room before speaking. "I don't think so."

"You want one what be perfect for a carriage ride!"

Alice's startled eyes flashed in Mary's direction, and she remembered mentioning to Mary a dress suitable for a carriage ride. She waltzed across the room. "That *is* what I want. Something perfect for a carriage ride, but you cannot say a word to anybody about it. You hear?"

Hanging the blue dress back in the cabinet, Mary said, "I just don't know what you be getting at, but I'll look for another dress. What about that red one?"

"Red *is* for me today. Do you have second sight?" Anticipating the ride with Whit had made Alice's mind absolutely giddy.

Mary shook out the dress of red tulle with skirt and sleeves that ended in double ruffles. "If I had second sight, I'd know what you're talking about."

"And get the shawl, Mary, please. There might be a nip in the air today."

Alice slyly moved her ring back over her heart, and began to fix her hair. When she heard her mother's voice calling her from the bottom of the stairs, she grabbed a red hat and flew from the room. Today she did not want to antagonize her family in any way. When they returned from All Saints Church, and Whit arrived dressed like an English gentleman in the new carriage to take her riding in the countryside, Mrs. Flagg and Allard would have to be in the perfect mood in order to accept what was happening.

17

Dr. Alexander Glennie chose for his Scripture the fifteenth chapter of St. Luke. His deep, resonant voice with the Scottish burr read:

> And he spake this parable unto them, saying, "What man of you, having an hundred sheep, if he lose one of them, doth not leave the ninety and nine in the wilderness, and go after that which is lost, until he find it? And when he cometh home, he calleth together *his* friends and neighbours, saying unto them Rejoice with me; for I have found my sheep which was lost. I say unto you, that likewise joy shall be in heaven over one sinner that repenteth, more than over ninety and nine just persons, which need no repentance."

And then Dr. Glennie began to describe why some sheep get lost, saying that when that particular animal eats grass, it keeps its head down as it nibbles, and the eyes did not always detect a change in the flock's direction. Thus, a sheep often wanders away from the rest of the herd, and the shepherd goes in search of the lost sheep.

Alice had not thought of it exactly like that before. Of course it was natural for sheep to become lost occasionally, as they moved about facing the grass, and could not see where they were going. In a sense, she was like a lost sheep, one who was moving in a direction that was different from the others in the group. But the head of the flock always came for the wandering sheep and rejoiced. It would be that way with her. When her mother and

119

Allard realized that she simply wanted to marry Whit and be his wife and live their own lives, but still be a part of their respective families, they would rejoice.

Sitting in the pew, Alice eyed the stained-glass windows, carved chancel rail, and hand-embroidered kneeling cushion which had all been given by the Wards, the Flaggs, and other rice planters. She listened to the soft words of Dr. Glennie and made a certain determination. She would be married in this very church, and Dr. Glennie would perform the ceremony.

She pictured herself holding onto Allard's arm as they slowly walked down the center aisle. Dr. Glennie, in his white robe, so pure and clean, would be waiting at the altar, and he would say the divine words:

> . . . Wilt thou . . . forsaking all others, keep thee only unto her, so long as ye both shall live? . . . To have and to hold from this day forward, for better for worse, for richer for poorer, in sickness and in health, to love and to cherish, till death us do part. . . . With this ring I thee wed.

Alice's hand went to her heart, *With this ring* . . .

Alice knew that her cheeks were scarlet, for never before had she been so deeply moved by the thoughts in her head.

And then she began to see herself as Whit's wife, as they stood outside the stucco church with Greek columns and greeted the guests. In her white wedding dress with matching picture hat, holding a nosegay of gardenias—gardenias absolutely, as they were her very favorite flower—she would be radiant, her eyes sparkling. Why, her wedding dress would be the stunning satin and lace creation she had bought in Charleston! And Whit, outrageously handsome, would receive endless compliments from the women, including the Wards.

And after the lovely All Saints wedding, her life would be jam-packed with days of gaiety and happiness, days like Christmas Eves, birthdays, family reunions. The house that Alice and Whit would build would be filled with gales of laughter.

Suddenly Dr. Glennie was leading the last hymn, and then the service was concluded. The parishioners followed him into the churchyard for what they called "dinner on the grounds." It was the usual practice, for the trip back home would take at least two hours, except for the planters who lived closest to the church.

It was a glorious afternoon, sunny and warm with a cloudless sky. Alice wandered over to her mother, who was removing a platter of chicken from her basket. "Take a plate, darling," Mrs. Flagg said, "and help yourself to the fried chicken, hog's head cheese, and drop biscuits."

Alice took a plate, but suddenly, although she had felt especially strong during the service, nervousness seemed to weaken her body. Realizing she could not tolerate all the food her mother had suggested, she took a piece of orange sponge cake from a platter. But she only nibbled at it. In a couple of hours she would be climbing into Whit's carriage, and that would be the first time anyone would witness their courtship. Although she had yearned for him constantly these last few weeks, now that she was about to show the world openly that he was the mystery man she had chosen for her future husband, she was a shambles. This case of the jitters, she fervently hoped, would soon pass.

18

FLUSHED AND BREATHING rapidly, Alice sat on the porch to await Whit's arrival. Her hat was on her lap. Fortunately, no one questioned why she was sitting alone, and no sounds came from inside the mansion. She assumed her mother was resting in her room, and Allard was probably working at the walnut secretary, perhaps still inventorying the Flaggs' assets.

Alice's eyes followed the winding road as far as she could see, but there was no sign of Whit. In her mind she traced its entire route, and she believed that Whit would be somewhere near the plantation by this time. She had only moments to wait. In her concentration on the road, she was completely relieved of the anxiety she had experienced just a short time ago. Oh, Whit, Whit, she thought, and her heart beat all the faster as it swelled with love. And then she saw him riding around the curve and into the yard, where he came to a stop before the house constructed of longleaf pine, with steps made of English brick that came to South Carolina as ballast in sailing vessels.

The carriage was black and as shiny as though it had been greased with lard. There was much brass, including two magnificent lamps at the doors. Whit sat on a velvet seat, and held the reins.

He was dressed in a blue suit with a wide wine-colored cravat neatly knotted above his waistcoat, which set off his frilled shirt to perfection. The cravat was fastened with a pearl pin. A groom suddenly appeared, and Whit tossed him the reins as he alighted. How brightly his boots shone! Merriment danced in his eyes, and he bowed from the waist as he said, "May I have the pleasure of the company of Miss Alice Flagg for a ride in my carriage?"

With a burst of energy she jumped up and hurried down the walkway between rows of boxwoods. "Miss Alice has been eagerly awaiting your arrival," she teased.

Whit helped her to the velvet seat, went around the carriage and took the reins from the groom, and climbed up. Alice instinctively knew that this was the first time Whit had formally called on a young woman, and although he was the very embodiment of courtesy, she felt that he wanted to grab her and squeeze her until she would lose her breath. His eyes were exuding the heat she had seen when Allard looked at Penelope and Arthur looked at Georgeanna. She would never forget this moment. The picture was etched on her mind forever.

"Wait!" It was Allard's voice, coming from the porch. That word, spoken so hatefully, pierced Alice's heart. She cleared her throat and touched Whit's arm lightly. "I am sorry. If he says anything to hurt you . . ." She stopped, searching for the right sentence of consolation.

"Get out of the coach," Allard screamed, now standing next to Whit, sitting on the velvet seat.

"But *I* have come to take Miss Alice for a ride," protested the young man, holding the reins. "And this is *my* carriage."

"Be it your coach or not, *get out,*" ordered Dr. Flagg. "I will drive your carriage and take Alice for a ride. You may ride my horse." He turned and motioned for a groom. "It is indeed a fine animal, as I bought it in Virginia as a yearling, and I paid nearly two thousand dollars for it."

"But you have no right to order me from my carriage," Whit stated, clearly exasperated.

"I may have no authority to order you from your coach," Dr. Flagg asserted. "But I am the head of the Wachesaw family seat, and I can remove my sister from your carriage. If you want to enjoy the afternoon ride and feel the sea breeze on your cheeks, you will ride my mount."

The lumberman sat quietly for a moment, contemplating, and then he glanced at Alice, but she did not respond right away. A stony look had spread across her face and he knew her well enough to see she was warring with anger and frustration. Frowning, Whit swung his long legs from the carriage. A groom brought Sylvan, and was waiting to help Whit to the saddle.

"Allard, don't!" Alice finally exploded, her face flushing.

"You were a simpleton to come up with this preposterous plan," Allard fired back at his sister.

"She did not make the plans. *I* did," Whit said, stepping up and returning Allard's cold look with an unblinking stare.

Alice felt her muscles stiffening on the carriage seat. Whit was an amazing model of self-control as he stood up to Allard, but he would be no match in manipulation. Allard was a master at the art and left no room for negotiation. Alice pushed herself from the velvet seat and walked slowly to Allard, still in his Sunday suit. Her life had been bound by him and her mother for as long as she could remember. Allard was the squire of Wachesaw and her mother submitted to it and expected Alice to do the same. Now, when she was coming to the best part of her life, she still had to bow and scrape to them and their selfish preoccupation with their station in life and the all-consuming love for the plantation. Grievous trouble was ahead, and she would do almost anything to avoid a violent confrontation.

"Allard, *please*. Let us go inside the house and talk about this." She focused all her attention on her brother, not surprised at the vindictive outburst, but she made an attempt to control her voice as she added, "Be fair. We will listen to your point, and you should listen to ours."

Allard regarded his sister and Whit alertly. What he saw was a daughter of the gentry—a privileged woman—and a common laborer. If one cared to look beyond the shiny carriage and new suit of clothes, there was no distinguished air, no culture or polish, no match for a woman of elegance. He turned to Whit, and his expression was condemning. "You have wasted your time in coming here. It was a silly thing to do."

Whit was rigid and met the accusatory glance. It was clear he was angry, seething. Alice shivered, wondering what was going to happen, when to her surprise she saw Whit bring a neutral expression to his face.

"You are looking at me, Dr. Flagg, as a mare about to be put to the test of being raced on the Jockey Club course, and as you see it, I do not have a chance," Whit said. "It *is* a demanding course, a supreme test for a man like me, competing against a man like you. The breeding is not there, you are thinking, but have you considered stamina? I want you to know who is in the saddle, and I am willing to take you at a full gallop anytime. You are a thoroughbred, but do not pass by this dark horse lightly. The prize is one I intend to win, for I love Miss Alice beyond reason. Because of my love for her and my concern for her place in this family, I will hand you the reins today and award you the trophy. But next time the race will be on *my* terms, and you will have to take your chances."

Alice was thinking that Whit was better at manipulation than she had believed. As she walked slowly back to the carriage, she thought that with calm deliberation Whit had put Allard on notice that there would be another carriage ride, at another time.

Alice and Allard climbed into the carriage. As he took the reins to Whit's horse, Allard looked at them and pictured a noose into which he wished to place Whit's head. He flapped the reins in the air, Whit's horse went into motion, and the carriage rolled away. Alice huddled herself into a corner of the seat, her altogether striking profile turned away from Allard in icy silence. Whit struck Sylvan with the crop and the horse fairly flew to the side of the carriage. Whit was now beside Alice, and his face was desolate. Suddenly, Allard shot ahead, leaving Whit behind. Again, Whit caught up, and Alice recognized the form the afternoon was settling into. Now and then, Alice maneuvered to get a glimpse of Whit, but there was no opportunity to call out to him, as Allard constantly raced ahead, then slowed down.

That night after Alice retired to her upstairs bedroom, Allard and his mother had a family consultation.

19

"I AM PUZZLED about Alice, I really am," Mrs. Flagg said.

"There is nothing to be puzzled about," Allard retorted. "That no-good lumberman has just discovered a way to try to work himself into a society where he doesn't belong. He will be the laughingstock of the Low Country."

"I don't know," Mrs. Flagg answered rather listlessly, as she pictured Whit Buck. "He seems to care for Alice."

"So what if he does? It is only a schooner ride into the good life. He is an opportunist, and Alice is naive enough to fall for his guile."

"We must save her, Allard. You and I are the ones to save her. Arthur might take her side, as she has always been closer to him. You and I are the guardians of this family, the bulwarks, protectors, and we must keep Alice for a proper husband."

"Her birthday is on November 29," Allard muttered, glancing at his mother.

"Yes, and she will expect to exercise some authority when it arrives."

"We must change her mind about that young Buck before she becomes fifteen," Allard responded. "We have a few weeks yet."

Mrs. Flagg went to a window and her eyes took in the barren landscape of a marsh at low tide. The mud banks were black in shadow, and shorebirds had gone to roost. No living thing moved. It was a lonely scene. Finally, the woman turned toward her son. "I wonder when she communicated with him. How did she know that he would be coming here today?"

Allard went to the walnut secretary and sat down. He absent-mindedly opened a ledger book, glanced at it, then pushed it away. "I have searched my brain, but I do not know. I don't believe he has been here before today."

"But they could meet at some other location," Mrs. Flagg said. "Where?"

The woman's eyes widened as an idea came to her. "It is the seabeach. That is the only place. Alice has been enjoying frequent outings there. Alone."

"But she *hasn't* been alone," Allard added ironically.

"What ruin the Flaggs will come to if it isn't stopped. But how? We cannot watch her every move."

"No, and we cannot depend on others to do it for us. Mary One would lie and cheat for Alice," Allard surmised.

Just then Mrs. Flagg turned and her face showed desperation. "Alice has needed a father for ten years. I have not been all to her that she needed."

"Stop blaming yourself this instant," Allard snapped. "*I* am the head of this household, and I have taken the place of a father for her. She has not confided in me one iota."

"Alice and I just have not been as close as most mothers and daughters," Mrs. Flagg went on, torturing herself aloud.

"I told you to stop that. I will not stand for it!" Allard all but shouted.

"Please keep your voice down. The last thing we need is for Alice to hear us. We do not want to confront her before we decide what to do."

"Has anything come to your mind that we *can* do?"

Mrs. Flagg thought about it. "We could have Dr. Glennie talk with her."

"And what would *he* say?" Allard wanted to know. "Would he point out that she is from a wealthy family and she must marry a man of means in order to live a dignified life?" Without awaiting an answer he went on. "No. He would tell her that she should find a good Christian man with whom she could live her life, and settle down to having babies and raising them in his church."

"Allard!"

"Isn't that the truth?"

Mrs. Flagg was silent and stiff as a statue. Finally she said, "It is true. We cannot go to Dr. Glennie. But there is something else we can do."

"And that is?"

"You can take her to Charleston and enroll her in a good school, where she will be continuing her education and mingling with people of her own kind."

Allard stood up. "That is an excellent idea, Mother. I wish I had thought of it." He rubbed his palms together and smiled.

"Do you know of such an institution?" Mrs. Flagg asked.

Allard went to a window and looked out, but his eyes were unseeing. He was racking his brain. After a few moments, he turned. "I believe I have heard of a place that would be perfect. There has been some mention of it lately."

"What is the place?"

"Madame Talvande's School on Legare Street."

"I have heard of that place myself, but I know little of it," Mrs. Flagg stated.

"Robert Francis Withers Allston of Matanzas Plantation on the Pee Dee River has two small daughters, Adele and Elizabeth. He told me at the Pee Dee Gun Club that he plans to send them to boarding school when they reach nine. I believe the older of those girls is six now."

Mrs. Flagg shook her head in dismay. "Nine is too early to be sent away from home."

"But fifteen is the perfect age," Allard said, his mind racing as he stole a quick look at his mother.

"And what do you know of this Madame Talvande's School?"

"As I remember it, Robert Allston said that a Madame Togno is going to open a French school on Tradd Street, where all of the students will have to speak French."

Mrs. Flagg winced. "Alice could not attend. She does not speak French."

"Of course. But Robert hopes that his daughters will be ready to attend the French school when they are nine. However, he went on to say that if the French school has not opened by the time he needs it, he will send Elizabeth and Adele to Madame Talvande's, which is in quite a well-placed house on Legare Street."

"What else did Robert say?"

"That most of the planters who produce sea island cotton on Edisto Island send their daughters to Madame Talvande's, and their sons to the College of Charleston. It seems to be the prestigious thing to do. Madame Talvande teaches music and dancing as well as a full curriculum of studies. Her students are chaperoned, and they cannot leave the building, even to walk across the garden, without wearing a hat."

"Thank God for that!" Mrs. Flagg looked relieved. The black waves of shock that had engulfed her when Whit Buck arrived at the Hermitage were now subsiding. "How soon can you see Robert Allston and get further information?"

"I shall see Robert tomorrow, and will send a communication to Madame Talvande. Then, and only then, at the very last minute, we will tell Alice."

"We will tell her there will be no balking, that we are making a special effort for her," Mrs. Flagg said.

"And we will tell her without preamble," Allard said. "There will be no time for argument."

"Actually, Alice should love residing in Charleston," her mother reasoned. "The gardens, pathways, and avenues of the town are ablaze with glorious color in springtime. All manner of variegated greens border the lawns this time of year. Going to Madame Talvande's School will be a privilege *any* woman should desire."

"But just any woman hasn't fallen in love with a common lumberman, Mother, and I am sure you have taken that into consideration."

"Our hands *are* tied in the current situation, but sending Alice to Charleston will release the bonds. There simply isn't anything else we can do."

"And the quicker the better!"

"Classes would already be in session, would they not?" Mrs. Flagg asked.

"I understand that the students are on a brief recess at the moment, and a new term will begin shortly. But Madame Talvande is a businesswoman. She would be pleased to have a paying boarder for a week or two before classes actually begin again. And such a period of orientation would help Alice adjust before the other students return."

Mrs. Flagg's gaze was contemplative, as she endeavored to work out the disquieting question of sending Alice off to Charleston before she had time boisterously to object. "You must see Robert Allston tomorrow, and leave early. If anyone asks for you, I shall say you had business matters to attend to in Georgetown."

"By the time Alice arises tomorrow, I will be well on my way."

"Well on your way where?" Mrs. Flagg's sister, with her usual bubbling enthusiasm for everything, came into the room with a flourish.

Mrs. Flagg returned her sister's smile, delighted with the unexpected visit. But Allard viewed his aunt, the one who had been born with a caul over her face, with a sudden flash of embarrassment. Aunt Blane was arriving at a most inopportune time.

"I was speaking of being well on my way to visit Robert Allston tomorrow," Allard answered.

"Give Robert my regards," Aunt Blane said, and added, "and let me say quickly that I am not here for a visit, but simply stopped in on my way to Georgetown. I shall be leaving in a moment."

"You do not have to leave so soon," Mrs. Flagg protested, a little taken aback. She rushed to her sister and took her arm. "You have just arrived."

"I cannot stay at this time. I am going to make a late arrival in Georgetown as it is."

Mrs. Flagg and her son observed her closely and noticed a troubled expression settling on her face. Then her eyes opened wide.

"What is wrong?" Mrs. Flagg asked.

Her sister removed her hatpin, took off her hat, and rubbed her forehead. "I cannot quite define it, but something terrible is going to happen to Alice, and I believe it takes place in Charleston. I can feel it to the marrow of my bones, but I cannot see it clearly."

After a short pause, Allard said, "I know you have our interests at heart, but we do not intend to listen to any words of doom."

Aunt Blane pulled herself up sharply, made a clucking noise, and shook her head. As she positioned her hat on her head, she replied, "Very frankly, Allard, you should pay close attention to my intuition, but I do not have the time to convince you of it today." She jabbed the hatpin through the straw hat and secured it. "I must leave at once."

After her sister departed, Mrs. Flagg mulled over her words, and finally said, "You know she was born with the veil and she *does* have second sight."

"Believing in that old superstition is revolting," Allard snapped. "Alice is going to Charleston, and that is the end of it."

20

"MOTHER! YOU CANNOT be serious about sending me to Charleston!" Alice screamed.

"Do not be selfish and irresponsible, darling," the elder woman said. "You know that we are always at our home in Charleston for the social season until Lent. We will be there when you attend the St. Cecilia ball as well as the races at the Jockey Club."

Oh, that is all they think about, Alice fumed to herself. There were more important things in life than Charleston's "social season." Being near Whit was what mattered most to her now. Did her family honestly believe that she would accept the luxuries of Charleston in place of Whit, and be happy?

Alice wondered passionately what was going to happen to her. With a sickening drop of her stomach, she realized that her mother and brother *could* force her to go to Charleston. Suddenly her shoulders became heavy, her thin, tapering fingers trembled, and she shivered with cold from the clammy sweat that dampened her back and neck.

Alice looked about, considering the best course of action to take. It would be easier on all concerned if she bowed under the pressure and went along with the move, but she would have to live with herself, and she knew that in the days ahead she would not be pleased with herself if she did not make her feelings crystal clear. If she ever confronted her mother and made her true feelings known, now was the time. Abruptly, she said, "Mother, the bone of contention is my wedding, is it not?"

"Of course not," Mrs. Flagg answered directly. "I did not know you were planning a wedding."

"You and Allard are afraid that I will one day stand at the altar with Whit Buck. *I* know that if I married a rice planter the wedding would be a grand event, and you would be pleased. But such a wedding day would be the saddest day of my life, for I would not be marrying the man I loved."

"We are not asking you to marry anyone against your wishes," Mrs. Flagg answered quietly. "All we ask is that you go to Charleston and attend Madame Talvande's School for the winter term, and then we shall discuss a wedding, if that is your choice at that time."

"Why do I have a strange feeling that you think I shall change my mind about Whit Buck while I am in Charleston?" Alice asked as she lifted her skirts and ran upstairs to her room, where Mary One was packing clothes for the trip.

"Oh, Mary, why do I have to go?" Alice wailed.

"Well, chile, you knows better than me why your mother and brother want you far away from here," Mary replied.

"Well, it will not do any good. I am not going to forget him or quit loving him just because I am a hundred miles away. And if either one of them really knew me, they would realize it!" Alice stamped her foot in frustration.

Mary took her time to respond. She folded another dress and placed it carefully in the trunk. "Hard as it be for such a willful one as you to understand, your family believe they know a mite more 'bout life than a fourteen-year-old girl."

"Maybe about some things, but not about this. All they see is that Whit is not their 'social equal.' He is not a rice planter. You know and I know that is all they care about."

"Your mother done told me the whole story. I think just maybe she seen the results of such unions before. After all, you not be the first pretty young girl to fall in love with someone who's not part of her family's world, not an equal part anyway," Mary said sharply. "Love just don't conquer all, chile," she added in a softer tone.

"Mary!" Alice's voice was disbelieving. "How can you talk like that? You, better than anyone, ought to understand me. This love is more important than such things as money and status. It simply has to be!" Alice turned, holding back tears, and walked to the window. "Otherwise, what is the point of love?" she finished quietly.

Mary walked over to Alice, touched her shoulder gently, then moved away to resume packing.

"What are they so afraid of?" Alice asked.

Mary, not really sure if Alice was talking to herself, chose an obvious rather than a philosophical response. "I did hear them say something 'bout bringing the family 'pecuniary embarrassments' if'n you marry your lumberman."

"You don't really believe I should do as they want, do you?" Alice asked, still staring out the window.

"No," the servant answered quickly. Then, afraid her charge might interpret that as approval for disobeying her family, she amended her answer. "But that's not for me to say. Besides, it surely would make things a sight easier if'n you'd follow their guidance."

"Oh, yes," Alice said, lifting her skirts and twirling across the room. "If I should marry a rice planter, the wedding would be the event of the Waccamaw Neck, and everything would be very grand." Alice stopped her twirling, and her voice took on a strange, singsong quality. Her eyes were glazed, unseeing.

"Mother and Allard would want me to be married here at the Hermitage. I would glide down the stairway and across the carpet into the drawing room. Sunlight would filter through the tall windows and, for a moment, the only sound would be the ticking of the clock on the stairway landing and the lapping of the water in the inlet. Then the excited murmurs of the guests would rise up. Oh, such a wedding would be elegant and glorious for everyone . . . everyone but me."

Mary had stopped packing and was watching Alice carefully, a little afraid of her mood. When Alice resumed her narrative, her voice was barely audible. "No, for me it would be fearful and oppressive. The empty eyes in all those dark portraits of Flaggs and Belins that Mother is so proud of but has never even met would stare down at me, pinning me to the floor, daring me to risk censure. It would be the saddest day of my life."

Mary shook herself out of her lethargy and made a determined effort to continue packing and rid Alice of her despondency. "There be no point in frettin' 'bout things what may never happen.

Besides, you can't very well get married to no man—be he rich or
be he poor—till you come back from Charleston. You got a while
yet 'fore you needs to be carrying on so. And a sight can happen
between now and then."

"Oh, I know, Mary. And I know they will not *force* me to marry a
rice planter. But they *can* keep me from marrying a lumberman.
A woman is no better than a piece of property. Sometimes I wish I
had been born a boy and could make all my own decisions and go
where I want, when I want, with whom I want—"

"Humph," the servant interrupted. "Now that'd sure be fine.
But I don't think your Buck fella would be awantin' to marry you
if'n you be wearing britches and smoking a pipe."

"No," Alice laughed, responding to Mary's effort to cheer her.
"I guess I should be careful what I wish for—" Alice abruptly
stopped talking, as the gravity of her situation again weighed
upon her mind. *There is nothing I can do to stop it now. Everything
Mary said, as well as Mother's words, indicate that the matter is settled.*

Alice went on thinking that her stay in Charleston would be
only an interval, one term of classes. Her ring would give her
courage while away, and she would keep the picture of her beloved in her mind always. They could make her go to Charleston,
but they would never extinguish her love for Whit Buck, not in a
million years. And hadn't Whit recently gone to Charleston on
business? It was likely she would see him there from time to time,
and that would be unutterably more satisfying than meeting in
secret on the seabeach. Alice gave Mary a quick peck on the cheek.
"I am going to miss you so much," she said, then turned quickly
and ran out of the bedroom.

In a few hours Mary One had completed the packing and
closed the doors to Alice's armoire. The packed trunk was pushed
into the hallway at the top of the stairs, and all was in readiness for
the journey to Charleston, which would begin early the following
morning.

Murrells Inlet is especially dark and quiet on moonless nights, and
on such nights screech owls sometimes come near a house and sing.
Many believe that when a screech owl sings near a house on black
nights, death will follow. Alice and Mary both heard the screech owl
that night. And both tried to shake off the oppressive feeling that
overcame them, whispering of things dark and inevitable.

21

ALICE TREMBLED; FEAR was a jagged blade in her heart as she climbed into Allard's carriage with her brother. Some of her luggage was strapped to the top. Arthur stood beside the carriage sadly, and Mrs. Flagg, lightly weeping, was saying something about going down to Charleston and conducting herself with propriety and dignity and charm and grace. Alice did not answer, so the driver flipped the reins and the horse sprang forward. Alice did not look back.

The first ferry to be negotiated was the Georgetown Ferry at Winyah Bay, where four great rivers merged. As the ferryman was usually on duty there, Alice and her brother were spared any waiting for him to come from his fields. Ferrymen were usually farmers in the district, and they were not always at the river when needed. The ferryman directed the carriage onto the flat. Then the man rolled several barrels of sand on board and picked up two long poles just before he jumped on the boat. Alice and Allard were in the coach, and the coachman was on the box while they were propelled across the water. The ferryman maneuvered the barrels of sand with the poles to affect the flat's balance, and in forty-five minutes they were on the other side and moving into the roadway.

Allard insisted on going to the burial ground at Prince George Winyah Episcopal Church to see if the grave marker for Elizabeth Gause had been set in place. Allard often visited Elizabeth's husband, Ben Gause, to get the latest news of England, as well as the most recent methods of producing rice. The driver stopped the carriage when they reached the ancient church, and Allard walked into the walled-in-brick burial ground and viewed the marker. Alice, in a sort of daze, did not even bother to leave the coach.

Finally they were again on their way to Charleston, and Allard and Alice sat stiffly, looking neither to the right nor left, so silent that they could have been mistaken for ghosts on a midnight ride. Alice was thinking how much she hated Allard, hating him with such intensity that her fear of the unknown in Charleston subsided temporarily. She thought of Whit, and wondered how much time would pass before he realized she had been taken away. It may be days before he would have the chance to go to the seabeach and look for her. And days, weeks perhaps, would pass before he would know the truth, if he ever would. Her eyes burned with disgust for Allard.

A river emerged in the distance, and Alice knew that they would again stop and make arrangements to cross on a ferry. But the ferryman was nowhere in sight when they reached the water. Dr. Flagg got out of the coach, found two pieces of an old iron plow, and struck them together to attract attention. Just then a man poked his head from the door of a cabin, and he waved his arms frantically to indicate he had gotten the message.

"In a couple of hours we will cross the North Santee River, and after that the delta portion of Hampton Plantation, then the South Santee," Allard explained when they had been ferried across. "We shall spend the night at the inn located on the south side of that river."

Alice tried to stir herself. "Who operates that inn?" she asked, not really interested.

"A Mrs. Williams," he answered, remembering the woman's reputation for being a superb hostess.

Alice stretched, and took a deep breath. "I trust we will get some relaxation there."

"Some hot food and peaceful rest is what we both need," her brother answered.

That night at the inn, everything was pleasant enough, but the next morning, Allard told Alice they would spend that night at the Thirty Two Mile House. "Is that the place where several murders have taken place?" she asked sarcastically.

"Oh be serious. That was a long time ago and its ownership has changed several times since then."

Of the many tales of murder at the Thirty Two Mile House, the one that had intrigued Alice most was the one involving a minister. He had heard unusual noises coming from the next room and pulled a chair to his transom window to look. The proprietors of the inn were standing by a folding bed from which arms and legs protruded. For a few moments the arms and legs moved, and gurgling noises came from the fold of the bed. But suddenly the limbs were still and all sounds ceased.

The next day the minister reported what he had seen to the law, and an investigation was made. A further search disclosed skeletons of others who had been guests at the inn. The proprietors of the inn were charged with the murder of several of their customers. It was a gruesome story, and Alice shuddered at the thought of it.

Alice wished to know more about the notorious inn, but not enough to open the lines of communication with her brother. She would rather face murder than converse with Allard. Any chitchat they had enjoyed was in the past, never to be experienced again, she hoped.

As she had done the day before, Alice turned herself toward the carriage window so she would not face her brother, as he was responsible for this move that was surely breaking her heart. He may as well have taken a rice hook and ripped at her insides.

"Don't look so glum," Allard scolded. "Everyone in the world loves Charleston. You will be no different from anyone else."

"Oh, but I am different," she shot back. "I have become the black sheep of the Flagg family, and that is different enough."

"You needn't be the black sheep. You could conform to our expectations of you."

"Oh no, I cannot."

"No? You are a part of the family, whether you like it or not."

"Since I will not, as you have pointed out, conform to the Flagg family, it is unlikely I will conform to Charleston," Alice said, indicating that she had no intention of changing while away from home. "From what I have seen of that city, it is just like the Flagg family, only larger. The people there are required to do this and that, only because they have always been done that way. It is senseless." She paused, then added, "And as I think about it, I shall probably meet some boring fool whom you expect me to marry, and because I will refuse, things will go from horrible to unbearable."

"You certainly *are* different from any Flagg I have ever known," Allard said slowly, his voice raw with emotion.

Alice glared at him. "When I think of my family living in Murrells Inlet, that quiet place that I love, and I in Charleston, with those sacred cows and their stodgy St. Cecilia ball and races and gossip, it just tears my insides out."

"You talk like a wharfman," Allard scolded.

"Just you wait until you again see me. I will have been exposed to so many wharfmen, I may look like one!"

Each remark became more shocking and infuriating as Allard and Alice jostled toward the inn where they would stay the night. When they arrived there, they were so weary that they had ceased bickering. The coachman took the horses to be attended to, and Allard paid for two rooms.

The inn was a homey gathering place, more homespun in motif than elegant. A red and green tartan blanket was casually thrown over a pine bench, and the aroma of orange and cinnamon floated on the air. A bucket of large pinecones sat by the hearth, and a murex seashell, in seemingly perfect condition, lay on the mantel. The ambiance could have been pleasing under different circumstances.

Before dinner was served, Allard met Alice in the parlor. He seated himself and crossed his long legs. "There will be no murders committed here tonight. There is a transom window over each hallway door, and if anything frightens you, pull a chair to the door and scream for me through the transom. I will hear you if you call."

Alice did not comment again on the murders, and when the guests were summoned to the dining room, she quietly followed Allard and took a seat beside him. They were offered choices of oyster pie, fish, wild turkey, duck, venison, and vegetables. Dessert was a concoction called Westminster Fool.

That night Alice slept fitfully. Sometime during the lonely hours after midnight, she thought she heard a ghostly gurgling sound, filling her mind with eerie thoughts of death. In the morning she felt as though she had always been awake.

This would be the day she would begin her life in Charleston, whether she desired it or not. She dressed quickly and met Allard in the dining room, where, as he waited for her, he thumbed through a newly published book, *The Carolina Housewife*.

"This book was written by a Charleston lady," he said as his sister entered the room.

"I thought real ladies had their names in print only three times," Alice said coolly. "When they are born, when they marry, and when they die."

"The book is published anonymously, likely for the very reason you have mentioned, but the proprietor of this inn just told me that in actuality the book was written by Sarah Rutledge, a daughter of Edward Rutledge."

"The *signer*," Alice said mockingly.

"He did sign the Declaration," Allard replied tartly.

"Well, please do not impose that book on me," Alice replied. "I am sure that when Edward Rutledge dies, his name on the grave marker will be in capital letters, and if the Almighty is mentioned, His name will be in lower case."

A servant now placed a crystal bowl of quince jelly on the table and asked what Alice and Allard would like for breakfast. They ordered fricasseed eggs, cheese pudding, and spoon bread. All was served, along with a pot of steaming coffee.

Before arriving at Madame Talvande's, Allard insisted on visiting the market, one of the his favorite Charleston landmarks. Only after the carriage stopped on Meeting Street did Alice agree to accompany him on a stroll through the market. *Anything to delay the arrival at her new home.* Allard stepped from the carriage first in order to assist Alice. Her tiny feet went down to the one step, where she paused to press in her skirts and pull the rest of the large hoop through the door. She looked around, noticing a rather pleasant "feel" or "air" about the city that she had failed to perceive on former visits. The pace was leisurely.

Unlike the street, the market was abuzz with activity, as it was almost three o'clock and the gentlemen who walked home at that time usually ate their meal at the market and went home for a short nap before returning to their offices on Broad Street. Market stalls were jam-packed with produce which had come from the islands, "Hungry Neck," and the rivers and parishes. Boats arrived daily with fish, shrimp, oysters, and vegetables, and other foods came by the wagonload. While some of the wagons were tidy, others had wobbly wheels and were pulled by swayback horses.

Alice studied the produce and the people selling it. The market was the most colorful place she had ever seen, with tall, straight, thin, dark-skinned women balancing huge baskets on their heads. Some of the baskets held vegetables, fruits, and some even transported turtle eggs.

Sea turtles were sold there, and they were not to be confused with terrapin, or cooters. Most country people, like Old Mr. Magood, sold cooters at the market. Allard and Alice watched with rapt attention as Old Mr. Magood attempted to decapitate a cooter. The reptile was in a large tub, but the owner was having trouble catching it with its head extended from the shell. Finally, the head came out, there was a quick whack, and the job was done.

All of it made Alice squeamish and she passed to the next booth. Maum Phyllis was making stuffing for fowl, using eggs that had been taken from hens before the eggs had been laid. The next booth held barrels of oysters, and bowls of hot oyster stew were being served. Alice declined, although Allard paid for a bowl of the thick, white, simmering soup. When the last of his soup had been consumed, Allard was ready to go to Madame Talvande's.

22

THE CARRIAGE ROLLED into the driveway between the white, four-story frame house and a ten-foot-high red brick wall and stopped in the garden. Small gardens lay behind most Charleston homes, and gardeners kept lawns, flowers, and fruit trees in perfect order. As soon as Alice was out of the carriage she went over to a walkway that was lined with small orange trees common to the South Carolina Low Country. Although the oranges were too bitter to be eaten, they made a most marvelous marmalade.

"That tree is *Citrus aurantium*," Allard explained, "and it has been known in England since the twelfth century, although it is believed to be a native of southern China or Burma." Alice did not answer, but turned her attention to three servants who had suddenly appeared and were introducing themselves as Kit and Cudjo, husband and wife, and a man named Moses, who said he was the gardener. As Moses began to remove Alice's trunk from the top of the coach, Kit suggested that Alice and Allard present themselves at the front door where they would be greeted by a butler, Fraser.

Alice and Allard were ushered into the drawing room where they waited only a moment before Madame Talvande came in, walking across the carpet. She wore a gown of an unusual nutmeg shade that enhanced the mellowed-brick color of her hair, and although the dress was narrow about the knees, there was a flare at the hem that rustled as she walked.

With the brightest of smiles, the woman extended a small, white

143

hand ringed in lace ruffles. "I am Madame Talvande." Her voice had just the slightest accent, and she tilted her head in a rather coquettish way. Alice was thinking that there was something flamboyant about her, something of the stage actress.

"I am Dr. Flagg, and this is Alice."

Madame took Alice's hands in hers. "Alice, my dear, welcome to my house and my school. You will be very happy here." With a sort of flourish, she let go of Alice's hands and gestured toward the ceiling. "You can see that this house is special. Large rooms with fourteen-foot ceilings. Our cornices are of gold leaf, and the damask came from England. The tapestries are from a Bonaparte sale in New York."

Alice was thinking that if she had expected to feel institutionalized at this school, she had been mistaken. She had never in her life seen such lovely surroundings.

Madame went on with her flourishes. "We dance in the ballroom, a grand room just above this one. You will sleep on the fourth floor. But allow me to show you the dining room." Without awaiting a response, Madame turned on a heel and Allard was right behind her. Alice followed.

From the doorway a mahogany table stretched almost out of sight, and Chippendale chairs lined the sides. "Although my students have not arrived as yet," Madame pointed out, "my table is always set with the Crown Derby china. It is twenty-four carat, you know." Gleaming silver pieces also graced the table as well as a sideboard which held tureens, serving pieces of every description, and pitchers.

Alice looked up. The chandelier was as large as a foal, the prisms sparkling in the late-afternoon sun. The fireplace, with trompe l'oeil and gold leaf, seemed large enough to walk inside. Although Alice didn't sanction the life-style such a house indicated, she had to admit to herself that everything she had seen was exquisite.

"Now allow me to show you the garden, Alice," Madame Talvande said, "where you will be served tea and biscuits while your brother and I get settled down to business at my desk."

Alice realized that Madame was getting rid of her with amazing cleverness so that she and Allard could conduct business, some of which they had no intention of letting Alice hear.

Alice eased her slender body into a wrought-iron chair on the brick extension of a piazza and looked around. It was a snug harbor for schoolgirls, she thought as she took in the several tables and chairs. Just then Fraser came with a tray of tea and cookies, and Alice had no thought of the conversation going on in the drawing room.

"I should tell you that we are bringing Alice here somewhat against her will," Allard explained.

"Against her will? My goodness, most women consider it a rare entitlement."

"Yes. Well, you see, Alice has chosen to turn her back on the wishes of her family for the attentions of a common man, one who is beneath her station in life."

Madame suddenly became even more alive, and endeavored to choose the very words that Allard hoped would fall on his ears. "Some are born to an exceptional family like the Flaggs, and others are not. But those who are fortunate to have been born into such a family sometimes court catastrophe by allowing their attentions to be diverted. They put themselves in danger with quick decisions. Fortunately, they usually discover that someone in the family was busily turning the chain of events to save them and lead them back to the safe and familiar regions of a prosperous and dedicated family. I am sure that you are leading Alice safely back to your family, and I shall see that none of the horror you fear will befall her. When you again see her, she will be a polished Charleston woman, one who is proud of her privileged family." Madame stopped for a second, and then added with emphasis, "When you see her, you will notice that she has withdrawn into the halls of her impeccable breeding."

"I trust you are right, Madame," Allard said. "And I should tell you that we have no desire that this man, Whit Buck, a Waccamaw River lumberman, see Alice while she is here."

Madame rose, took Allard by the arm, and slowly walked him to a window. She did not look out, but faced Allard. "We cannot of course keep our students locked up, but we have had only one infraction of such that you speak."

"Oh?"

"Yes. Marie Whaley, the daughter of an Edisto Island cotton planter, was attracted to the affections of Mr. George F. Morris, who, although he owned property in Charleston, was a native New Yorker."

"And what happened?"

"Marie was enrolled in my school, for many of the same reasons that you have brought Alice. But I am sure that Alice has no such intentions in her pretty head."

"What happened to Marie Whaley?" Allard asked, giving Madame Talvande his undivided attention.

"She left my home and met Mr. Morris at St. Michael's Episcopal Church on Meeting Street, and they were married."

"Did you find out immediately?" Allard asked.

Madame held up a hand. "Not immediately. The couple decided that Marie would secretly return here, and that they would wait until the light of day to announce the big event."

"And?"

Madame Talvande's voice took on a quality that made it plain she was ready to cease the story about Marie Whaley. "Suffice it to say that no such thing will happen to Alice Flagg," she said with authority. "Needless to say I am most determined that such an event will never happen again."

"But you allow the women to leave the premises?"

"Each afternoon we allow our students—with a chaperone—to take a two-hour break and walk to the region of the Battery. Fresh air and exercise are important to a woman's development, I believe. But you may rest assured that we will do everything possible to see that Alice has no liaison with the lumberman."

"I have complete confidence in your word," Allard said, turning his head toward the window as he became deep in thought. "And for my part, I shall see that Whit Buck never learns of Alice's whereabouts."

"Of course he would not be welcomed in this house," Madame continued. "None of the women have male guests here. And you may be interested to know that I am now in the process of having a ten-foot-high gate cast by Christopher Werner, the most renowned ironworker in the city. When the gate is stationed in the brick wall, we will be in a position to regulate the students even more."

"I must admit that I feel a little less than positive of Alice's security here, Madame Talvande."

"I think you should say farewell to your sister now," Madame Talvande said. "As the other women have not arrived as yet, you may go to the fourth floor and see where Alice will be living. I am sure each of you has something to say to the other." Madame rang for Fraser and asked him to bring Alice to the drawing room, and when she arrived, Madame explained to her that she would be shown to the room where she would sleep, and Allard could also see that room.

Alice followed Allard upstairs, but they said nothing. The room that served as communal sleeping quarters for the students had beds and bedside tables lining one wall, and armoires along another side of the long, rectangular room. Alice wandered over to a window, where she looked out at Charleston, and in a moment her brother joined her. It was obvious that neither one knew what to say. When Allard left for his journey home, he would be traveling to a house where he would now live with his aging mother and his brother. Nothing would be the same as it had been. And Alice would be left alone in Charleston, to face the new life that stretched before her, a time that now seemed mysterious and frightening. Each in their own thoughts, they continued to stare from the window. After a period of time, almost without realizing it, Allard and Alice actually began to see what their eyes had been taking in.

What they now viewed was quite unlike anything they had seen during their journey. They had traveled through fields and meadows, swamps and valuable estates, and they had seen thousands of acres of cultivated rice fields by the rivers. Charleston, so different from all of that, was a city where the planters kept elegant town houses, staffed year-around, although they spent precious little time there. Planter families came for "the social season" and occasionally the planters brought their rice to their agents to sell to English markets. But for the most part, the exquisite houses were showplaces, although there were some business establishments in the city, and the artisans and merchants lived in the city throughout the year.

Allard finally spoke. "You cannot see the Cooper River from this house, but I can tell you that nearly every conceivable kind of vessel is putting to anchor now, vessels carrying all sorts of products. Some of the hulls are filled with pitch, provisions, rice. Other craft are bringing people to this port."

Alice remained quiet, and as her brother observed her in the afternoon light from the window, she looked almost gaunt, the color drained from her face. He decided he should leave before either of them became emotional, and he put an arm around her shoulders. "We shall miss you."

She turned to him, her eyes wide and questioning. "You are *really* going to leave me here?"

"It is not as though I were subjecting you to hard labor. Any woman worth her salt would love to be in your shoes."

"Think of *your* shoes," Alice answered, weakly. "You have just taken your toe and pushed a potato into the ashes."

"Do try to bear it a little better, Alice," Allard pleaded. "Look around you. This house is special. And you will be pampered every minute by Kit."

"You think you are removing me from the Hermitage, and that I shall find a planter, someone of whom you and Mother approve, and marry him and never return to that house," she said, staring at her brother coldly.

Allard's mouth was stiff and white-lipped. "We have good reasons. We want to protect you."

Alice thought of Whit, and the optimism that came from that thought surfaced, and she managed to put on a brave front. She took a deliberate step toward Allard. "You and Mother have not shown one shred of tenderness or devotion to me since this entire thing happened. You think you have just taken my only love away from me. There are very few things you cannot do, Allard, when you set your mind to it. You are wealthy enough, and visible enough as a Flagg, to receive special consideration in almost any way you desire, such as enrolling me in school at this eminent school." Alice turned and walked to the door, her hand on the knob. "But before you go there is something I want you to know, because I assure you it is so valid I would declare it under oath. It will stand the test, because I am going to see that it is all but writ in stone. *I will be living at the Hermitage when you are dead and gone.*"

And Alice's words had the ring of prophecy to them.

23

THE NEXT MORNING Alice awoke to the sound of church bells and wondered what time it was, although it really did not matter until next week, when courses started. She lay limply on the four-poster bed thinking about her life and before she knew it the bells of St. Michael's Church were chiming another hour. It was eight o'clock. She got up quickly and dressed to the sounds of the street vendors outside her windows.

"Swimpy-raw-raw," came the call of the shrimp vendor, advertising his raw shrimp, and almost at the same time came the vegetable vendor's voice calling, "Vege-tuble! Vege-tuble!" She wondered if she would have to listen to such calls all day long. She remembered from former visits to Charleston that the street calls had always been an important part of the city, but she did not remember how noisy it was at night. It was so unlike Murrells Inlet, where everything was as dark as pitch at night and the only sounds came from lapping water, or wildlife calls, such as a bull alligator summoning his mate. Oh well. She would try to make the best of it by keeping her mind on the next time she saw Whit.

After splashing some of her favorite gardenia cologne on her forehead and neck, Alice started down the long corridor leading to the staircase. When she reached the second floor, she paused as her eyes took in the splendid ballroom, the ceiling of which she believed to be higher than the usual fourteen feet. The cornices of hand-carved walnut depicted rope moldings set with heads of

Muses, and the Regency chandelier of green overlaid glass was exquisite. In spite of its grandness and rich furnishings, the house filled Alice with a nameless terror. There was something oppressive about standing in a mansion such as that which her brother and mother expected her to oversee one day as mistress. Her lumberman could never afford anything close to such a house, and she had no reason to set her heart on it.

She placed a hand on the staircase leading down to the drawing room and admired the framework more for its design than its size. The curve was broken with a landing so as not to cut across the Palladian window which lighted the hall. When she reached the drawing room, Alice's nostrils perked to the smell of beeswax and a peculiar moist odor that spoke of the sea, and it reminded her of home. *Home.* She held her hand at her chest as she entered the dining room, and under her hand-embroidered white taffeta dress, she felt the strength the ring sent flowing into every recess of her body.

"Will you be having your tea and bacon now?" Kit called out.

"Yes. I am ready to eat now."Alice chose a chair near a window and sat down, but Kit poked her head around a door leading into the pantry and motioned that Alice should go to the sideboard and select her food.

"Thank you," she murmured as she took her plate to the silver services that held breakfast foods. The monotonous ticking of a clock reminded Alice that she did not wish to waste much time in the house. She planned to get out by herself and explore the surroundings. After choosing barely a mouthful of egg pye, bacon, and orange marmalade, she selected a biscuit and went back to the table.

Kit came into the room and looked at Alice's plate. "You be a light eater."

"I am just not very hungry, Kit."

"You should at least taste the mango muskmelons. They're the last of the season."

"I do not think I can eat more than I have on my plate, but I thank you," Alice said, as she sat down. Before beginning the meal, she smoothed her dress with a yellow satin sash.

"You be pretty frail," Kit said. Realizing that Kit was scrutinizing her appearance, Alice hurried with her meal, then rushed upstairs to her room, where she clapped a straw hat with yellow streamers on her hair. When she returned, Madame Talvande was standing at the foot of the stairs.

Madame smiled her brilliant smile that showed off to the best advantage two rows of pearly teeth, the likes of which Alice had never seen in her life. "And did you sleep soundly all alone in that large room?"

"With no difficulty at all," Alice lied, thinking on the night noises to which she was completely unaccustomed.

Madame put a dainty hand ringed, as always, in ruffles, to her forehead as though she were thinking. "Would you, Alice, care to join me in the drawing room? I have some accounts to work on, but we could talk."

"No, thank you," Alice said, remindful that it was kind of Madame Talvande to offer to spend some time with her. She was anxious, however, to go to the docks and begin searching for Whit. "But I plan to walk near the Battery."

Madame took Alice's arm, and slowly walked her into the drawing room, much as she had done with Allard yesterday. "Do you know, Alice, that it is a rule of this school that young women not go out alone?" She didn't await a reply before she added, "And only for a short time during the afternoon on any occasion?"

"No. I did not know that."

"If you will wait until the allotted time, after four o'clock, I shall accompany you on your stroll. It would do both of us good to get a whiff or two of the seabreeze."

"Uh, Madame," Alice began, a little hesitantly, "you know that we, the Flaggs that is, own a home near this place, on Tradd Street."

"I *am* aware of that."

"My brother had no plans to go there, and my mother would be vastly upset if I did not check on the staff and let her know how things are being carried out."

Madame Talvande hesitated before she answered. She straightened up and her gaze rested on Alice. "Your brother mentioned no such thing to me."

"My brother's plans were to return to the Hermitage as soon as possible," Alice said, a thoughtful expression on her face.

Madame Talvande was silent, her mouth tightly drawn, her face a picture of gravity. She sighed and looked directly at Alice. "Are you sure your mother would want you to go to the Flagg mansion and call on the servants?"

"Of course! If Mother were here she would do it herself."

Madame cleared her throat nervously. "Well all right. I have things to attend to now, but I suppose April, one of my servants, could be your chaperone if you are anxious to go. But, remember, be back here in two hours."

Madame clearly instructed April to accompany Alice only to the Flagg mansion and back, but Alice had the servant girl's ear as soon as they set off down Legare Street. She advised April of her situation, or most of it. She told the part about being sent to Charleston against her will, but then invented some imaginary cousin who owned ships at the dock. She claimed the cousin would be sympathetic to her cause and therefore had not been notified of her arrival. Therefore she would need to visit the docks to find him, so he could convince her family to take her back home.

April pitied the poor girl and decided there would be no harm in "chaperoning" her to the docks. She could not imagine why anyone should have to be forced into Madame Talvande's school, no matter how much she liked the woman.

Once they reached the corner of Tradd Alice flew to King, turned right, and almost ran to the Battery, with April hurrying behind. Passing by the Miles Brewton House Alice remembered what her mother had told her about "King Billy" Alston living there, and she thought back on how the Alston twins had talked of it. But Alice did not slow down to contemplate the mansion.

Scads of people crowded the streets and Alice looked about, her eyes darting from side to side. The streets appeared mean, and she observed the shadowy alleys and tiny courtyards, and wondered if she dare take refuge in one of them. Just then she was pushed against a brick wall by a solid phalanx of bodies and was separated from April.

"Who are you?" Alice shouted out.

"You don't know who we are?" a strange-looking man chided.

Alice looked about at so many men with beards and large round hats and long coats. She noticed only a few women and even fewer children. "No. Who are all of you?"

"Prospectors."

"Prospectors?"

"Indeed. You've heard of the Gold Rush, have you not?"

"As a matter of fact, no."

"Why, miss, where have you been?" Alice did not bother to answer, as the man quickly explained the mission. "Eight thousand gold seekers have boarded ninety ships and are on their way to the Pacific by way of Cape Horn." Pointing to a group of people gathered nearby, he said, "We boarded the *Crescent City,* a paddle-wheeler, in New York. Most of us will travel steerage, and a steerage ticket is eighty dollars."

"Where are you bound for in the Pacific?" Alice asked, now becoming interested.

"San Francisco!"

"California?"

"The one and the same," the man said, excitedly. "There's a fortune to be made there. If we could travel the shortcut through the Isthmus of Panama that is used by mail carriers, we could arrive there even sooner, and it might be possible to reduce the lead of the prospectors that are ahead of us."

"How do you know you will find gold?" Alice asked.

"Because everybody's talking it. Fortunes have been made in a day. In an hour, for that matter." For a moment the man closed his eyes, and Alice could see that he was envisioning a treasure trove.

"And why are you here?" Alice queried.

"For supplies, miss. We make many stops." The broad-shouldered man, all six foot plus of him, breathed deeply of the salt air. "When we leave here," he added, "the *Crescent City* will head for the Republica de Panama, a little smaller than South Carolina, and with fewer people than this state."

"How do you know?"

"Miss, there's little that we don't know. All of us. The gold, and getting to it, well, that's all we speak of."

"Have a safe trip," Alice said, moving away from the stranger.

"Yes, miss. We'll be safe, I think. Although the Republica de anama won't be civilized like Charleston. It's a steaming jungle, I hear. Undoubtedly alive with tigers, boa constrictors, crocodiles, monkeys, and natives who live by a code of superstition and cannibalism. But it will all be worth it when I get my hands on the gold."

Alice spotted April and took her leave, believing the man hardly noticed her departure. She had never seen anyone so obsessed with anything before. Were there actually people who idolized gold so much? She could hardly believe it. And what else was she to learn? She realized she had been so sheltered in Murrells Inlet that she had no idea what was going on in the world away from the Waccamaw Neck.

24

ALICE STOOD IN the middle of the bedroom and pressed her hands to her face. She was exhausted; she had slept hardly at all, and seemed cursed with interminable nights. She hoped that when her classes started tomorrow she would settle down to a regular schedule and relax a little.

She pulled her ring up over the neck of her cornflower-blue blouse and pressed it between her thumb and forefinger as she paced the room, lost in contemplation. Her green eyes, without the amber streaks that shone in most green eyes, were incandescent in the morning light coming from the ceiling-to-floor windows. Although she had brushed her hair and pinned it into a bun, loose strands played around her face and neck.

After a few minutes she sat down at a ladies' desk, pulled a piece of paper from a pigeonhole, and looked at it, thinking. Should she write Whit? What would she tell him? How could she explain what had happened? She studied the paper, thinking that she was locked in the jaws of a vise. There was nothing for her. Nothing, nothing, nothing but long days and sleepless nights away from her beloved.

"I simply don't know what to do," she moaned. "If I send him a communication it will only upset his timetable and his work. He could not take the time away from his business to make the long trip to Charleston and back. And if he did, what good would it do?" He would only stay a day or two and have to return to the

155

sawmill, and the short visit would make them long for each other all the more.

But if he would come to Charleston on business now and then, and they could see each other, declare their love and make plans for their future, the time would surely fly by and she could return to the Hermitage and make arrangements for her wedding. Allard and her mother would in all decency at least make a pretense of giving their blessing, Alice concluded. After all, she had consented to come to Charleston and attend the winter term of school. She pushed the paper back into the pigeonhole, deciding she wouldn't communicate with anybody just now.

But as she continued to think on these things, it came to Alice that someday she would want to tell her man how she had come to live in Charleston for a school session, and she would want to describe her feelings, and the city, to him. Suddenly she realized that she should record the events of her days in a journal. Not only would her future husband find pleasure in such a narrative, but someday she would have children who would read the account of their mother once floundering unhappily in one of the world's most beautiful cities. She quickly dropped the ring on the white velvet ribbon under the neck of her blouse and went to the armoire for her purse. She would go to King Street and purchase a journal in which to record her story.

This time Madame easily granted permission for Alice and April to leave the house. Madame recognized the advantage of having a proper journal in which to record the day's activities.

King Street, the main shopping artery in the city, was bustling with activity. From the shining carriages in front of each store, Alice was reminded that Charleston matrons had voracious appetites for shopping at the exclusive shops. Footmen, coachmen, and spirited horses awaited the women who leisurely made their selections.

April soon went off to purchase a few things for the house, and arranged to meet Alice a few houses away from the school so that they could arrive at Madame Talvande's together. Alice strolled into an emporium at the corner of Broad and King streets. She thought that she had never seen the likes of this merchandise in her life. Dresses of lace, satin, and silks of every hue were here and there, and hats fashioned of plumes and artificial roses accented the dresses. A black lace shawl lay on a chair with a fan as translucent as onion skin resting on it. Brooches and cameos on velvet ribbons were everywhere.

All of it was wonderful, Alice admitted to herself. But it was not for her. She had turned her back on the life lived by the rich when she accepted Whit's ring. She was annoyed at herself for being attracted to these extravagant items, and quickly went to the stationery portion of the store.

There were journals and scrapbooks with the most beautiful covers in existence, Alice believed. She chose one of black, with pictures of young women as decoration. One lady had lustrous brown hair wreathed in roses and greenery. Her necklace was of gold, and an off-the-shoulder dress revealed creamy white shoulders. Another woman wore a blue velvet jacket adorned in silver braid. Her hat of blue velvet was embellished with a pink plume that extended from front to back, and underneath the brim were three pink roses. A face encircled by thick braids looked into a mirror framed with blood-red roses. Although Alice knew that she would never be as beautifully attired as the ladies on the cover of the journal, she chose to buy it for her notes. She was thinking that it would be one of the most beautiful things she would ever own.

When outside, Alice looked around. It was a chilly but clear day, with a hint of the sea in the air, and the prospectors were gone. Although Alice was filled with compassion for Whit, and conscious of their suffering as they longed to be together, she decided to fill herself with happiness by her own determination and will. For this one day she would forget a broken heart and loneliness and look on the mansions she had passed, and as the years went by, perhaps someone would get pleasure by reading her thoughts. Just then she remembered seeing a small booklet listing the owners of the Charleston houses, and she rushed back inside the store and bought it. Using it as her guide, she set out on a stroll that would help get her mind off her worries.

The homes were a puzzle of banisters, eaves, and intricate scrollwork, but the craftsmanship that most caught Alice's eye was the ironwork. Gates and fences and other decorations were all different. They had obviously been especially designed for each owner by the craftsmen.

One house that intrigued her was located at 110 Broad Street, and the book told her that a famous South Carolinian had lived there. Joel Roberts Poinsett, a Charlestonian who served in the

United States foreign service, introduced the poinsettia to this country while he was ambassador to Mexico. Finding this information interesting, Alice paused and leaned against a gas-lamp post and read from the book. Drawing-room mantels were of grained Italian marble with delicately carved figures, including animals and a central scene in which Ceres, goddess of the harvest, was the main figure. Alice closed the book, gave the house another glance, then passed on to 116 Broad Street, where a governor of the state had lived.

"Dictator John" Rutledge, who had served as president of the Republic of South Carolina, governor of the state, associate justice and chief justice of the United States Supreme Court, had lived in the house where the ironwork was by Christopher Werner. The state's palmetto tree and the federal eagle were among the ironwork designs. In the dwelling were eight carved mantels, the most outstanding one being in the ballroom and carved in the likenesses of angels, cherubs, and a tiny owl.

Alice decided it was time to walk back to her new home, if she could ever call it that. On the way, she read from the booklet and made mental notes of places she would try to visit before she became too burdened with her schoolwork. One house she would surely see was being built for Thomas A. Coffin, a member of a well-known Charleston and Beaufort clan. When completed, that house would occupy the most desirable location in the city, giving a commanding view of both the Cooper and Ashley rivers, the entire harbor, and the sea beyond.

The book informed Alice that the Coffin house would look directly at White Point, a spot where the pirate Stede Bonnet and his men went to the gallows in 1718. Bonnet was a retired British army officer, but became a pirate in order to escape his nagging wife in Barbados. He bought and fitted out a ship, the *Revenge*, sailed away from his plantation, and plundered ships along the Carolina coast. He was one of the few pirates who forced his prisoners to walk the plank to their death. Bonnet once received a king's pardon, but soon returned to pirating under an assumed name, and he surrendered when all of his ships ran aground during a battle. The bodies of Bonnet and his men hung from the gallows for a time as warning to those who might wish to fly the Jolly Roger. Then they were buried below the high-tide mark.

Tired now, Alice was almost home and soon met up with April. When they arrived at the house on Legare Street, Madame was writing a letter. Alice removed her hat, walked toward Madame's ornate desk, and sat down.

Madame Talvande put aside her pen and faced Alice. "My dear, I am so pleased that you always wear a hat when you leave this house. It is a rule of the school that all women wear hats, even when they walk only in the garden."

"I have hats to match everything," Alice said.

"One more thing, Alice," Madame went on. "The students will be arriving today. During this season we have twenty women, sixteen boarders and four day students. After they arrive, you must never leave the premises alone." Madame paused, and then added with a flourish, "There will always be a friend to accompany you on your daily walks."

She hoped she could find a friend, Alice was thinking, but it would be unlikely that she would confide in anyone about her love for Whit. Alice was staring at the hat in her lap as she thought how difficult it would be to find Whit at the docks. But difficult or not, she would visit the docks as often as possible, and when she saw her beloved, her dismal life would quickly change.

Madame pushed a sheet of paper toward Alice. "Perchance you would like to read what I am writing, as these communications deal with my students and their work."

Alice reached for the letter.

"If you have any questions, do not hesitate to ask me anything," Madame Talvande said.

Madame's handwriting was filled with coils, spirals, and other curlicues. As Alice read, she believed the letter to be to the father of a student named Elizabeth:

> I am happy to inform you, as Elizabeth has indicated that her wish is to continue all of her studies except arithmetic, and she is desirous of relinquishing that subject, she shall certainly be gratified in that respect.
>
> ROSE TALVANDE

"Did Elizabeth have trouble learning arithmetic?" Alice asked.

Madame again put aside her pen. "Some women have a great deal of trouble with that subject, while they show great promise in others," Madame explained. "It is my theory that if Elizabeth is worrying about the arithmetic, then we shall relax that subject for her and lift her spirits in others."

Madame Talvande certainly knew a lot about human nature, Alice thought. It was possible that when Elizabeth returned to the study of arithmetic she would approach it with a fresh mind and even find it to her liking, without having to continue in her present state of anxiety over the subject.

Madame passed to Alice a note of thanks to two Columbia students named Nancy and Rebecca, for "the elegant souvenir." And the next letter was one that intrigued Alice:

Charleston
November 1848
Madame Rose Talvande to her friend Harriet

Your letter, Harriet, requires an answer to solve what I call no difficulty. "This pair of silk stockings is yet good" is perfectly correct. The verb "is" agrees with the nominative "pair" which, although a noun of multitude, signifies *one* particular pair. So the verb is properly put in the singular. I am almost certain that the sentence penned by my dear Harriet is her way of deciding the point.

Alice read and reread the letter and put it back on the desk. "You assist your students in every way," she said, thinking how very much she liked Madame Talvande. She stood, looked over Madame's shoulder, and took note of a statement she was preparing for the father of two students:

Current bill from Madame Rose Talvande.	
Five and a half months' board and tuition for Sarah and Margaret	$282.86
Grimshaws U. S. and Greece with questions	$2.00
Two cyphering books and one ancient atlas	$2.00
Dancing lessons	$34.00
Total	$320.86

"Madame Talvande, may I look over some of the books I shall be studying this term?" Alice asked.

The expression on Madame's face indicated that she was not pleased with the request—she was fearful that Alice would not find the curriculum to her liking—but finally she acquiesced. Alice followed Madame into the library, where the teacher took several books from a shelf. With the books under her arm and holding her hat, Alice went upstairs to the fourth floor, and to the bed by a window which she had staked out as hers. She placed the books on the bed and her hat in the armoire.

Just looking at the books that would be a part of her curriculum worried her. Had the tutor Allard had brought from Germany prepared her for this more formal study, in Charleston? She lay across the bed and opened the first book. Before she gave her attention to the pages before her, Alice glanced toward the window and wondered if there would ever be time to read some of the novels she had seen in the library. Some of them looked absolutely delicious, books like *The Captain of the Vulture* and *Lady Audley's Secret*.

But now looking back at the books scattered about her bed, Alice doubted there would be much time for novels. Besides classes, she had to go to the docks every time she could find an excuse to go there. For any day that she missed going could be the day that Whit would anchor a vessel carrying lumber!

The first book Alice perused was one on the French language: *An Introduction for the French Language, With classical, analytical and synthetical elucidations.* The book was copyrighted in 1830. Alice pushed that book aside and pulled another to her.

A Catechism of the History and Chronology of South Carolina was its title. Alice flipped through the pages. Although there were no illustrations, the paper, print, and binding were excellent.

She glanced at the title pages of a couple of other books, including one on Elizabethan and other early English and Continental literature, W. H. Timrod's journal—in part—during the expedition to St. Augustine in 1836, and one on geography: *Geography with a brief view of the Solar System, by way of question and answer.* Shining words on the cover read, "Next to religion, what study is so important to youth, as the study of the earth we inhabit, and of that glorious system, of which our earth forms a part?"

Alice gathered the books together and went back to the library. Madame was nowhere in sight, and she decided to steal a glance at some of the novels that interested her. There was an old printing of Sebastian Brant's *Ship of Fools,* printed at Strasburg in 1497, and Milton's *Paradise Lost,* a poem in two books, and there were limited editions *de luxe* of some living authors like Thackeray and Dickens.

But the book that caught Alice's eye most was *The Tryals of Major Stede Bonnet, and other Pirates,* a book printed in London. Although she selected no book to read that day, Alice was totally convinced that Allard had chosen a wonderful school for her, and if she applied herself, she would be educated as well as any woman in South Carolina. She could withstand one term, she decided, as she could do worse than be taught by Madame Rose Talvande of Charleston.

When her family came to Charleston for the social season, however, she would return home with them. Regardless of whether or not she had seen Whit Buck by that time, she would take up her life with him where she left off. She would live up to her part of the bargain, and the breach of common decency if Allard and her mother failed to live up to theirs would be grounds for taking her leave from the family and marrying Whit without their consent. Having made up her mind now as to what she would do, Alice was pleased when she heard the commotion of several students arriving at the mansion.

25

ELLA RAVENEL AND Rutledge Dupre came into the mansion as though they were accustomed to the life there. They were familiar with the school and Madame Talvande, for they were from Charleston and had attended Madame Talvande's School for two years prior to this one.

Various daughters of rice planters came in a great flurry of excitement, with many trunks being carried to the fourth floor and everyone talking at once as their billowy skirts filled stairways and halls. But the thing that surprised Alice most was the number of women whose fathers were cotton planters on the sea islands, and if their carriages and clothing meant anything as a scale of wealth, these were the ones accustomed to the most luxurious of lives. Yet they were friendly, and Alice became enchanted with Frances Whaley of Edisto. She was thrilled when Frances chose the bed next to hers.

"Alice, are you one of the Flaggs of Wachesaw Plantation?"

"Yes," Alice said, surprised that Frances had heard of her family when she herself was not familiar with any of the cotton planters on Edisto Island. And everything that Alice knew about the production of cotton could be written on a pinhead! "I wish I knew more of Edisto," Alice added, "but we have a whole term for you to tell me everything."

"I will tell you one thing," Frances began. "I am surprised that Madame allows a Whaley to attend her school." She paused a moment, then added, "But she is aware that Papa is a wealthy cotton planter and paying the expenses is no burden on him, and if I know *her,* that is the sort of student she seeks."

"Why would she not admit a Whaley?" Alice asked, her eyes wide with wonder.

"Oh, it all dates back to the time that Marie eloped."

"Marie who?" Alice asked.

"Marie Whaley, my aunt. You know of course that eloping with a man not approved by one's family is a sin black enough to keep one out of heaven!"

"You mean Marie Whaley came here for school and eloped with a man of whom the family did not approve?" Alice asked.

"That is so. Isn't it scandalous?" Frances giggled.

Alice joined her friend in giggling though she wasn't sure why. It was *not* funny. Marie was obviously in love with the man forbidden to her, and she took the responsibility of her life away from her family and made a new life for herself. But it *was* sort of amusing that she would have the nerve to walk away from Madame Talvande and do such a thing. By now, Alice was bending over with laughter and looking forward to many more talks with Frances Whaley.

Alice thought that in all her born days she had never seen a woman as interesting as Frances. Strands of blond hair played about her face, which had a few freckles on the nose and was slightly sun-bronzed, displaying a blush. Alice detected in this girl a mite of stubbornness, a trait that could be tolerated if one had a sense of humor. Frances had that too. Frances Whaley was simply herself, not caring one iota to be like anyone else, and Alice thought she could not keep the laughter out of her voice if she tried.

Just at that moment Mary Margaret Seabrook, also of Edisto Island, came over to say something to Frances, and as Alice turned away so they could speak in private, she realized just how shaken she was by the Marie Whaley story. *A woman had actually come here for schooling and walked out the door and married the man she loved.* Alice could hardly wait to hear the rest of the story.

"Alice," Frances called. "I want you to meet Mary Margaret Seabrook, a daughter of the great Whitmarsh B. Seabrook!"

"Stop it, Frances," Mary Margaret scolded. "You are being sarcastic."

"I am *not* being sarcastic. Everyone in South Carolina knows about your father. He is a gentleman planter of great wealth, a graduate of Princeton, and a member of the legislature. He is most impressive."

"Do not listen to her, Alice," Mary Margaret said. "If Madame hears her going on so, she shall be expelled."

"Not me," Frances squealed. "Not unless I elope with a common man." Both Mary Margaret and Frances went into gales of laughter, and Alice pressed Frances for more details of Marie's story. But Frances said she would have to wait until after the lights were extinguished.

"How can we talk then?"

"Simple. After Madame is asleep in her own bed, we will whisper until dawn."

That was scandalous, Alice was thinking, but she was satisfied. Frances and Mary Margaret still needed to unpack their trunks, so Alice wandered downstairs, where the most delectable aroma came from the small brick kitchen building. Alice strolled in that direction, being certain to take her hat even for the short walk across the garden, and thought how much she liked Frances Whaley. She fervently hoped that Frances was not so attached to Mary Margaret that they would be expected to include her in their strolls and gossips. It was true, that old saying, that two is company, but three is a crowd!

"Miss Alice," Kit said. "Come in. I be making orange marmalade."

Alice untied the bow under her chin and laid her hat on a chair. "Would you show me how you make it?"

Kit looked at Alice oddly. "You be sure about that? No grand lady s'posed to be working in the kitchen."

Alice scrutinized Kit. She was a tall, scrawny woman, but her eyes showed honesty and warmth, and Alice seemed drawn to her in an odd way, surely something akin to the way she felt about Mary One and Frances Whaley. "I am not a grand lady, Kit, and I never shall be."

"Nobody who goes to Madame Talvande's School be anything less than a grand lady," Kit explained.

"Then perhaps I shall be the first. I would truly like to learn to make orange marmalade."

With a wary expression on her face, Kit said, "First you weigh the fruit, and every part of it will be used in the process." She indicated the scales on which she had weighed the oranges. "Then the oranges be cut in half and the juice squeezed through a sieve." The dark-skinned woman gazed at Alice to see that she had her attention, and added, "Peels be set aside, and seed be put in a bowl of water, which after a time jells around the seed."

"You mean something in the orange seeds actually makes the water jell?" Alice asked incredulously.

"That be the sure enough truth," Kit answered.

Alice realized that Kit had just finished that process. "Later today, Kit, I am going to record in a journal all that I have seen today, but the most important record will be the recipe for making your delicious orange marmalade. What is the next step?"

Kit went to a cupboard and removed a loaf of sugar. "Sugar be added to the juice, and when the seed jelly be formed, it be added to the sugar and juice mixture."

The next step was to boil the peels, changing the water five times, until the bitterness had been sufficiently extracted and the peels were tender. Several peels were set aside and the remainder were pounded with a marble pestle until they were soft. The peel mass was added to the juice and sugar mixture and cooked until it was thick, and during this process, Kit allowed Alice to stir the pot. At the last minute, Kit added to the jelly several pieces of peel she had reserved for extra texture and flavor.

"Kit, I cannot believe it. I have actually cooked something," Alice said, laughing. "And I loved doing it." She wished that Whit knew how well she had done in the kitchen.

Kit smiled, but it was clear she did not comprehend what had happened. She had never seen a plantation woman perform a kitchen chore.

"Oh, Kit," Alice said, "I had looked on my stay here in Charleston as a brief sojourn to be patiently endured. But for the first time I feel that I am not going to be simply marking time while I am here. Instead, I am going to learn everything I can to prepare me for my life when I am married. It will be a plan, Kit, a *secret* plan. While I am here, I want you to teach me everything you know about cooking, and keeping a house in superior arrangement."

"Oh Cudjo, he keep the house."

"Then I shall observe Cudjo, and when the term is over, I will be perfectly trained, and ready to become a wife." Alice picked up her hat, and just before she left the kitchen she looked at Kit, who was dipping some of the marmalade from the pot and putting it into a crystal container. Alice suddenly felt as glowing and warm as the yellow-orange marmalade in the crystal jar, which was sparkling from a slant of sunshine coming through a window.

Alice looked around the garden and not a soul was in sight. On impulse she decided that now would be a perfect time to run to the docks for a quick look. It wasn't beyond possibility that she would see Whit. Within minutes she was on Bay Street, and it was quite a sight.

Although she had seen many kinds of carriages in Charleston before, Alice had not really noticed them until now. There were carriages of every conceivable kind, and no two seemed alike. She knew something of the different kinds of carriages, from Wachesaw, but the ones she now gazed at were even more elegant. From the variety of styles, she attempted to identify as many as she could. The appearance of the vehicles, and the number of horses pulling them, gave her some clues. There were barouches, landaus, victorias, tandems, four-in-hands, pony phaetons, governess carts, dogcarts, and T carts. Every horse had been groomed in the same careful manner—brushed and currycombed—and the man on the box of each carriage wore livery. One of them wore dazzling black boots, and the whitest of britches, and his coat was adorned with gold buttons.

Alice realized that if the coaches were so distinctive, the sailing vessels would be even more so. As she neared the docks, she worried that Whit probably would not be in Charleston on business now, as he had recently come and bought his carriage. Still, she did not want to risk missing him. She would inquire as to where the lumber vessels tied up, and she would do her best to make these visits a part of her daily schedule.

Alice felt renewed as she bounced along toward the docks, picturing a reunion with her fiancé. When it happened, they would have the moment all to themselves, with no fear of Allard spying them. They would not have to concern themselves about him in Charleston.

Alice began to be aware of a constant movement around her. Men in business clothing, accompanying ladies with umbrellas over their heads, walked among the wharfmen who were shouting to one another in a most profane way. When Alice turned a cor-

ner, and was near the water, barrels were stacked one upon another, all around.

She worked her way to a pier and saw every kind of vessel she
had ever heard of, and more. There were barkantines, snows,
three-masted schooners, and all kinds of sea-going craft. She instantly hated this filthy place, but her eyes searched, just in case
she would see anyone from the Waccamaw River region. In her
mind she cursed herself for failing to question Whit on his business in Charleston. How many times a year did he come here?
How long did he stay? With whom did he make deals for his
prime lumber?

She didn't have an answer to a single question. And then she
noticed a group of seamen who had come off a three-masted
schooner. They shuffled, trying to get their land legs, and they
bumped along until Alice found herself in the midst of them.
Finally she was away from that mob, but just then a wobbly man
with watery eyes seized her in his arms and kissed her passionately, running a scarred hand down her back caressingly. "You're
the first lass I've seen in over a year," he wheezed. She pulled
herself away and ran, wondering if the man possessed one of the
deadly fevers that was said to land at this dock with some of the
passengers. She wiped her mouth and spat several times, and
fervently hoped that she would not contract anything from that
obnoxious seaman.

Alice strode swiftly away from the docks, lost in a multitude of
thoughts. It wasn't safe for a young woman to visit the docks
alone, and even if she saw Whit there, it wouldn't be as wonderful
as their meetings on the seabeach at Murrells Inlet. Murrells Inlet
was so different from all of this, with the freshest of air, and the
sky so wide and clear that all of heaven looked down on you. Alice
wished that she were there at this very moment, and the agony of
being in Charleston was almost more than she could bear. She
thought of Whit, and wondered how she would ever see him
again, and when, and then she knew with certainty that even
though she hated the Charleston docks she would have to go
there, and continue to search for any knowledge of her beloved.
Surely, one day she would see someone from the Waccamaw River
region who would have knowledge of the Buck sawmills.

Still shaken by the rude man who had kissed her with such
crushing desire, Alice now felt unclean and had a great urge to rid

herself of all the demons that seemed to hover around her. A picture of Dr. Glennie came to her mind, pure, clean Dr. Glennie, and All Saints Church, where one day she would stand as a bride with Whit. *Church.* Alice would go to church and find more strength. In the quiet and calm of a church she could sort things out, make some meaning of all the things cramming her mind.

Alice rushed back to the house on Legare Street, and as she passed through the drawing room she stopped to speak to Cudjo, who was dusting the tables. His hands were thin, his fingers long, and there was nothing clumsy or awkward about him. He could wash the urn-shaped Chinese vases and replace them on the tables with a swift assurance. Fraser soon came into the room, saying, "Miss Alice, Madame Talvande is looking for you."

Alice's heart came to her throat. *Did Madame know that she had gone out alone—and to the docks?*

26

"ALICE FLAGG! *Where* have you been?" Alice had never seen Madame Talvande so angry. She was trembling, and her eyes flashed. "I have been worried to death."

Alice hesitated, somewhat breathless. What could she say?

Just then Kit came into the room. "I want to pay my respects to you, Miss Alice, for helping me make the marmalade."

Madame turned to Kit, a look of surprise on her face. "Has Alice been helping you, Kit?"

"Yes ma'am. I don't know if I could've done all that without her help. I be so busy and exhausted, and Miss Alice, she stir the pot."

Madame Talvande looked defeated. Her hands went to her forehead. "Alice, why did you not let us know where you were?"

"I did not think it mattered," she said softly, still reeling from what she had just heard. Kit had come to her defense at a time when she most needed a friend. How could she ever thank her?

"You should have known that we do not know what is going on in the kitchen. That building is away from the main house," Madame explained. Then, in an effort to dismiss the matter, she said, "All of the students have arrived, and we have gathered in the ballroom to discuss the plans for this term."

Alice untied her hat and held it as she quickly followed Madame up the stairs. When they entered the ballroom, the women were sitting in chairs that had been placed along a wall by the windows.

As Alice's eyes searched for a chair, Frances Whaley motioned. "Come over here, Alice. I have saved a chair for you."

Still feeling rather sheepish about what she had done, Alice quietly went to her friend and sat down beside her.

"Where were you?" Frances asked. "Madame was frantic."

"I, uh, helped Kit make orange marmalade."

"Alice Flagg! Aren't you the clever one! Whoever heard of doing that."

"I am going to start this term's curriculum on a rather elementary scale," Madame began in a clear voice. "Your first studies will only be arithmetic, history, diction, and spelling. Of course there will be piano lessons twice a week for each of you, and dancing every day."

Madame went to a table and picked up several books. "You will become familiar with this volume," she said, holding one up for all to see. "It is *A Vocabulary of English Words,* by Charles Motte Lide." Putting that book aside, she held up another. "This is the third edition of *History of South Carolina,* from its first European discovery to its establishment as a republic, with a supplementary chronicle of events to the present time." She set down that one and took another. *"The Southern First Spelling Book* is as good as any, and it is my choice to begin the term. *Elements of Plain Mathematics* will start you toward a more advanced study of arithmetic."

"I shall never survive," Frances whispered to Alice.

"Before the term is over," Madame added, "you will be studying French, literature, geography, as well as John Waldo's books, *The Rudiments of English Grammar* and *A Latin Grammar.*"

"Latin!" Frances said. "Can you believe it?"

"Hardly," Alice said, still half-dazed over the seaman who had kissed her at the docks. Now that Kit had covered up for her, Alice knew that she could never tell that the horrible man had kissed her. No matter what happened, she could not say anything about it.

"What will be our first dancing class, Madame?" Frances asked.

"Although you will never dance anything at the St. Cecilia balls other than the waltz," Madame explained, "I am going to introduce you to the 'round dances,' such as the polka and the mazurka."

"Oh, that is just heavenly," Frances chirped.

That night the formal dinner training began, with each woman being helped to her chair. Madame had gone to the fullest extent in having a well-planned dinner, and when it was over the students were fairly stuffed.

"Alice," Frances began in a low voice, "tonight I will tell you the story of Marie Whaley. But we must be careful. Sometimes Madame pokes her head into the room to see if we are all sleeping. After she drifts off, we may talk all we like. I don't think an earthquake would awaken Madame Talvande after eleven o'clock."

Soon Alice had completed her daily entry in her journal and was settled down in her nightgown in bed, ready for a night's rest after hearing the story of Marie Whaley. She could hardly wait to hear the details, for if ever there was a woman with whom she could identify, it was Marie.

Frances, from her bed, began her narrative by telling Alice just what and where Edisto Island was. Edisto Island, about forty miles southwest of Charleston, is bounded by the Atlantic Ocean on the southeast, by the North and South Edisto rivers, and on the northwest by Dahaw River, which connects the waters of South Edisto or Pon Pon River with those of the north inlet. Indented by a variety of creeks, Edisto is extremely irregular, and is really two islands separated by a small creek. The island is twelve miles long, and in the broadest part is between four and five miles wide, with an area of more than twenty-eight thousand acres.

"The more elevated parts," Frances explained, "consist of a light, sandy soil. When the settlers, which were from Scotland and Wales, discovered that the soil was not suited to the production of rice, they turned to indigo and cotton. If the land was perfect for indigo, and it must have been, as the dye extracted from this weed was in greater demand than that from any other part of the state, it was even more perfect for cotton. But do you know, Alice, that Edisto cotton never goes to market?"

"I cannot believe that!"

"It is true. French lace mills contract for the product before the seed ever is sown."

"They make lace of it?"

"For the most part, although the cotton is also used in the manufacture of silks and all of the finer classes of cloths."

"And that is how you became so wealthy?"

"Yes," Frances answered without false pretenses. "The Whaleys and the Seabrooks are perhaps the foremost cotton planters, although there are others worthy of note, including the Jenkinses and Mikells, and many more. The Whaley clan is said to be the most prolific and prosperous."

"All right," Alice said. "I am now acquainted with the clan. Let us get to Marie and her story."

"Marie—my father's sister—was fifteen in 1829, and she had fallen in love with Mr. George F. Morris, a native New Yorker. He owned property on Edisto as well as a lovely home here in Charleston."

"Why was he not acceptable to your grandparents?" Alice asked.

"Because he was from New York! They wanted her to marry a Southern planter!"

"Oh, the indignity of it all!" Alice said, with more emphasis than she intended.

"Shush!" Frances cautioned. "If you awaken Madame we shall be punished."

Alice leaned her head over near Frances's bed. "Go on."

"Are you familiar with those broken bottles on the top of the ten-foot brick wall?" Frances asked.

"No."

"Well, tomorrow take a good look. That is when Madame put them there."

"Go on with the story. What happened?"

"George Morris was so infatuated with Marie that he set out to become best friends with the planter family whose cotton plantation adjoined the Whaley plantation. He visited his friends frequently so that he could secretly meet with Marie. They were so-o-o in love."

Alice was now thinking what a superb move that was. If Whit could have befriended someone who lived near the Hermitage, she could have seen him more frequently. "That was brilliant," Alice said.

"Brilliant, my foot! It was the most foolish move he ever made. My grandfather found him out, and he threatened the neighbors—if they ever allowed George on their property again he would retaliate."

"What did the neighbors do?"

"They refused George admittance to their house. And do you

know what? He pitched a tent on their property so that he could see Marie."

"He must have adored Marie," Alice said, dreamily.

"Oh, there is no question about that. And that is when my grandfather sent her here, to Madame Talvande's School," Frances added.

Alice sucked in her breath, as she could scarcely believe her ears. The story of Marie Whaley equated precisely with hers. All the time that Frances was describing George Morris, Alice was seeing Whit Buck.

"But George Morris followed Marie to Charleston, and she secretly rendezvoused with him."

"Did Madame Talvande find out?"

"Not just then," Frances said, "and that is a curiosity to me, for Madame Talvande's husband, Andre, was living then, and he helped her with this school. Isn't it curious that he did not discover that Marie was seeing George on the sly?"

"It is, really. Even today, uh, when I was not so far away," Alice said, "she was very upset when she missed me."

"It was in the spring when Marie dressed herself in her finest silk dress and left the school, without Madame noticing. Marie and George went to St. Michael's Church and were married."

"Oh my," Alice said, flopping her head on the pillow and picturing herself standing at the chancel in that beautiful church with Whit. "How perfectly marvelous."

"But Marie came back to Madame Talvande's that night, and she told not a word of her wedding."

"And her friends knew nothing of it at all?"

"Nothing. They would have questioned her to death if they had."

"And she did not spend her wedding night with her husband?"

"No."

"Go on," Alice urged. "I can hardly wait to hear what happened next."

"You aren't getting sleepy?" Frances asked.

"Oh good heavens no. Continue."

"The next morning, George Morris was dying to see his bride. After all, they were now married, and he had been kept away from Marie for so long. So he took things into his own hands and came here, to Madame Talvande's."

"And?" Alice was leaning out of her bed, with her head as close to Frances as she could hold it.

"As was the custom, he sent in a note."

"What did it say?"

"Very to the point. That he had come for his wife, Marie Whaley Morris."

Alice moved back on her own bed. Staring at the ceiling, she said, "Oh, I know that Madame Talvande died right there on the spot."

"I think she very nearly did. And do you know what?"

"No. What?" Alice was again hanging from her bed.

"Madame told her students, and she paraded them right down the walkway between the rows of magnolia trees, and they watched as the 'matron' Marie Whaley Morris greeted her husband and left with him."

"And that is when she put broken bottles on the wall?"

"Yes," Frances said. "Because although Marie would never tell about it, everyone believes that she scaled the wall in order that she not be seen if she had walked down the walkway and left by the opening in the wall."

"Do you think she climbed that high wall?" Alice asked.

"I do. I believe it. Because she would have been detected if she had left by the usual route."

"Oh, isn't it all so wonderful? Can you imagine how it would be to elope with the man you really love and be married in St. Michael's Church?" Alice asked.

Frances did not seem to grasp Alice's zest for the romantic story. "You can be married in St. Michael's Church if you desire."

"I do not know that I would choose St. Michael's for my own wedding. I might select a small church nearer home. Such as All Saints."

"Well, that would be just as thrilling."

"But I cannot actually choose where I would like to be married," Alice said, before she realized she was speaking her thoughts.

"Why not?"

"I don't know. Who knows what will happen? I might never marry."

"Silly egret. You shall be married this time next year."

The words spoken so innocently by Frances Whaley filled Alice with a warm softness, like honey oozing through her neck, arms, and body. "Let us go to sleep now," she said. "I want to think how splendid it would be if, as you say, I would be married this time next year."

"Are you in love with someone, Alice?" Frances asked. Alice did not answer, as she was thinking of Whit. Frances turned over, her back toward Alice. "We had better get some sleep. Tomorrow is our first day of school, and Madame will, as usual, begin by telling us all about herself, and then about this house. And only then will she start our lessons."

But Alice was deep in her own thoughts, and she did not hear what Frances had said.

27

UNDISGUISED CURIOSITY FLICKERED onto Alice's face as Madame Talvande began her first lecture, one in which she was to explain the customs and regulations at the school. Madame radiated her usual warmth, and her face was wreathed in smiles as her eyes roamed around the drawing room, lingering on some of the treasures she had collected during her life. Sunshine filtered through the tall, leaded windows.

"In this house," she began her address, "it would not be difficult to forget that there is a world outside." She clapped her hands, and held them together. "But there *is* a world out there, and when you have completed your education here you will be prepared to enter that life as a proper woman, one who is acquainted with all of the social graces." A trail of perfume heavy in the scent of lilies of the valley followed as Madame slowly moved about the room.

For some reason Alice suddenly thought of the seaman who had kissed her so passionately, and the idea came to her that the world outside this house was ugly and filled with pain. Her heart ached with wistfulness for Murrells Inlet, where there was such gentle peace with no disruptions.

Alice brought her attention back to Madame, who she thought resembled a character in one of the portraits on the wall. Madame was wearing a dress the shade of copper, with lacy folds around her delicate wrists and a high ruffled collar at the back of her neck. The color of the dress intensified her eyes, which were pools

179

of cool brown in an alabaster face. Her slick black hair was pulled
severely back and held in place by a tortoiseshell comb, and her
only jewelry was a pendant of diamonds that dropped to her
waist. She was so beautiful, Alice was thinking.

"But my life has not been a bed of roses," Madame said, as
though reading Alice's mind. "I came here from Santo Domingo
after the uprising. My husband and I were refugees, and it was a
difficult time for us. In Charleston we were referred to as 'the
exotic group.' But I shall speak no more of that time except to say
that Andre and I were fortunate to be in a position to purchase
this lot and build this home."

Frances mouthed to Alice, "Here we go. She is going to tell us
about this house." Alice nodded.

"This lot was originally granted to James LaRoche and James
Lardant on the grand model of the Charles Town project in
1694," Madame went on. "Its first owners were French
Huguenots, the Solomon Legare family. Andre and I built the
house in 1819," she continued, "and after my husband's death, I
became the sole owner. If there is anything I can do to add to your
pleasure while in my house, only let me know."

"She can give us more free time away from it," Frances whispered to Alice. Alice wholeheartedly agreed, but kept quiet in
order to hear Madame's next words.

"And now," Madame said, "a bit about your curriculum. You
shall study from the books I exhibited to you yesterday, and twice
each week we shall join in conversation about current events.
Some very important things are happening in South Carolina,
and you should be equipped with the facts so that you can discuss
them when you attend a social event. And speaking of social
events," Madame went on, "I have taken the liberty of having
cards printed with your names, and when they are delivered to
me, I shall distribute them."

A girl whom Alice did not know raised her hand. "Madame
Talvande?"

"Yes, Catherine?"

"What will be the use of these cards?"

"When you call at someone's home, you shall go to the door and
present your card to the butler, who in turn will take it to the
person on whom you are calling. That, Catherine, is the only way
to properly present yourself, and you should have your cards in a

few days." Then Madame added, "And if you should answer any invitation by writing, your communication should never be written in the first person."

"But how should it be written?" Alice asked, surprised to find herself participating in the dialogue.

"You should write, 'Miss Flagg regrets that she will not be able to ride with Mr. Blank this afternoon.'"

"Oh," Alice answered.

"All will not be grueling work here," Madame explained. "We shall attend the theater twice each month."

"Oh," Catherine cut in, "please tell us about that, Madame Talvande."

"As it is important that you meet some theatrical people and learn something of the Charleston stage, we shall leave by carriages and arrive at the theater to view a play, after which we will go backstage and be introduced to the actors."

"Shall we attend the Old Theater?" Mary Margaret Seabrook asked.

"Yes."

"Tell us a theater story, Madame, please," Frances begged.

Madame Talvande smiled, and it was clear that she was pleased with the request. Her eyes lighted as she moved toward the women lined up before her. "Many of the elder Charlestonians remember old Tam O'Shanter. He was a good creature, an especial favorite for a long time here, and he was featured at many glittering parties. But I remember 'Old Faulkner,' as we called him—Thomas Faulkner—who died a number of years ago. He also went to parties, and I recall one in particular. He sang, 'St. Patrick Was a Gentleman' and 'To Be Sure I Can't Sing an Oration.'

"For a long time here in Charleston, he reserved the night of Easter Monday for his Benefit. He always had a good Benefit, so popular with every class of people. The first one I saw was called *The Manager in Distress*."

Madame Talvande straightened, a satisfied glint in her eyes. "I am impressed with you, all of you, all of you," she said, "and I predict a successful school term."

"Are we excused?" Frances asked.

"In a moment, Frances," Madame replied. "Before you go, there is something I must warn you about, and this is extremely important. There are three types of fevers raging in South Carolina at this time, and you must be careful that you do not contract one of them."

"What are they, besides malaria?" Mary Margaret asked.

"Yes, Mary Margaret, malaria fever is a dreaded one. And yellow fever is ever so deadly. Hundreds of people in Savannah have lost their lives to it. Like malaria, it too could be spread by a type of mosquito, although no one knows for sure."

"And what other fever is there?" Frances asked.

"Probably the most deadly of all," Madame answered soberly. "Hemorrhagic fever."

"Is that the fever called 'the black vomit'?" Catherine asked.

"Yes. It is referred to as the black vomit, as the patient vomits black blood. And as dreadful as it is for me to say the word, that fever is fatal. There is no cure."

"Mercy," Alice heard herself say.

The grandfather clock in the hall was striking the hour at precisely the same time St. Michael's church bells were chiming. "Be very careful," Madame cautioned. "Stay away from the boat people, and keep yourselves healthy." She dismissed the group by saying that they would have a lesson on the history of South Carolina in thirty minutes, and there would be music lessons in the afternoon, including one for Alice.

On the way upstairs, Frances said, "Alice, I want you to go to a wedding dinner with me."

"A wedding dinner?"

"Yes, at the country's most prestigious address."

Alice stopped walking. "What could possibly be the whole country's most prestigious address?"

"Number One Meeting Street," Frances responded. "You know of course that Charleston's Meeting Street is the most desirable street on which to live and the lower the number the more prominent the address. And this wedding dinner will be held there, in that very house."

A wedding dinner. That would be interesting, Alice thought. "Do you think that Madame will allow us to go?"

"Of course. My parents sent a written request and they asked that I choose a friend to accompany me."

"What about Mary Margaret Seabrook? She is from Edisto Island, and you are good friends. Will she be offended if she is not invited?"

"Think nothing of that stuffy goose. She is so carried away with herself she will never notice our absence!"

Frances's statement brought relief to Alice. She wanted Frances for her best friend, but she had feared there was a bond between Frances and Mary Margaret. Now perhaps Frances and Alice could become like sisters, confiding in each other. And Alice was beginning to feel that she did need a confidante.

They walked up the steps to the fourth floor, and Alice removed the sheet music for the Polonaise from her armoire to look over. She sighed heavily and strived to control herself as she noticed the words written by Madame Le Conte: *Allegro 1/16*. Where was Madame Le Conte now, she wondered. Could she be back at Brookgreen Plantation? Suddenly Alice was racked with longing as she pictured herself in the vessel, beside Mary One, on the way to Brookgreen. And there on the bluff was Whit, so handsome and dear. For a moment she thought that her heart would break. Although she liked Madame Talvande and the new friends she was making in Charleston, she would give anything to be back home, preparing for her music lesson at Brookgreen.

Frances noticed that Alice was somewhat shaken and asked her if she wished to lie down. "No," Alice said, trying to appear cheerful again. She took Frances's arm. "Let us go back downstairs."

"Columbus discovered America in the year 1492, but it was not settled by white people until more than a hundred years after its discovery," Madame began her history lecture. "At first the whole southern country was considered as one place, and it had several names. It was first called Florida—which means *blooming*—by the Spaniards. The French called it generally by the same name, but sometimes they called it New France. The English first called it Southern Virginia, but afterwards they named it Carolina, after their king, Charles. These three nations, England, Spain, and France, all claimed this southern country as their own, but at last the English ruled most of it."

"She gives this same lecture every term," Frances murmured to Alice.

"The English claimed this beautiful southern country because John Cabot was sent over to America by King Henry VII in 1497. The Spaniards claimed it because Ponce de Leon, in 1512, came from Spain to Florida and named it. Eight years after this, Velasquez de Ayllon, a Spaniard, came over in two ships to South

Carolina. He navigated the Combahee River, and treated the Indians kindly, until they went aboard his ships to see all the strange things there. When there was a great crowd of them on board, he suddenly sailed away! He took the poor savages to Santo Domingo, *my* country, and there sold them as slaves. After that, there were some unusual people there. They were called 'half-castes.'"

"Do you think she, Madame, is half-caste?" Alice whispered to Frances. She was not sure what the word "half-caste" meant, but she could guess. It was probably a mixture of Santo Domingans and the slaves sent there.

"I don't know," Frances answered. "But there *was* a half-caste here in Charleston once, and there are many stories about her. She was absolutely beautiful, and her name was Madame Margot."

"I don't care if Madame is a half-caste; I think she is wonderful," Alice declared. What did it matter if she was a half-caste? Alice knew that she would never look down on anyone who was believed to be less than she was. Everyone was equal, especially in the sight of God. She thought of Whit, and how very appropriate he would be as her husband, and yet her mother and Allard looked down on him, as though he were a half-caste. The very thought of their attitude disgusted her.

"The French claimed the land because Verrazano, in 1524, was sent over to the northern part of this southern country by Francis I of France," Madame continued. "Now this is very important," she emphasized. "Please remember this, for you will hear these words many times in your lives, and you will need to go back to your foundation lesson to know the very meaning. The Indians called this part of South Carolina 'Chicola.' That word has been corrupted over the years to 'Chicora.' Remember that, and tomorrow I shall tell you about the Lords Proprietors. There will be a diction lesson after dinner, and then the music lessons for today. Following that, your walk in the fresh air. But remember the fevers, and *do not walk alone*." Madame quickly left the drawing room.

"Madame! Madame!" Frances called, running after her. Alice was hurrying to keep up with Frances, who said, "I must ask her about the wedding dinner. It is to be held tomorrow night."

Madame turned, and held Frances by the shoulders. "What is it, my dear?"

"Madame, my father gave you a written request that someone

accompany me to a wedding dinner tomorrow night at Number One Meeting Street. May Alice Flagg go with me?"

Madame pondered the two women who faced her. She was fond of them both, but in totally different ways. Although Frances knew everything of the social graces, she was not sure about Alice, and it would do Alice a world of good to attend a wedding dinner at Number One Meeting Street.

Madame stole a look at Alice. There she was, all porcelain fragility—quiet, spiritual Alice. What an event this wedding dinner would be. Madame had heard about the wedding dinner, and wished that she herself could attend. It would be such a large wedding party, the bride being of an Edisto Island cotton planter family, a Mikell woman, she believed.

"Of course Alice may go with you, Frances. I am sure you will be in excellent company at Number One Meeting Street, and there shall be no restriction on the time of your return to this house."

28

THE DAY OF the wedding dinner, Alice chose to wear the gown she had worn to the Brookgreen affair, as she liked the tassels on the bodice. Of all the dresses she had seen in Charleston, none had that particular feature. Frances had many gowns from which to choose, and she rather nonchalantly picked one from her armoire and threw it across her bed. Madame Talvande had dispatched a servant girl to help each of them prepare for the dinner. Alice felt uncommonly attached to the woman holding up the dress for her to wiggle into, as though the girl were Mary One. Finally Alice and Frances were ready to leave and Alice seemed quite in awe of Frances as she observed her.

Frances's gown was of tulle with tiny pleatings from waist to floor of white tulle and then pink tulle, and long garlands of silver leaves. A short garland was attached to her hair. Although Frances Whaley was a great belle, she seemed not to care for attention at all, and that made Alice love her all the more. The other students had formed a ring of spectators and stood back as Alice and Frances descended the stairway to the drawing room.

The butler escorted them to the carriage, and Madame Talvande also walked to the street entrance with Alice and Frances. Just before they climbed into the carriage, Madame said, "I have something for you."

"What is it?" Frances asked.

Madame pressed a card into Alice's hand and extended one to Frances. Alice studied hers:

Miss Alice Flagg
Murrells Inlet, South Carolina

Frances was also reading hers.

"I hurriedly got your cards as I knew you would need them tonight," Madame said. "Just hand it to the butler when you arrive."

"Oh thank you, Madame Talvande," Alice said, holding the card in her white-gloved hand and stepping into the coach.

Madame helped arrange the huge hooped skirts in the carriage, and they were on their way, and she hoped desperately they would behave properly and give her school a silent recommendation.

Frances and Alice handed the butler their cards, and he ushered them into the drawing room of the spacious house. Alice's first thought was that she had never in her life seen so many beautifully gowned women and handsome men, who were gathered in groups everywhere. She and Frances were escorted into a hallway that was as large as many homes Alice knew, and to the stairs that swept grandly upward to a huge open-spaced room, obviously constructed with large entertainments in mind.

When Frances and Alice reached the upper piazza, Alice took in the magnificent view of the harbor. She wanted to stretch her arms and feel the seabreeze flow under them, but tonight she must play the part of a grand lady. "This truly is America's most prestigious address," Alice said.

"I told you," Frances replied.

Just then Alice and Frances got their first glimpse of the wedding party. In the midst of twenty-four happy attendants were the bride and groom. The bride gave the groom an adoring look as they made their way into one of the dining rooms. Alice was silent, filled with an aching sadness. Would she ever be married to the man she loved? she wondered. This bride obviously loved the man she would live her life with. And everyone was happy for them, wishing them well, laughing and talking. It could never be that way at Alice's wedding, she thought, picturing Allard's scowling face and her mother's disapproval showing plainly.

What had these people done to be so fortunate? Did they know how blessed they were? As Alice looked around, she believed that everyone there, the whole multitude of guests, had known such happiness. If there had ever been any jealousies, hatred, and differences, they had long ago been buried, or they were well concealed behind the smiling facades.

Alice hoped that Frances had not detected her tension. Frances fit so perfectly into this crowd. She was one of them, that was clear. Although Alice felt she had been amiable enough she was somewhat reserved, and there was even a veiled hostility when she thought of how she and Whit could never be as happy with her family as the bride and groom she had just seen. She didn't want Frances to see beneath the surface and know that she was truly a misfit. Yes, as she thought about it, that was exactly what she was, a misfit! She felt she no longer belonged to this aristocratic group of planters. But for tonight, she must hide her true feelings. It seemed to Alice that she was always having to suppress her true feelings in deference to someone or something else.

Frances, who had been fluttering around a woman she knew, came back to Alice so they could amuse themselves by watching the wedding party, now enjoying toasts and congratulations. Champagne was being poured, and soon Alice found herself with a glass of the wine in her hand. Now, in the candlelight, she sipped the champagne and felt uplifted. Even if she was not the happiest person in the world, she should not impose her discomfiture on anyone else. The bride was a stunning beauty who was unutterably happy, and the groom had not a flaw that she could see. She lifted her glass when a toast was given, and soon the dinner menus, engraved in gold on parchment, were handed out.

When Alice read the page, she could not believe her eyes:

Bridal Cake	Groom's Cake
Bridal Palace	
Pyramids of Oranges Christalisee	
Pyramids of Almonds Christalisee	
Tout au Fruit	Harlequin
Bisquit Glassee	Russian Charlotte
Italian Cream	Wine Jelly
Maraschino Jelly	Orange Jelly with Oranges
Spanish Maringo	Blanc Mangee
Spanish Kisses	Strawberry Ice Cream
Orange Sherbert	Fancy Cake
French Wafers	French Bonbon

French Dragee au Liquer

Boned Turkey with truffles		Pheasant
Woodcock	Capon	Grouse
Canvas Back Duck	Currant Jelly	Wild Turkey
Venison		Oysters Stewed
Oyster Patte		Gélatine de l'Inde

Chicken Salad a la Mayonaise
Pattie de Fois Gras
Prepared by
W. Guillard, successor to A. J. Rutjes

After looking over the menu, glances were exchanged by some, but they all did as asked and seated themselves. Alice settled down to enjoy the feast. During the meal her glance caught that of a man seated on the opposite side of the table.

"Where are you from?" he questioned brusquely.

"Wachesaw Plantation, at Murrells Inlet."

"Oh, you are from up on the Neck," he said.

"That is correct."

"Do you know my friend, Joshua John Ward?"

"I know him well," Alice answered. "My brothers are engaged to his daughters, Penelope and Georgeanna."

"One by one, the younger generation are planting on their own," the man answered.

Alice was relieved when someone else spoke to the man, and he turned his attention elsewhere. Something about him reminded her of Allard. The last thing in the world she needed right now was to feel the scrutinizing eyes of Allard or her mother on her.

As the buzz of conversation continued, Alice thought back on the day, which had been unusually pleasant. She was carving out a place for herself at Madame Talvande's, and she actually enjoyed the classes. Besides that, she believed that Madame Talvande was an even better music teacher than Madame Le Conte. All in all, things were going well for her in Charleston.

When the man sitting across from Alice directed his attention at Frances, Alice noticed how astutely she handled the situation, letting him know at once how well acquainted she was with her island. She was perfectly at ease as she spoke. "The Spanish first named it Oristo," she explained, "but the English renamed it for the Indians when they reclaimed the land for the crown."

Alice wished for a moment that she could tell Allard about the dinner conversation, until she remembered he was now practically her enemy. Still she felt pangs of loneliness, being so far removed from her home, and wondered if she would be strong enough to continue spurning her own family for a life with Whit.

On the way back to Madame Talvande's that night, Alice asked Frances if she was going to go home for Christmas or remain in Charleston. Thanksgiving would come first, but that was not a time that the students traveled long distances to go home. Frances was expected to go home for Christmas, she said, as the island was so nearby. But Alice mentioned that she was thinking of staying in Charleston—she told herself it would be a good way to test her independence. Her family would be coming to Charleston for the social season soon afterward in any case.

"Are you going to the St. Cecilia ball?" Alice asked.

"Oh, of course. I have never missed that," Frances answered.

Alice thought that she would attend the St. Cecilia as well as the Jockey Club races and make Allard and her mother happy. When this school term was over she was going to exercise some will of her own, but she would go along with them during this winter season. And she decided that she would also call on a dressmaker and have some new gowns fashioned for her. After all, if she was going to hobnob with Frances Whaley of Edisto Island she had better prepare herself for the most glowing entertainments.

Alice could hardly believe how extraordinary the wedding dinner had been that night. Even her mother and Allard would have been astonished. Although she had no aspirations to ascend Charleston's social ladder, it had been nice to go to dinner at America's most prestigious address. Even Allard and her mother had never done that!

When the carriage arrived at Madame Talvande's, Madame was at the door to welcome her students, and Alice was as excited as Frances as they told Madame every detail of the evening.

29

As ALICE HAD been tired after returning from the wedding dinner the night before, she recorded all of it in her journal the next morning, just seconds before going into Madame Talvande's first class.

"Today I will talk about the proprietary government," Madame said, beginning the history class. "It came about this way: eight English noblemen received a charter from Charles II, King of England, for an immense tract of land—more than North Carolina, South Carolina, and Georgia all together. These noblemen were the Earl of Clarendon, the Duke of Albemarle, Lord Craven, Lord Berkeley, Lord Ashley, Sir George Carteret, Sir William Berkeley, and Sir John Colleton. Every one of these noblemen is remembered in the name of some place in this state."

"Were they not called the lords proprietors of the colony?" Catherine asked.

"They were," Madame confirmed, then with a hint of devilishness in her eyes she added, "and they pretended to wish to convert the Indians into Christians, but their real object was no doubt to make money. They did not mean to come to settle in America themselves, but they encouraged people to come over and settle the country, who were to pay them money for the land."

"And that was called the proprietary government?" Alice asked.

"Precisely."

After Madame Talvande had completed the history lesson, she

helped the students with arithmetic, which most of them found tedious, but the teacher promised that before long they would find it fascinating. During that class, Alice asked Frances if she would accompany her and April on a walk that afternoon, as she had some free time. She was pleased that Frances agreed, as Alice believed that the time had come for her to tell Frances about Whit.

"You cannot mean this!" Frances said as they meandered along the Battery, ahead of April. "Surely you are not planning to marry someone your family believes is beneath you, just like Marie Whaley!"

"I am," Alice said with authority. "He is the man I love, and I shall never love another."

"How do you know that?"

"I *know* it!"

"What do you plan to do?" Frances asked.

"Today I plan to go to the docks and see if he would by chance be there with a load of lumber, and I want you to go with me."

"Oh, Alice Flagg. You are not the girl I thought I knew. You are a cuckoo! How do you expect to live without the support of your brother and mother?"

"What happened to Marie after she married George Morris?"

Frances was surprised by the question. "I do not know. I suppose they are living happily, but nobody ever hears from them."

"See there? The worst that can happen is that you go off and live happily with the man you love."

"You might look at it that way, but I do not think I could ever turn my back on my family," Frances said. "Besides, George Morris was a man of some means, and Marie could still enjoy a luxurious life with him. Your lumberman would not be able to provide you with the pretty things and fine amusements you have always had. Haven't you considered that?"

Alice shrugged casually, not wishing to reply. Of course she had considered that, she thought to herself. In fact, being here in Charleston was beginning to threaten her resolve to be with Whit, what with all the lovely clothes and houses, the fascinating people, and their glorious parties. She was enjoying her life of privilege more than she cared to admit. But she wanted her heart to stay true to her humble Whit, and tried to push Charleston's seductive charms back out of her mind.

They had now reached the docks, which were mercifully quiet

on this day. Alice looked around but saw no vessel that had lumber stacked on it. She stopped a wharfman and asked him if any Carolina lumber had arrived from the Waccamaw region, and he said not that week.

"Alice! Don't you remember what Madame cautioned us about?" Frances asked. "She said not to talk to seamen."

"That is not a man of the sea. That is a Charleston man who works on the docks," Alice said shortly.

"There is very little difference if you ask me," Frances said. "We should go back to Madame's."

But just at that moment Alice saw dark clouds boiling up across the bay. "Let's not go quite yet," she said.

"I really need to be getting back," Frances objected.

"Have you ever seen a storm, Frances? I mean *really* watched it?"

"Mercy no. There are so many lovely things to put my attention to."

"Well, I want you to watch this one. Look at it now. It is over there, across the bay, and you can see lightning flashing."

"And it is dark over there, but the sun is shining here," Frances observed.

"Exactly. In a few minutes you will see the storm start across the bay."

"And that is when I am running back to Madame's!"

"You will have plenty of time," Alice said. "The storm still needs to build up to its fullest capacity."

"I do not want to see a storm at its fullest capacity," Frances said.

In an effort to divert her attention for a moment, Alice remarked, "Frances, I want to find a very exclusive dressmaker in Charleston. I have a heavenly white gown for the St. Cecilia ball, but would like some more made for the other functions of the season. Who is your dressmaker?"

"There is one on King Street," Frances said, and Alice believed she was talking about the same person who had made her white gown, the one in which she pictured herself as a bride. "I shall be happy to go with you to my dressmaker and select some materials," Frances said. "Oh, she has the most heavenly cloth, and of all shades."

"When can we go?" Alice asked.

"Any day that you choose."

"Now that I have seen your gowns, I would like more, and there is no limit on the amount of clothes I can buy. My mother has never believed I had enough."

"The same with my parents. They want their daughter always to make a good impression."

Alice laughed. "I have heard that remark before."

"We shall go tomorrow," Frances said.

Alice agreed. Just then her attention was brought back to the storm. "Frances, look now. The storm is beginning to come onto the bay. Can you tell where?"

Frances squinted her eyes. "There is a band of water, and it is not the same color as the rest of the water, and the wind is picking at it."

"It is choppy, and dark gray," Alice said. "Whereas the other water, over there in the sunshine, is very blue."

"We had better start on our way," Frances said.

"Not just yet. Wait a few minutes, and notice the change in the surface of the bay."

"But it is coming faster now, and we must go."

"No! I am not going yet," Alice said determinedly. "I want to watch the storm."

"Is storm watching one of your pastimes?" Frances asked.

"Not usually," Alice admitted.

"Then don't start adding that to your activities now," Frances said. "I am going."

Just then there was a great vibration that shocked the people on the dock to attention, and thunder roared. "We'd better get every-thing tied down," a dock worker said. "This gale's coming in fast."

"Did you hear what he said, Alice? The storm is coming fast."

"It is not coming that fast," Alice said, holding her ground. "Just a little longer, Frances."

The whole bay was now navy blue and brilliant lightning came in great rods, extending from the clouds to the surface of the water. People were running inside, and those who were on boats were checking their ropes to see that they were securely tied. A chill came to the air, and it became very dark. Rain came in large droplets and a moment later in sheets. Darkness enveloped them and lightning popped all around.

"I am leaving," Frances said as she started running.

"Wait for me," Alice yelled. "I am coming!"

Alice and Frances ran so hard they were gasping for breath. April, who had been standing aside to leave the girls to their conversation, chased after them in the downpour toward the school. Although the girls held them up, parts of their skirts were dragging in riverlets of water gushing down the street. Alice's wet hair clung to her scalp and neck, and water dripped off the end of her nose. They ran along East Bay to Tradd, turned there and ran all the way to Legare Street, where they turned left. When they reached the brick wall surrounding Madame Talvande's house, the sun came out, and the storm had passed. Frances, nearly out of breath, leaned against the wall. Finally, she spoke. "Alice, why did you do that?"

Alice, also breathless, answered, "I simply wanted to see if I could stand up to something fearsome that was against me. Something fighting me. I was uncertain if I had the capacity and dignity to stand up to *anything* or *anybody* who was against me, tooth and nail."

"And what conclusion did you come to?" Frances asked.

"I *can* do it. I could have stood there through the whole storm!"

30

ALICE AWOKE TO the sound of St. Michael's church bells. It was Sunday, and the day that stretched before her would be a leisurely one. She made no move to hurry as she pulled the journal from a bedside table and read the entries she had made the night before. She could hardly remember writing those words:

> My birthday comes on November 29, a little over a week away. Fifteen. I shall be fifteen, and can become my own person then. Immediately after completing the school term I shall find Whit Buck and be married. I feel now as though I am about to explode as I fly ahead with plans. If gold is the dream of the prospectors, then marriage to Whit is *my ultimate measure of happiness.*

Alice read the words again, and once more after that. She had to bite her lip to control herself as she thought of Whit, envisioning her marriage to him.

She raised up on an elbow, thinking about her future. Some people never knew true happiness, while others had plenty but allowed it to slip away unawares. She would find happiness and keep it. And she would be willing to make sacrifices beyond belief. Alice could think of no other person who would be giving up as much as she in order to marry the man of her choice. Her children would never ascend the stairway at Number One Meeting Street as if in a dream and dine on delicacies most people in the world had never heard of. But on the other hand, her children would not be taught to accumulate wealth, and work even harder to add to the pile. Her situation was almost like a profit and loss statement, and one thing balanced against another.

Finally Alice moved her arm and eased her head down to the pillow, realizing that every bone in her body ached from severe concentration. But she could not rest long, as Frances was soon awake and saying that they didn't have all the time in the world to get dressed, have breakfast, and go to St. Michael's Church for services. Alice rose, sponged off with water, and splashed gardenia cologne on her neck and arms. She shimmied into pantalets and a chemise, and selected a dress of green, her favorite color. When the women were ready to leave for church services, Madame Talvande had coaches lined up at the entrance on Legare Street.

Many of the boat people had sailed away, and it was a typical Sunday morning, quiet and peaceful. The large mansion of Nathaniel Russell caught Alice's attention as she rode by. Surely it was one of Charleston's finest. She had read of it in the book, and knew something of its construction and the family who lived there.

The builder was a businessman, not a planter. Nathaniel Russell, Esq., came to Charleston from Bristol, Rhode Island, and had engaged in a long and successful business career. One of his daughters had married Arthur Middleton, and the other married Bishop Theodore Dehon, a native of Boston. Bishop Dehon had been rector of Trinity Church at Newport, a post from which he resigned to take charge of St. Michael's in Charleston. Although he was now dead, his widow still lived in the mansion.

Alice's eyes left that house and came to rest on St. Michael's Church, across the street. Something about the architecture reminded her of All Saints Church, except St. Michael's was larger, and much grander. In a moment the women were out of their carriages and were walking down the aisle, led by Madame Talvande in a lavender gown and gloves, and hat of deepest purple with lavender plume.

Sitting on the pew beside Frances came as a great relief to Alice, as she had spent a tense night. During its early hours, the clanking of the milk cans had been an annoyance. Alice had become accustomed to hearing the voices of the street vendors during the day, somewhat in the manner that one ignores the regular chiming of a clock unless one wonders what time it is, but these night noises were a nuisance. While lying awake, Alice became worried that she had been exposed to one of the contagious fevers said to be carried by the boatmen and others.

Although she did not have her usual zip, dash, and vigor this morning, she attributed it to her lack of sleep. All she needed was a good night's sleep, free from the jangle of noisy milk cans. As her attention came back to the words being spoken by the minister, Alice suddenly realized that this very church was the one in which Marie Whaley had married George Morris. They had stood at the front of the church, before a minister in a white robe, like the one there now.

"Frances," Alice whispered, "isn't this the church where Marie married George Morris?"

"Yes. I can almost see them now. Can't you?" Frances giggled.

Following the service, the students filed back into the carriages. As she rode back to Legare Street, Alice began to feel a little weak, and her face was flushed. "Frances," Alice said, "when we get home I am going to take off my dress and rest. I slept fitfully last night."

"What was the trouble?"

"Those harsh, jangling milk cans. Did they not disturb your rest?"

"Nothing disturbs my rest," Frances replied. "Sometimes I am asleep before my head touches the pillow."

Alice removed a glove and felt her face. "It is usually the same with me. But now . . . I don't know. Just when I am about to drop off, I am suddenly wide awake, and a bit nervous."

"I think you are just in love," Frances commented. "I am still thinking on all that you told me."

Alice's hand automatically went to her chest where she felt the ring, and her mind was on the commitment she had made to herself only this morning. "Does love actually make one ill?"

"Indeed it does, sometimes," Frances said. "When one of my sisters was planning her wedding, she could not eat anything other than cold foods."

"Cold foods? I never heard the like."

"It is true. Anything hot or well seasoned just made her woozy."

"Well, I am woozy," Alice sighed, leaning her head back on the seat.

Madame Talvande stood aside while the women alighted from the coaches, and she came immediately to Alice. "You look a little wilted, dear. Have you lost some of your carefree girlish air?"

"I believe I have, Madame."

"Well, go to your room and get comfortable, and I shall be there in due time to attend to you."

In the room, Alice removed her dress, hung it in the armoire, and waited there, in her chemise and pantalets.

"Alice Flagg!" Frances all but shouted. Alice didn't move. "Alice, you are wearing a ring on a ribbon. Did the man you want to marry give you the ring?"

Alice abstractedly placed a pale hand over her chest. This was the first time she had been careless enough to allow someone to notice the ring on the velvet ribbon.

"Well, tell me. I cannot wait!"

"Yes," Alice said, not caring now if the whole world knew of Whit Buck. "It was a gift."

Frances came over and looked at the ring carefully. "You *are* serious about that man, and you haven't told me his name."

"It is Whit Buck." She hid the ring under her hair.

"Well, Whit Buck is a very fortunate man," Frances said seriously, "for you, Alice, are one of the most exceptional women I have ever known."

Alice flopped on her bed as Madame Talvande came into the room, the wide skirts of a dress into which she had changed rustling around her ankles. She strode quickly and purposefully to Alice's bed. "Alice, are you ill?"

Alice turned over. "No. It is only that I did not sleep well last night. I think the moving of the milk cans kept me awake."

Madame picked up Alice's hand and looked at it. "Your hand feels warm. I believe I had better summon a physician."

"Oh, no, Madame, that is not necessary."

"But Alice, you may be coming down with something."

Alice raised herself up. "My brother is a physician, and he treats me for this illness often," she lied.

"What does he call the illness?"

"Dyspepsia."

"How does he treat you for dyspepsia?"

Alice thought back quickly to a time when she had overeaten and made herself sick. Allard was at home from medical school, and he forced her to drink a pot of warm water. "He treats me with warm water."

"That doesn't sound like a very good treatment to me," Madame said.

"It is successful on me," Alice responded weakly. "If you will send up a pot of warm water, I will drink all of it, and tomorrow I will be as fit as ever."

"The warm water will be right up," Madame Talvande answered brightly, but the expression on her face showed that she was worried about Alice. "And I do trust you will be up to your usual energy tomorrow, Alice. We are having our first lecture on Latin as well as the first instruction on dancing the mazurka."

"I won't miss them, Madame Talvande. I promise," Alice said, but she knew that she would not feel up to dancing a mazurka soon.

Alice slept most of the afternoon, and that evening when Madame Talvande came to her bed to check on her condition, Madame decided to have a bottle of old wine brought to the room. Alice indulged as much as possible, but found that cold artesian water pepped her up more than the wine. The next morning, she believed she felt a little stronger.

If the next day had not been Alice's fifteenth birthday, she would have preferred to let it pass with little notice, but being the day that gave her some measure of independence from her mother and Allard, it was cause for extra exertion. The very arrival of the day brought her anxiety. It was *strange*, there were no two ways about it. To be fifteen was different.

Alice's senses were floating as she poured water into a bowl and splashed it on her face. She leaned against the washstand and closed her eyes, assessing. *Fifteen.* She wished she had time to be alone just then, and think back on her family and their battles. Sometimes she wondered if they realized how deeply they had hurt her. And now she was all grown up and one of them. She had a new weapon with which to fight. Although she wished desperately that things could be smoothed over, it was out of the question. They would never change, and now that she was fifteen she intended to act fiercely. If it came down to it, she would simply withdraw from the family. Or would she?

Not having the time or privacy calmly to consider these nagging questions, Alice sighed and decided to abandon such thoughts until she could think more objectively. Just becoming fifteen was enough for one day. She raced to Frances's bed, pulled back the sheet, and said, "Miracle of miracles! I am fifteen."

Later that day a package arrived from Wachesaw. Gifts from her mother, Allard, and Arthur included an elaborate gold cross on a chain. Alice looked at it and laid it back into the box. She already had something to wear around her neck.

Several days later, when Alice came downstairs for classes, Madame handed her a letter. It was the first real communication she'd had from Murrells Inlet. She quickly ripped open the envelope.

Murrells Inlet, S. C.
December 1848

My dear sister,

I assume you are some sort settled in your own quarters; that you are pleased with yourself and grateful for the opportunity to study in Charleston. We hope your birthday was pleasant and that our gifts were well received.

If you desire the volumes of the *American Encyclopedia*, I will send them to you. You have used them in the past, and if the lack of them is causing any deficiencies in your lessons, pray let me know.

I have seen none of your acquaintances save the Wards. Penelope and Georgeanna send their love.

I am extremely anxious to hear from you. God bless thee.

Your affectionate brother,
ALLARD FLAGG

Thoughts of home flashed in Alice's mind and the letter fell from her hand and lay on the rug. Allard hadn't mentioned Whit, so obviously they had not talked. She groaned, then fought the urge to answer the letter immediately and tell Allard how much she hated to be uprooted. Flushing, she picked up the letter and reread it. So short. So lacking. Laughing a mirthless laugh she went to class, with no intention of answering it.

A few days later a sort of transformation took place. Alice felt better. Her face glowed with the freshness of health, and she was filled with energy. During the conversational part of the classes that day the talk got around to the ailing John Calhoun. Alice jotted down everything that was said. She had come to look upon John Calhoun as South Carolina's greatest statesman, and regretted to learn of his poor health. There was a chance he might die. It was tragic.

As she left the drawing room, Alice asked Madame Talvande if she could take a walk in the fresh air.

"I believe it would help restore you from the recent deterioration of your health," Madame said. "You and April may take Frances Whaley with you. It is rather sunny for December, fortunately."

When Alice told Frances about their outing, she added, "Of course, Frances, I want to walk to the docks."

"What a fabricator you are, Alice Flagg! You didn't need the stroll to boost your health."

"But that is our secret," Alice quipped.

It was late afternoon, and there wasn't so much activity at the docks as in the mornings. Alice asked a wharfman if he knew anything of the Waccamaw River boats, and he said that since the rice season was over he saw only a few of them. When she asked him about vessels carrying lumber, he remembered that, yes, a boat had arrived from one of the Buck sawmills.

"A boat came here from a Buck sawmill on the Waccamaw?" Alice asked.

The wharfman, who was rolling barrels to a worker several feet away, didn't look up. "Yes'm. Believe that vessel came in yesterday, but as soon as it was unloaded, it shoved off." He straightened up and looked around. "And that yellow pine went out pretty fast, too. It's on its way to Liverpool."

Alice fixed the wharfman with a fierce stare and said, "Who came down with the lumber? Was it a young man? Tall? Of muscular build?"

The wharfman scratched his head. "That sounds about right. Right smart looking young man. But he was in a big hurry. Had to get back, for some reason. Worked real hard. Yes sirree. He worked real hard. Not a lazy bone in his body, I'd say."

Alice went weak in the knees and rocked back and forth in her shoes.

"You feeling all right?" the wharfman asked, putting an arm around her shoulders to steady her.

Her eyes felt as though they were sinking into her head, and she couldn't answer. Whit had come to Charleston, and she had missed him. She was attending classes, and he didn't know she was in Charleston, or he would have found her. Alice wrapped her arms around herself, trying to be steady. She had never felt so sick in her entire life.

"Thank you," she murmured to the wharfman and turned to go. Somewhere between the docks and the school on Legare Street, Alice began to shake uncontrollably, and Frances ran ahead to tell Madame that Alice had taken ill again. When April and Alice entered the garden, Alice did not bother to nod to Moses, who was picking up limbs and twigs. She labored up the stairs to her bedroom, pulling herself forward on the handrails.

"I think I am going to freeze to death," Alice said to Madame as she came into the room. "May I have some quilts?"

Madame raced to the hallway, where quilts were stored in an armoire. Returning with two comforters, Madame declared, "I am going to send for a physician."

"No," Alice managed to answer. "I will be better soon. Please leave me alone so I may rest."

Madame backed out of the room, her eyes on Alice and a look of horror on her face. Alice did not notice Madame's expression, as she was trying to keep her mind on Whit. But there was something more important to think about. Survival.

31

ALLARD WAS STANDING on the front porch when he heard hooves coming around the bend. Whit pranced Bootblack to a stop, slid off the horse, and threw the reins to a groom who had suddenly appeared. "Where's Miss Alice?" he shouted.

"What are you talking about?" Allard asked, coolly.

"You have sent her away, and I demand that you tell me where she is." Daggers were flying from Whit's eyes.

"What makes you think she isn't here?"

"I don't have to explain anything to you. But I will say that I know she has not been here for some weeks. You cannot deny that she has not attended divine services on Sundays."

Allard realized that Whit Buck had watched the Flaggs go to All Saints Church in order to see if Alice was with them, and felt he did not have to tolerate such actions. It would be a simple matter to order the man off his property, and there was plenty of backup help if the Buck fellow was too strong for him. But what would be gained by that action? Whit Buck would come here again, and again. There must be a sensible way to handle this situation. *A way that would be infallible.* Suddenly a plan evolved in his thoughts. "You are right. Alice is *not* here. If you will come inside and have a glass of sherry with me, I will tell you about it."

Mary One was in the hallway, and Allard asked her to have a servant serve sherry in the drawing room. Whit followed Allard into the high-ceilinged room, where they took seats facing each other.

"Where is Alice?" Whit repeated. "If you don't tell me, I'll find out anyway."

Allard cleared his throat and said in his gentlest voice, "It was clear to us that Alice hadn't received enough education to prepare her for her life as the wife of a rice planter."

"She is educated," Whit said. "And for all you know, she may not choose to become the wife of a rice planter."

Allard stood and walked across the room, holding his head high. "Alice seems, somehow, unpolished for her age, and we felt it was in her best interest to send her where her mind would be faultlessly cultivated."

"And where is that place?" Whit shifted in the chair and there was a mournful expression on his face. His eyes burned with hostility.

Allard paused, and decided he would tease this young Buck before he gave him the information he was seeking. "We thought that England was the proper place."

"England! You *didn't* send her to England," Whit cried in disbelief.

"No," Allard said as he turned to face Whit. "We did not send her to England, although we should have given the schools there more consideration. Alice is in Charleston."

Just then a servant named Tillie came into the room with a silver tray bearing a bottle of sherry and two small crystal glasses.

"Tillie," Allard said, "I believe this talk is going to be serious, man-to-man. Please take away the sherry and bring bourbon." Without answering, Tillie took the tray and hurried from the room. "I believe you said your family calls you Whit," Allard resumed. "May I do the same?"

Whit nodded, a scowl on his face.

"Whit, when the skies of your mind clear, you will see that we did the right thing."

"That's nonsense. A fairy tale. You took Alice away because of my attentions to her, and you have ruined her life, as well as my own."

"I can understand in a measure your consternation, but it is because you were not prepared for Alice's leave-taking. When you consider the reasons for the move, you will thoroughly understand."

Tillie returned, and Allard poured two glasses of bourbon and added a little artesian water. He handed a glass to Whit, who downed it quickly, as his host was now doing.

"I do not deny, Whit, that Alice is indebted to you for a very great portion of her happiness, but she has now reached a point in her life where she must give her attention to improving her mind. Alice has been possessed with a strange indecision and timidity, which is unlike a woman of her position. Her refusal to adhere to the pride and glory of the planter aristocracy reminds us of no one we've ever known. In recent months she has abandoned all preparation for her life as a plantation heiress."

"Her conduct is highly honorable," Whit cut in.

"Highly honorable, indeed, but her independence of mind is leading her to a different result than that which is expected of her."

"You are denying her everything she loves," Whit said. "Charleston is not to her liking, and she must be the unhappiest person in the world."

"On the contrary," Allard snarled, then remembered that he must display the best behavior possible. "Alice has embarked on a new stage of her life, and she laughs about it with good humor."

Whit looked at Allard worriedly. "That cannot be true."

"Of course it is true," Allard lied. "I accompanied her myself. We traveled the road, choosing not to go by the ocean route, and we of course visited the best tavern in the state." As Whit was listening intently and his eyes were wide, Allard continued the fabrication. "She made me promise I would not tell you of her whereabouts, so that she may pursue her studies in peace."

Whit put his face in his hands.

"We are in touch with her now, and she is not only developing her mind, but she is *amused,* more *social.*"

Appearing to be overcome with exhaustion, Whit did not protest the information.

"Imagine to yourself the feelings of this woman who was once spiritless and delicate," Allard urged. "She is now rewarded with happiness and intelligence, and she is making plans for the St. Cecilia ball and the races. Also, imagine to yourself that you should contact her at this crucial time in her development and reduce her again to feeling no pride, a debility to be treated seriously." He looked at Whit, and their eyes met. "Pray muster up enough courage to go your way and allow Alice to aspire to hers.

She realizes now that she is a product of Wachesaw Plantation, and she no longer harbors doubt and impatience. She belongs to a life that would always be strange to you. If you are enamored of Alice, you will not risk her future happiness."

Whit sat very still, thinking, and Allard said nothing to invade his thoughts. Finally, Whit rose slowly. His face tightened and darkened and he left the room. Allard went to a window and watched as Whit rode away, slumped on his horse. Just then Mrs. Flagg came into the drawing room.

"What are you looking at?" Mrs. Flagg asked.

"A funeral procession."

"Oh, don't try to be amusing!"

Allard turned to face his mother. "But it *is* a funeral procession. Whit Buck has just buried his love for Alice."

32

FRANCES LOOKED DOWN the long expanse of white linen until she caught Alice's eye. "You are *not* in love," she mouthed.

"What do you mean?" Alice asked, not raising her voice.

"I have always heard that women in that state lose their appetites. I have been watching you, and you have an excellent one."

Alice laughed. She had eaten a substantial dinner.

Just then Madame Talvande arose from her chair at the head of the table. "I have some happy news for you." All chatter stopped and every eye was on Madame. "We are going to the theater tomorrow night."

"Oh," Frances squealed. "The theater. What play shall we see, Madame?"

"An actor by the name of Kenyon has been a member for several successive seasons of a company that performs in the Old Theater. I saw him once at the Drury Lane in London and he was superb in a Christmas holiday play, a sort of fairy spectacle. It was an extraordinary success. And there is something else I want to announce today."

"What is that, Madame?" Catherine asked.

"In the spring, near the end of the school term, I will have a raffle here at this house, and although all of Charleston will desire to attend, visitors will be admitted only by invitation."

"Just what *is* a raffle?" Alice asked.

"It is like a fair, Alice. I shall spread the things out in the drawing room, and there will be a pair of little sugar pistols, candle snuffers, a sugar ham, pasteboard dolls that are the prettiest things, and pin cushions, and there shall be a sylph!"

"And you raffle these things?" someone asked.

"Of course, and the money is given to charity. But the fun comes not from the money, but the twitter and hoopla of it all."

The women at the table looked at one another, and they began to chatter about a raffle. It would be the most titillating thing, and one that was entirely new to them.

"But give me your attention," Madame broke in. "Although I shall be preparing for the raffle during the next months, there are other events to be looked forward to, not the least of which is the theater tomorrow night. You must be attired in your most elegant gowns and gloves, and we shall leave by carriage at eight o'clock." Alice was as entranced by Madame's words as were the other women, and they began to talk of what they would wear to the theater.

The women were adorned in their finest gowns when they gathered around the first coach as Madame Talvande was helped inside. She wore a gown, gloves, and hat of red velvet, and her students were completely dazzled by her. Just before she took her seat, she told her charges that she would be at the Old Theater to greet them when they arrived, and they must all stay together and not scatter.

The Talvande carriages arrived along with a host of others, and Alice felt as though she would be crushed in the stampede of people rushing into the theater. Madame was in the midst of the throng, flailing her arms, calling out, gathering together her little herd, and getting them into the building and down the aisle to their seats. When she was finally in place, Alice took a deep breath and looked around.

The play was a sellout, as hordes of people were crowding into the gallery, second tier, boxes, and pit. Finally the music began, and the lights dimmed, and the curtain parted. It was a moment of tingling excitement to all but Alice. Her head was throbbing. She rested it on the back of the chair for a few moments, and when she again looked at the stage, the actors were slightly out of focus. She forced herself to get through the next hour, and when there was an intermission between acts and the other women left their seats, Alice remained in hers. Never in her life had she longed so to be in her bed. But another hour and a half passed before she was there.

The next morning Alice moved her leaden legs and did not know if she could pull herself from the bed. "I am tempted to ask Madame if I may stay in bed today," she called out to Frances.

"Are you too weak to go to classes?"

"I hope not," Alice answered, forcing her legs over a side of the mattress. "We have discussions of current events today, and I quite enjoy that part of our studies. I am being introduced to new ideas, and some of them are to my liking."

Frances came over to Alice. "You look pale. Why don't you lie down and let me get you a tray." It was clear that Frances didn't believe Alice was well enough to attend classes that day.

"I'll go," Alice said, sliding off the bed. She splashed water on her face. Patting it with a towel, she realized she *did* feel stronger. Whatever her ailment had been, she hoped it was now abating, and in order to goad herself on to vigor, she would force herself to keep up a regular schedule.

Later that day, during the discussion of current events, a Grimke girl mentioned slavery, and Alice felt pushed to voice her opinion. "If it were not for slaves, there would be no rice plantations," she said.

"Then there should be no rice plantations!" the Grimke girl snapped. "Do you know, Miss Flagg, that slaves are whipped and sent to the Work House and made to walk treadmills to grind corn?"

"I know of no such thing," Alice said.

"For God's sake, *where* have you been?"

"We have a plantation, Wachesaw," Alice explained, "and it extends from the Waccamaw River to the sea marsh. It is absolutely necessary for my brother to have a large labor force to maintain so much property and to produce rice. But we do not whip our slaves."

Madame was pale, and gaping at the Grimke girl. "We at this school support slavery."

"Well I do not, and I think it is your duty to explore both sides of the subject."

"If slavery were abolished, that would put an end to the Southern way of life," Madame said firmly.

Alice was fascinated. She had never thought seriously about

slavery before. Although she did not oppose it, she wanted to learn why others did.

When Madame felt enough had been said on this subject, she ended the discussion by saying, "Slavery is an impossible situation and should have been corrected long ago, but that time has passed. Ingenuity has been exhausted in the fruitless search for a practical remedy. The institution is firmly established."

All of this made Alice think. Actually she did *not* approve of slavery. She just happened to like the slaves on her brother's plantation, and she didn't know what she would do without them. As she pictured Wachesaw in her mind, she could not imagine what it would be like without the Ones. But clearly many slaves on other plantations were whipped by cruel overseers, and nothing could be more against her will. Quite unexpectedly she realized that slavery was not as harmless as she had supposed. It was as bad as, or worse than, the half-caste situation, and even existed at Wachesaw. She wanted her brother to know that she had become aware of its horrors, and it had happened in Charleston, of all places. It was time to write him a letter.

Charleston, South Carolina

Dear Allard:

Your letter from Murrells Inlet was received not long ago. This is the first time I have put pen to paper to you, but I have been busy, with my schoolwork. I am learning more than I expected. How much of your taste is displayed in my taste! Too much! And not all of it is suitable and respectable.

Recently I had a lesson not to be forgotten. Slavery is an abomination to the Lord! I am so horrified at the punishments that some slaves receive in the Work House that it makes me ill. They are whipped and made to walk treadmills to grind corn.

This may be falling on deaf ears, but I can tell you this: within a few years this rice and cotton economy and its attendant evils will come to an end, and that will be the end of you, too.

You should diversify. Have you thought of going into the lumber business?

Your affectionate sister,
ALICE FLAGG

The slavery matter was a heavy one for Alice, and as she thought about it she again experienced sleepless nights. So many thoughts had employed her mind—Whit, first of all. She had been to the docks several times, and the one time that he had been there she had missed him. Although she longed to see him, she now was setting her sights on the spring when she would return to Wachesaw as a fifteen-year-old woman. She would put in motion the plans for her wedding then.

Other thoughts that nagged at her included John Calhoun's failing health, as well as the evils of a rupture in the relationship with one's family. And not the least of her worries was her own health. If she should die this year it would be under the worst of circumstances. But if she lived another few years, it was probable things would be better. She wondered what was wrong with her. Could it be that Charleston had a bad effect on her? Even if that were true, there was nothing she could do about it. Allard would never let her come home. Not even at Christmas, which was at hand.

33

CLASSES HAD BEEN terminated to reconvene after Christmas and many of the students had gone home for the holidays. Rules were less stringent now, and Alice took daily strolls with April to the docks, a heavy shawl over her hair and shoulders. She had now become a regular visitor to the wharves and some of the workers spoke to her. Others simply shook their heads and mumbled that no vessel carrying Carolina pine, cypress, or oak had docked, at least none from the Waccamaw River region.

After one such unsuccessful search, Alice leaned against a heavy crate and gazed toward the sea with a heart full of questions. "Oh Whit, Whit! What are you doing at this very minute? Do you miss me? Do you even know that I was taken against my will from the Hermitage? I have never cared for anyone as much as I care for you right now. Just cling to what we had, and in the spring I shall return and we shall be married." Finally Alice pulled the shawl tightly around her shoulders and left the docks. She knew that her heart was nearer breaking than it had ever been.

Alice's face was drained of its rosy tints and paled to ashy gray, and her hair was hanging loosely over her shoulders. Although she was barely fifteen, she looked twelve. Alice and April had to fight their way along the street, as it was jam-packed with prospectors as well as with people who had come in on other vessels. All sorts of languages were being spoken, and in the midst of it were the street vendors with their familiar calls.

Suddenly Alice found herself in the midst of a throng of jabbering foreigners, and she stepped into an alcove where she could take refuge and hopefully let April catch up. As Alice leaned against a wall to brace herself, a dark-skinned woman came from the adjoining house. When she saw Alice, she stopped in her tracks.

"You be a very sick lady," she said.

"How do you know?" Alice asked.

"I know," the woman answered. "I know about things like that. I been born with a caul over my face."

Alice nodded at these words, but remained suspicious.

"I tell you what you need to know," the woman said, in an unemotional tone. "You better find place to lay your weary head."

"You say that as though it is an omen!" Alice said irritably. "I do not appreciate your innuendo."

"This be your home?"

"No. My home is at Murrells Inlet, several days' journey from Charleston."

"Then go home. People should be buried on home ground."

"I cannot go home until spring. I am enrolled in school here in Charleston. When my classes are concluded, my brother will come and take me home."

"Lissen good," the woman said, backing away. "Go home."

Alice left the alcove and rushed in the direction of the school. April spotted her and called out. Alice eventually slowed her pace and thought back on what the woman had said, and she played absently with her hair, lifting it above her head and letting it fall to her shoulders. She knew better than to dismiss the warning.

It was almost twilight when she and April returned to Legare Street. Moses was standing in the street, inspecting Christmas trees on a cart hitched to an ox. He pulled each tree off the cart, held it up, and examined it for perfect symmetry. Finally he found one that he chose for the drawing room.

"What a bee-oo-tiful tree," Kit crooned as Moses stationed the tree on a stand, near a drawing-room window.

"It is a perfect picture," Madame agreed.

Alice joined Kit and Madame in decorating the tree with handmade decorations of wood, and tiny oranges from the trees in the garden. Moses mentioned that this year was a "holly year," meaning that the crop of holly berries was unusually good. Alice soon forgot the frightening woman in the alcove and became filled with the spirit of the season. It could be a wonderful Christmas, except for her absence from Whit, and her other nagging worries.

After awhile, the tree was completely trimmed, and the drawing room and hallway were decorated with red partridgeberry, mistletoe, smilax, cedar, and pine. Cudjo lighted a fire on the hearth, and in the midst of the warmth and wildwood fragrances, Alice became happy for the first moment in a very long time, it seemed.

The next day Kit was busy cooking Christmas foods, but Alice was not in the mood to learn from her so she read novels in her room. Finally, she decided to walk with April to the docks. There was little activity. Probably most of the boat people were at home, celebrating with their families. *Family.* The very word stuck in Alice's heart. In spite of what they had done to her, she missed her mother and brothers. Was it a sign that blood was thicker than water? She thought of them on the way back to Legare Street, where a letter from her mother was awaiting her.

Christmas 1848

My darling daughter:

Christmas is here, and I miss you dreadfully. You are fifteen now, and when I see you again you will not be my "wee one" any longer.

Arrangements are being made for us to come to Charleston for the season, and we shall be attending the St. Cecilia ball. As all will be bustle and hurry, I am perking up your favorite white dress, but if you choose to buy a new one, please purchase one of excellent detail.

It will be glorious to again be attending the St. Cecilia ball, at the usual time, on a Thursday evening, at nine o'clock. The St. Cecilia is as fixed as if ordered by the heavenly bodies.

You must give some thought to the ball, as to be on the list is a distinction, and to be dropped from the list would be a disgrace. I understand one of the Izard boys will be playing violin this year. What do you know of it?

Your devoted mother,
Margaret Elizabeth Belin Flagg

Deciding not to answer the letter until after Christmas, Alice carefully folded it and placed it in her journal. Answering the letter, and allowing old pains to resurface, would shake her to her very soul. She did not want to do anything to dampen Christmas Day.

Three other women besides Alice had chosen to remain at the school rather than go home for the holidays, and Christmas morning at the house on Legare Street began much in the same manner as it did at Wachesaw Plantation. The sideboard was laden with fluffy hominy, cold wild turkey, venison sausages, biscuits, crumbly corn breads, orange marmalade, and coffee. Making the coffee was a solemn rite with Kit, and Alice had never known any that had such a strong aroma.

Cudjo had lighted a fire in the dining room, and the mingling of the fragrances of burning oak wood and the greenery hanging from the ceiling and chandelier gave pleasure to those at the table. Madame Talvande asked Alice to relate a Christmas story of Wachesaw. Alice explained how her father had risen early on Christmas morning, gotten the staghounds ready, and tuned up the hunting horns in preparation for the Wachesaw Hunt, which began immediately after dinner.

Even during the sumptuous meal, Alice could not get Whit out of her mind, and she was filled with a sort of melancholy. But Madame did not allow anyone to be in a gloomy mood, and she told Alice that the two of them along with the other three students who had remained at the school would attend services at St. Michael's. As she spoke, her voice so lyrical and filled with joy, Alice actually forgot her worries. But only temporarily.

Attending Christmas Day services at St. Michael's Church was a wonderful decision, as a grand opera star was visiting, and the large church was filled with the most amazing music. Alice sat in the huge sanctuary, next to Madame Talvande in her dress, gloves, and plumed hat of brilliant red. Alice looked down at her own dress, and although she was trying to be polite and attentive to the sermon, something about the bell-shaped skirt and jacket of ivory, faced and edged with forest-green velvet, reminded her of the garden at the Hermitage. The minister was now talking animatedly of the star of Bethlehem, but Alice's mind was on the green leaves of the orange trees, mingled with wax myrtle and other shrubbery in hedgerows, and the ivory blooms in the shape of tiny stars. How those blossoms filled the springtime air with the sweetest of scents, second only to gardenias.

Now that she thought about it, the ensemble she wore was the very same hue of gardenias—soft white petals accented with rich green leaves. Alice smoothed the creamy white velvet skirt, and her heart tightened. She loved the Hermitage very much and was lucky to have been born there. She would do anything to go home again, and perhaps she should do whatever her family asked of her. . . .

34

WHEN SCHOOL RECONVENED after the holidays, the talk was still of John Calhoun's failing health. South Carolina had never given a president to the country; the nearest the state had come was a vice-president, John Calhoun. He had exhibited great wisdom and ability in dealing with important public issues, and that night, reclining on her bed, Alice recorded in her journal a few sentences of the plans for the funeral:

> John Calhoun will soon leave this world and go to his heavenly reward. Although I disagree with him on his stand on slavery, he has been a son that South Carolina has cherished with pride, and his funeral will be a state occasion.
>
> His body will arrive by steamer, and it will be accompanied by dignitaries and congressional committees. The remains will be placed on a funeral car modeled after the funeral car that bore Napoleon's remains, and it will be drawn by six horses in mourning trappings trailing on the ground, each to be attended by a groom in black livery. To the accompaniment of muffled drums, the body will slowly move to the Citadel Square on Boundary Street, where it will be formally surrendered to Governor Seabrook, and by him to Mayor Hutchinson.

When Alice had finished the record, she put the journal on the bedside table and turned down her lamp. Madame tiptoed to the door of the room, and in silhouette, Alice could see that she wore a silk dressing gown, and her hair was hanging loose, nearly to her waist. It was the first time Alice had seen Madame with her hair not in a twist at the back of her head. Seeing that all was quiet, Madame softly left the doorway.

Alice got up and went to a window, where she gazed out at the city. Rooftops were of every conceivable material and style, including gable, gambrel, hip, and mansard. The buildings under the roofs were splendid by design and construction, and, in a curious way, reminded her of Murrells Inlet, for these towers of craftsmanship seemed just as implacable and everlasting as the marsh and moss-draped oaks, and the ever-recurring tides. Whereas she had drawn incomparable strength from the marshes and trees and sea, now she was compelled to obtain it from her new environment. But this newly gained strength, if indeed she had gained it from anything in Charleston, was of a temporary nature. When she returned to Murrells Inlet she would instantly go back to her old values and hopefully her vibrant health. But there had been scarcely a day that she hadn't worried about her physical condition. Finally she went to bed, but sleep did not come.

Staring into the darkness, Alice craved counsel on the cause of her restlessness. Before coming to Charleston she had had the services of her brother or Dr. Blythe of Georgetown, but now she had no one even to confide in. Even as friendly as Frances Whaley was, Alice was reluctant to discuss with her the vaguest thing about her declining health. Although many people blamed the low-lying rice fields for the malarial fever, so prevalent in the Low Country, there were no rice fields in Charleston. If she could only sleep, refresh and uplift herself, all would *seem* well.

A few days later Madame Talvande told each of the students to take on a research project. Alice pushed herself to think up a topic, and asked if she could write a paper on the St. Cecilia Society.

"That would be perfect," Madame purred. "The St. Cecilia Society has been important to Charleston since its inception, and I would like to have its history recorded."

That night Alice set pen to paper on the assignment. As the Flaggs had always taken pride in their membership in that society, Alice could pull from her memory nearly everything she needed to prepare her paper. She began the project by simply making notes, planning to rewrite all of it later. She would research, correct, and polish it as needed.

There were a number of social clubs in the city, but the St. Cecilia Society was the most important. Second to it was the Jockey Club, which brought races and the Jockey Ball. As Alice jotted down bits and pieces coming to her from the preachments of her mother, she saw how the St. Cecilias, the Dancing assemblies, the Philharmonic concerts, and even the races and Jockey Ball were considered almost sacred occasions.

The St. Cecilia Society began in 1737 with a concert given on a Thursday, which was called "St. Cecilia's Day." Any true St. Cecilia ball was held on a Thursday. The St. Cecilia admitted only men, and later on only men whose fathers or older brothers were members. No publicity was permitted, and the society existed to give concerts and a ball. For many years the concerts were the most important part of the society, and in 1773 a Frenchman received 500 guineas to play with several amateurs.

Members, their cousins, aunts, wives, sons, and daughters gathered, sipped sherry and coffee punch, and nothing else. Women had to be escorted, even to the ladies' room. They waltzed to the accompaniment of the one grand pianoforte and twenty pounds' worth of the best modern concert music, that had been ordered from England.

After verifying some of these details from books, Alice completed her report on the St. Cecilia Society and turned it in to Madame Talvande, who was extremely pleased with her project and gave her a high grade for her work. The exercise brought Alice more than a good mark in school, however. It confirmed for her that, although she may be forced to attend the St. Cecilia ball with her family, she would never in a hundred years approve of the snobbery such an organization represented.

35

CIRROCUMULAR CLOUDS PUNCTUATED a cobalt sky on the day the Flaggs arrived from Murrells Inlet for the social season. Hearing the commotion of the arrival, Alice came downstairs with a certain nervousness. She did not feel up to all that stretched ahead, and would have ignored it all except for the fact that she desired to endear herself to her family as much as possible before the defiant act of marrying Whit. Alice was relieved to see Moses, Kit, and Cudjo gathered in the garden as a sort of three-person welcoming committee.

While Mrs. Flagg and Allard rode in the carriage that bore the family's coat of arms, the carriage that followed was filled with trunks. Mrs. Flagg emerged from the coach, came straight to Alice, and touched her cheek. "How are you, my darling?"

"I am well, Mother."

Now scrutinizing her daughter, Mrs. Flagg added, "But you seem to have lost weight. Your arms, and face, they have somewhat fallen off."

"Just you wait until you see me in my white ball gown," Alice said, ignoring her mother's appraisal.

"You will be the fulfillment of my soaring dreams and expectations at the ball, Alice. I can hardly wait to see you on that evening, dancing in the cotillion."

"Of course, Mother." Alice turned to Allard and they kissed each other lightly on the lips. No words were spoken between them, and Alice thought that things had not changed. Facing her mother, she suggested that they take a tour of her school.

Mrs. Flagg and Allard soon went on to the Flagg residence in town, and it was not long before Alice was reunited with the Wards too. The next few days passed in a haze of visits with the Ward girls, much chitchat about ball gowns, and wedding preparations that were now formulating at Brookgreen. Allard would marry Penelope in just about one year, on January 16, 1850. And Arthur would marry Georgeanna soon thereafter. They all were blindingly in love, and it was almost more than Alice could bear.

Pained by the sight of these happy couples, and knowing that Whit was far away and unaware of her present situation, Alice lost much sleep. She remained wide awake for most of the night prior to the St. Cecilia ball. She went to crouch at the window, as the other students slept, and observed the goings-on in the street below.

In the lamplight she could make out the profile of two milkmen, rattling the cans that disturbed her nightly rest. In the semidarkness they were gray-black characters, seemingly moving in slow motion. One wore a cap which he had placed on his head backward, and he rolled the filled can noisily to the back of the house, and made even more racket as he wheeled the empty one back to the wagon.

Suddenly, two chimney sweeps appeared, and as they carried on a conversation with the milkmen, Alice marveled at the little boys, dressed in black suits with cutaway coats, many sizes too large for them. The suits were castoffs of funeral directors, and they were the regular uniforms of Charleston's many chimney sweeps. Finally, Alice went back to bed, but sleep did not come.

After the day's classes, Alice went to the Flagg residence, where Arthur had brought the horses and jockey that would compete in the Jockey Club race at the Washington Course the next week. Others had already gathered. They were marveling over Schlatter, the horse that Allard's groom would ride.

Schlatter was dazzling, self-centered, and flighty, and as Alice observed Allard standing by her, she knew that the horse made him feel like a king. Schlatter could have been the steed of a conquering noble! As she thought about it, Alice decided that the other members of the landed gentry, such as the Singletons, Lowndes, and Heywards, who were famous for their thoroughbreds, would be hard put to beat Schlatter, who had a smooth way of moving.

Allard put his forehead against Schlatter's, and for a moment no one spoke, but allowed Allard and his horse a few seconds of close communion. And then Allard said, "My greatest pleasure comes when this horse flies so straight, true to the mark, and with such velocity on the Washington Course." Allard patted the horse's face. "Everything must be perfect. We shall blacken and shine the hoofs, trim leg hair to emphasize the fine bone structure, and add a little oil around the eyes to give prominence."

Mrs. Flagg came over and took her daughter's arm. "Physicians make the finest racers as they know everything to do to enhance the quality of the animal."

"True," Alice answered. "Allard's horse will win the race. What other horses did Arthur bring?"

"Bright Flagg and Handful of Stars, but you can be sure that every eye will be on Schlatter."

Alice, who hadn't had the time to speak to Arthur during the excitement over the horses, went over and pecked him on the cheek.

"Put my name on the number three slot on your card tonight," Arthur said. "Of course my first dance will be with Georgeanna, and the second with Mother, and the third is for you."

Alice became painfully conscious that tonight was the occasion of the St. Cecilia ball, and there was nothing she could do but attend. At that very moment she dreaded going. But that evening, as she left in the family carriage for the ball, she was perfectly groomed and beautiful.

Mrs. Flagg, sitting opposite Alice in the carriage, wore a gown of mauve silk, decorated with a large and beautiful cameo brooch and pearls that came from Paris. Alice, of course, was in her white creation, as all the young girls were required to wear white. Alice knew that Frances would be beautifully dressed too, and was wondering what the Ward girls' dresses were really like, as she had not seen them. She would find out soon, when they all arrived at the St. Cecilia meeting hall.

Alice's mother hadn't taken her eyes off Alice since the carriage ride began. "The young planters will be mesmerized by your sophisticated stylishness. I expect you to be asked to dance all the waltzes, and, of course, the cotillion."

Alice thought about it, then answered, "I do not expect to receive so many requests."

"Of course you will. That is what the St. Cecilia Society exists for. To give young men an opportunity to meet the young women at their finest moment."

"The St. Cecilia Society exists to exclude," Alice said in a voice that was almost a whisper.

"That simply isn't true," Mrs. Flagg protested. "But I refuse to become outraged. You have been blessed since girlhood to be connected with the society, and on this night you are going to enjoy that blessing, I will make sure of it."

Alice studied her mother. Mrs. Flagg's dark hair was swept up into an elaborate pompadour and the mauve dress cast a rosy glow on her face, giving her a fragile appearance. The long strand of pearls gleamed lustrously against mauve lace. Alice decided that her mother was lovely tonight, and she vowed to herself, for her mother's sake, not to ruin it all. Tomorrow, the St. Cecilia ball of 1849 would be over, and for tonight, she would do her best to appear to have a good time.

When they arrived at the hall, and Alice and her mother had been helped from their carriage, Alice noticed a huge coach pulling up behind them. Of course that elaborate vehicle belonged to Joshua John Ward, and Alice lifted her skirts and went over to chat for a moment with Penelope and Georgeanna. Alice thought, as Penelope and Georgeanna stepped out, that they looked like goddesses, in the most divine white silk gowns one could imagine. Allard and Arthur were equally dazzling. Mrs. Flagg, now beside Alice, stood back speechless and admired her sons and their intended brides. Penelope and Georgeanna were surely the belles of the ball.

The Ward-Flagg party was soon ushered into the building. Alice looked around and thought the hall had never looked more beautiful. Candles were everywhere. There were silver candelabra of many shapes and sizes, and candles in holders of porcelain, pewter, and crystal. Ropes of wild smilax were draped at the ceiling, chair railing, and around windows, and at one end of the hall a platform had been built with false Ionic columns, entwined with ivy. All of it was a fairyland. How the workmen must have labored to bring it to this special beauty, Alice thought.

The musicians were gathering behind a bower of grapevine, ivy, and smilax, and when the first hum of music started, they were completely hidden.

"Oh do let's have some coffee punch," Penelope said to Alice as her white-gloved hand came to rest on Alice's arm.

"Alice *is* ready for punch," her mother answered. She spoke so loudly that Penelope looked at her curiously. "And I shall make my way to the other end of the hall." That was where parents and grandparents sipped sherry and beamed with pride at the young members of their families who would become their heirs.

Just before the president of the society stood on the platform to announce the first dance, Frances ran over with her family, and her face lit up as she introduced the Whaleys and Alice introduced the Flaggs. It was clear that everyone approved of everyone else, but before there could be any exchange of words, musicians began playing a waltz. Suddenly Georgeanna was curtsying in front of Arthur and they were dancing between the rows of exquisite men and women. Now Penelope and Allard were doing the same. After a few moments, a young man identified himself as a Pinckney and asked Alice if that dance was filled on her card.

"Why, no. And I shall be happy to dance with you." She knew that by now her mother had certainly stopped talking about the latest fashions in England and was observing her daughter, and Alice intended to put on a good show. The Pinckneys had been among South Carolina's most elite families for many generations.

"You are a marvelous dancer," Alice's partner said.

"Thank you," she murmured as she stepped in 3/4 time: one-two-three, one-two-three, dip, sway, turn, one-two-three. "And what did you say your name is?"

"Fletcher Pinckney."

"You are not so bad yourself, Fletcher," Alice said, beginning to enjoy the rhythm of the movements. She noted to herself that he was rather good-looking, and was startled that she found any other man besides Whit attractive, most of all a planter. Why, she had not given her fiancé much thought since she had entered this magical place that just brimmed with beautiful people and things.

During the next waltz, while Arthur was revolving his mother in perpetual circles across the floor, taking one step to each beat, Allard was dancing with Alice. Her next dance was with Arthur, and after that, she and Fletcher whirled around the floor every time the music started. Finally, the cotillion was announced, and she moved into the quadrille with Fletcher.

At the end of the cotillion, the president of the society again stood among the columns to speak. Everyone gave him their undivided attention as he announced the most recent bride, and she quickly appeared beside him as he was saying that for the rest of her life she would be referred to as the St. Cecilia bride. The president took her arm, and they led the way to the tables on which a sumptuous supper was laid. Fletcher Pinckney escorted Alice as well as her mother, who made no effort to disguise her growing interest in him.

The meal began with turtle soup, followed by the fish course—sheephead and bass cutlets—then went on to Beef à la Mode and ragout of pigeon with vegetables, and ended with Gâteau à la Madeleine. Mrs. Flagg questioned Fletcher during the supper about the Reverend Charles Cotesworth Pinckney, who was a trustee of the Protestant Episcopal Church and who married a daughter of Henry Middleton, of Middleton Place, Ashley River. Alice found the topic a little boring, but Fletcher was a pleasant conversationalist and made good company at the table.

On the way home, as her mother expounded on the esteem of the Pinckneys, and said that the only true heroes were Thomas Jefferson, Francis Marion, Thomas Sumter, and Charles Cotesworth Pinckney, Alice thought she had never been so tired in her entire life. And the schedule ahead of her was daunting. She would be attending classes while her mother visited Charleston friends and shopped on Broad and King streets; her brothers would most probably be spending their time at the Ward residence. And the next important social event would take place the following week, with the Jockey Club functions. She might be able to offer excuses that would exempt her from attending the races on Wednesday and Thursday, but there could be no excuse for missing Friday's race, which was followed by another ball. Almost before she knew it, the day was there.

36

THE WASHINGTON COURSE was blessed with looks, charm, and open spaces. She was Charleston's hostess to the *haut monde* of horsedom, and a legend among racecourses. For several dazzling days each winter the quiet section of Charleston exploded in a rapturous whirl of dashing men, pedigreed women, and world-class horses. For more than a month now, every thought had been on the moment the horses bolted from the starting line, and all the talk had been of Schlatter, the horse owned by the Flaggs of Murrells Inlet.

All planter families had a trusted "race-rider" who was a great favorite, and Allard had chosen a man named James. Of his grooms, James was the most expert rider, and although Allard had deep faith in his abilities, his nerves were twanging like the strings on a thousand guitars. It was terribly important to win the Jockey Club race. Not only would a win boost the animal's value, but the owner would enjoy a certain celebrity.

As Schlatter was in perfect form, the other horses were not taken to the track, and early in the day Allard and Arthur, dressed in black trousers, cutaway coats, and tall cylindrical hats of black silk, arrived at the racecourse with James. Alice planned to arrive with her mother just before starting time. Madame Talvande had suspended classes for the occasion, and many of the students, including Frances, would be attending with their families too.

At a late breakfast at the Flagg residence, Mrs. Flagg cautioned
Alice to wear the family colors. "It is just as important that you
show your colors—red, white, and blue—as it is for the horse to
ride under the Wachesaw colors of the Stars and Stripes."

"You would think there would be enough to worry about con-
cerning the horse," Alice remarked, "without so much emphasis
on what the women wear."

"The men are perfectly dashing," her mother answered, "and
we must be a match for them." She sprang up and took her plate
back to the sideboard. "My hat, the most recent one from Paris,
has plumes of red and white, and my dress is blue."

Alice, who had simply rearranged the food on her plate instead
of eating, asked, "And what sort of jewelry will you be wearing?"

"Diamonds, of course."

From the moment breakfast was over until Alice and her mother were in the carriage ready to leave for the race, the hours were
a blur of activity, dealing with dresses, hats, and jewelry. But it all
came together in the most marvelous way—Mrs. Flagg was the
epitome of grace and elegance in her ensemble, and Alice was a
great beauty in a dress of brightest red, and wide-brimmed hat of
the same color. Her dress was adorned with a jabot of white and
blue. Finally, they were on their way.

A long line of vehicles of all sorts streamed in one direction.
"The road is becoming more thronged," Mrs. Flagg observed.
"The crowd will be especially thick today."

Alice was tense, but as the elaborate carriage pulled by four
matching bay horses entered the grounds of the Washington
Course, she leaned forward with interest. It was impossible not to
be intoxicated with the excitement.

A sea of people moved to and fro, on horseback, in carriages,
on foot, swaying this way and that as they hurried about. The
Jockey Club race was an affair of families: parents, children, sib-
lings, cousins, and only the closest of friends who had been
granted an admission pass by a member of the club. Genuine love
radiated from the smiles, greetings, hugs, and kisses, and there
was not the slightest indication of financial burden on anyone
attending the race.

Ladies stood in a galaxy of beauty. Although most had come to
see, some had come to be seen, and to compete with each other in
attracting the attention of some wealthy planter. The scene was

much like Merrie Olde England on a great field day, with every display of wealth and rank.

The Grand Stand, designed by Reichardt, an architect from Germany and a student of the great Schinckle, had been remodeled. Light wrought-iron posts substituted for the heavy pillars which had partially obscured the view of the course.

The entrance was from the rear, and spectators leaving their coaches were protected by an arched canopy. A handsome saloon was one flight up, and its balcony could accommodate hundreds of people, giving a panoramic view of the track. Refreshments were served in the saloon. On either side of that room were compartments reserved for the ladies, and these separate rooms were carpeted and furnished in good taste.

To the right of the Grand Stand was a separate stand for the officers of the club, and the starter of the horses had his own building. The course and all buildings were enclosed by a stout picket fence so that the spectators could enjoy the race in private with no interference from the public. The track was oval, of sandy soil, and exactly one mile.

Horses were not entitled to start without the owner producing a proper certificate of the animal's age. They took their ages from May Day; that is, a horse foaled any time during the year would be deemed a year old on the first of May the following year. The horse that had its head to the ending post first, won the heat.

When Alice and her mother arrived at the Grand Stand, they commented on the new coat of paint as well as a new set of Venetian blinds that would protect the women from wind, sun, and glare. They found a comfortable place to stand and watch the race, which would begin very soon, as the jockeys were now being weighed in the basement of the same building.

"I am so glad the schools adjourned for this day," Mrs. Flagg said. "Of course no one would have attended otherwise. All business has ceased in Charleston at this hour, and even the courts are not in session."

"And the businesses on Broad and King streets are closed," Alice added. "Who would there be to buy the merchandise? Anyone with a purse is here at the race."

Mrs. Flagg glanced around to see who was there. "You are correct. Everyone with a purse is here, and they shall all be at the ball tonight."

"The ball tonight," Alice echoed, wondering how she could find the strength to continue this round of social functions.

Mrs. Flagg looked around and saw the look of disquiet on her daughter's face. "What is worrying you?"

"Nothing serious," she lied expertly, while willing herself to relax about her health.

"Your spirits will lift when the race starts," her mother promised. "Just think of it now, from beginning to end. The saddling of the horses, the mounting of the jockeys, the anxiety of the owners, the giving of the word 'go,' and then—they are off!"

Hearing her mother's description, Alice pictured the race in her mind, and it was crystal clear: coursers were changing places and interest was increasing with each fresh struggle. Now the straining steeds were entering the last quarter stretch, the horses being urged to their peak of speed and exertion. Whips and spurs were doing their work. And suddenly there was a breathless moment of suspense when the horses all came together and it was anyone's race. Oh, how the earth was trembling! They flew by, passing the post, and it was over. In Alice's fantasy, Schlatter was the winning horse. "Oh, Mother," Alice squealed. "You *have* lifted my spirits. I can hardly wait."

"I pray our horse will win," Mrs. Flagg said, "but we must keep in mind that this race is closely contested, so much so that Joshua John Ward hasn't entered." She glanced around at the onlookers, all waiting in suspense. Mrs. Flagg smiled, nodded, and spoke to several people, and then she noticed Joshua John and Joanna Ward and their children. "I can see the Wards, but I cannot get their attention."

Alice too looked around and chatted with several of her classmates who had just arrived. Frances found her and they spoke excitedly about the event. The time for the race was approaching, and Frances took her leave to join her mother in the crowd. Alice stood idle for a moment, and then began to wonder if Fletcher Pinckney were out there somewhere. Perhaps she would run into him and have the opportunity to speak with him some more.

Suddenly the drumbeat for saddling was heard and then four horses made their appearance. In the crescendo of excitement, Alice heard someone behind her say, "Stuart's filly has many friends, but I take Schlatter against her." Mrs. Flagg nudged her daughter in the ribs to alert her to the conversation.

Schlatter was ready to dig her hoofs into the racetrack dirt.

Allard, as nervous as a cat in a tub of water, eyed the Wade Hampton thoroughbred, Millwood, sired by Monarch. And then his curious eyes went to James Tally's Thirteen of Trumps and W. H. Sinkler's Reciprocation, all magnificent animals.

"Aren't we fortunate to have this lovely winter weather?" Mrs. Flagg asked her daughter.

"It is absolutely favorable to racing, but be quiet, Mother. The clock is set to go."

As a last-minute gesture, James, his crop in his hand, stooped down to brush the hair on Schlatter's knees, and a sudden tremor rippled through the horse's flesh. The animal began biting James, as horses often do when being groomed. James, in an effort to save himself, accidentally hit the knees with the crop, and Schlatter buckled. James yelled for Allard. The men got the animal on its feet and into the lineup of horses, and everything seemed well, but there was still some confusion regarding Schlatter.

Arthur appeared, stroked the horse's neck, and said to Allard, "Don't let this accident upset you. She is very clever on the turf." But Allard was not so sure.

James, in his red, white, and blue "silks," was on the horse's back, ready to go. And in a moment, the drumbeat sounded and the horses were off.

Schlatter took an early lead, and all eyes were on the animal that had been predicted as the winner. But suddenly, Schlatter fell to the ground, throwing James over her head and into the path of oncoming horses. Miraculously, James was not injured and quickly got up. It was clear from the way he stood that he was devastated. He did not move until he heard the announcement that James Tally's Thirteen of Trumps had won the race.

Alice had screamed in terror when Schlatter fell. Mrs. Flagg leaned heavily on her daughter and said, "I am about to faint."

"Hold up for Allard's sake," Alice cried.

Allard saw at once that Schlatter was in terrible pain and he felt compelled from the bottom of his heart to do something to aid the stricken animal. For a moment, he looked around, wild-eyed. Then he flew to his leather case, which was lying behind a hedgerow. Fumbling through the contents, his hands came to a pistol. Like a madman he ran back to the scene where the suffering horse lay and a large number of people had gathered. At close range, Allard shot his favorite horse to put it out of its misery.

"What a mess," Alice screamed. "It's torture, heartbreaking.

Allard and Arthur have worked so hard and planned so carefully for several months. And it was all for naught. Not only did they lose the race, and that is not important, but they lost their favorite horse!"

Allard, pale and disheveled, made arrangements for the horse to be removed, and he asked Arthur to take care of the burial, in Charleston. And to his mother he announced that they would depart for home early the next day. Of course, the Flaggs would not be attending the festivities of the ball that night either.

On the carriage ride home, something happened that had never occurred before. While Mrs. Flagg was talking to her, Alice fell into a light slumber. Mrs. Flagg, terribly worried, had Alice carried up to her room at the school. Her mother followed and saw that she was settled comfortably. Then she backed out of the room, not taking her eyes off Alice.

The next morning, when Mrs. Flagg and Allard came to say goodbye and the last sound of wheels and hoofs died away, Alice went back to her room and thought about the rest of her life. There had been so many things these last days that she'd had to do; it seemed she never had a moment to herself. She got up and went to the looking glass. Her eyes were too large for her face, and her head, with the thick lustrous hair, was too large for her body. The only thing to do was to keep her mind on Whit and the Hermitage.

With a pang of guilt Alice remembered her eagerness to be with Fletcher Pinckney at the ball and race. She had come close to forgetting all about her love lately. She rebuked herself for letting time and distance—and the allure of wealth—turn her thoughts from Whit for one minute. Her family's plan had nearly worked, she realized with horror. But she knew that the pleasure she felt at the ball and the race was superficial. It was not the sort of life that would make her happy day in and day out.

Alice stared at her ghostly reflection in the mirror. She saw that life permitted no time for frivolous pursuits. Whit offered her something meaningful, and she must take it now and forever.

Alice was hungry for news of Whit, a little driven even, and that was all she thought about the next two weeks as she moved through her schedule almost unconsciously. On her face was a hurt look, a look of tired impotent anger, as she was in complete ignorance of what was going on in Murrells Inlet. She was beginning to regret that she allowed her family to visit with no confrontation about Whit. She had achieved what she had intended—allow the social season to pass with not even a drop of anger to stain it—but now her very insides were boiling for not pressing her family for news of Whit.

As soon as she could, she practically flew to the docks with poor April trailing behind. Little groups of people had gathered near the water, and they were talking of a storm at sea. Although one ship had made it safely through the storm, others had not been so fortunate, and as one vessel broke up, all hands took to sea. It was a horrible thought to Alice, for a winter storm could be so destructive. She knew many people who still remembered the violent storm that crashed ashore in 1822, when whole families had washed to sea, but that one had come during hurricane season.

Alice and April turned and headed back, and rain came in a torrent. They drew up their shoulders and stood under an over-hanging roof above a window of a fine Charleston house. Through a lace curtain Alice could see a black hand, dusting a mahogany table on which a candle was burning, and it reminded her of Mary One. *What was Mary doing right this minute?* Alice longed to see her and talk with her. Finally, when the rain stopped, and the sun appeared, they returned to Madame Talvande's. Alice went to the window in her room and stood thinking.

As bad as the word of the gale was, something else worried Alice more: her physical condition was disturbing. Although the Flaggs usually lived well into old age, she obviously had an unnamed affliction, and it nagged at her. Up to now she had halfway believed that the illness was brought on by the absence of her fiancé, but now the other half of her reason was taking over. For the first time it came to her that even if she were reunited with Whit, she would not be miraculously restored to good health.

The next morning Alice did not go down for breakfast, and Kit suddenly appeared at the door. "What be detaining you, Miss Alice?"

Alice did not answer, and when Kit saw the frail body lying askew on the bed, she ran from the room, her eyes wide with terror. Cudjo was polishing silver goblets that had been used during the visit of the students' parents for the social season. "Cudjo!" Kit screamed. "Go for the doctor."

"What?"

"Miss Alice. She be about dead."

"Oh, Massa Jesus," Cudjo said as he threw down a rag. Without another word, he ran from the house.

When the physician arrived, Alice was sitting up in bed, her back propped up against two pillows. As Kit went to her, Alice's eyes didn't focus, but stared straight ahead, vacant and unseeing. Kit moved aside, and just as the physician reached the bed, the patient's mouth mechanically opened, and without the slightest retch or clearing of the throat, a black substance rolled from her lips and spread across the bed.

"Oh, my God," the physician cried, his blood running cold. "The Black Vomit!"

Kit screamed hysterically. The doctor quickly recovered himself and said, "Kit, you must send Cudjo to locate a courier and get word to the Flagg family to come at once. Alice Flagg is not long for this world."

"Who will Cudjo get?" Kit asked, with the fear of death in her eyes.

The physician's anguished mind began to race. Finally he said, "I shall send my son. He owns one of the fastest horses in Charleston."

37

IT WAS A ghastly trip to Murrells Inlet for the courier. Although the storm had not come into shore, the fringes of it were causing wind damage. The messenger had to detour around fallen trees, and both he and his horse fought wind gusts. Even with the difficulties of traveling in such wretched weather, the man reached Murrells Inlet in two days, a journey that under normal circumstances would have taken another day, at least.

Word of the gale had now spread along the coast of South Carolina, and there was a feeling of danger in the air. The tide had not gone out that day and no oyster beds or sandbars showed above the tide line. Dr. Flagg was on the veranda of the Hermitage consulting the sky, and the marsh, which looked much like the ocean, with waves raging high and breaking into froth. Chunks of sea-foam were flying through the air. Dr. Flagg was just about to go inside when he caught sight of the figure slumped on a weather-beaten nag. The physician squinted his eyes to get a better look.

The man on the horse appeared too weak to get off without assistance, and Dr. Flagg ran to him and offered help. A groom came running to take the courier's horse to the stableyard for attention, and Dr. Flagg led the man into the drawing room and insisted that he partake of a glass of wine before speaking of his mission. Finally the courier regained enough strength to relay the message.

"Regret to inform you, Dr. Flagg, but your sister, Miss Alice Flagg, is ill."

"Ill?"

"Yes."

"With what disease?"

"My father is the physician who examined her, and he sent me to tell you that she is ill with the Black Vomit."

"Oh, my God," Allard said, throwing his hands over his face.

"My father asked me to tell you that although our prayers are for her safety and well-being, you should come for her immediately."

Suddenly, Allard began to pace the floor, thinking aloud. "My mother. She is not here. She left three days ago to inquire about obtaining a summer house in the North Carolina mountains. I cannot reach her."

"Dr. Flagg, my father suggested that you bring your sister home."

"Yes, of course. As difficult as the journey will be for her, there is no alternative." Dr. Flagg eased himself into a chair. "How bad is she?"

"Sir, it is with the greatest sympathy and regret that I must tell you that she is in such a weakened condition that she may not be alive when you reach Charleston."

"Oh, dear God in heaven." Although the young man went on to describe Alice's condition in some detail, the words blurred together as Dr. Flagg sat stunned, disbelieving. He rose and went to a window, his mouth trembling. Then he put his face in his hands and his shoulders shook uncontrollably. Eventually he brought himself to face the courier, and explained that he should spend the night at the Hermitage, and the next day he would be given a different horse on which to return to Charleston if his own horse had not fully recovered. But as for Dr. Flagg, he would leave immediately for Charleston. Arthur would ready the Hermitage.

When Allard arrived at the mansion on Legare Street he looked as though he had traveled day and night for a week. A stubble of beard was on his chin, and his eyes were bloodshot slits, nearly buried in puffs. His legs shook.

Madame Talvande told Dr. Flagg in a low, grieving voice that Alice's trunk had been packed, and the white dress that she had worn to the St. Cecilia ball was on the top. No schoolmates were in sight, as Madame had asked them to remain upstairs.

"This way," Madame said, leading the way to the bed that had been moved into a downstairs hallway. The Charleston physician was sitting next to the patient. Allard approached Alice tentatively, pausing, his fingers clutching his gold watch chain. At last he went to her.

Alice's black hair was spread over the pillow in soft curls and delicate tendrils, but her body was only a shell of the sister he had known. Despite her immense beauty, and the exquisite handmade nightgown she was wearing, she was a pathetic figure as she lay on the bed in the cavernous hallway. All about was an air of doom, of horrible tragedy.

"Alice," Allard said softly. There was not the slightest movement of any part of her body. "My dear sister, can you hear me?" There was no response.

The Charleston physician cleared his throat. "For the past three days she has been comatose."

"We must take her home," Allard said. "Even if she remains in a coma, we must get her back to the Hermitage."

Just then Alice's eyelashes fluttered slightly.

"Look," Madame called out.

"She is coming to," the Charleston doctor said.

"Alice? Can you hear me?" Allard asked.

She opened her eyes halfway. "My ring. Where is my ring?"

"What ring?" Allard asked. He looked at her fingers, but she was wearing no ring, and he had no idea that a ring was on a ribbon beneath her high-necked nightgown. Some of those who had been attending Alice had noticed the ring on the white velvet ribbon, but they thought nothing of it. Many of the students wore rings on ribbons around their necks, some of them being heirlooms that belonged to their mothers.

Alice shuddered slightly and went limp.

"She is delirious," the Charleston doctor said, as Kit brought a bottle of gardenia cologne and touched a drop to Alice's forehead.

Allard stood back and folded his arms, sadly assessing the situation. "We must leave immediately."

"If you wish your sister's last moments to be spent in the comfort of her own home," the other doctor advised, "you must go. I know you feel helpless and wretched, but that is really the most you can do to make her passing easier."

Those words, spoken so sadly, pierced Allard's brain and

touched him so profoundly that all bitterness he had ever had for his sister was replaced with compassion. "Alice is a nonconformist," he said softly, as much to himself as to anyone else. "Therefore I have been prey to feelings which someone else cannot imagine. When I sent her down here to attend school, I deemed myself no longer vulnerable, but I was wrong. Although I shall not allow feelings of guilt to overtake me, her fate haunts me."

Within minutes, the two doctors had carried the delicate fragment of a person to the carriage and tucked her in. Frances had been given special permission to see Alice off, and she could not hold back the tears as she saw her friend placed in the vehicle that might soon become her hearse. As the enclosed coach left the driveway, Frances, Madame Talvande, Cudjo, Kit, Moses, and the doctor stood in the garden, grief etched on their faces.

Only once during the next three days as they traveled to Murrells Inlet did Alice arouse. As the carriage was pulled onto a ferry, she almost shouted, "Where is my ring?"

38

THE SLAVES STOOD around the yard in groups, talking softly. Death was in the air, they believed.

"A little bird flewed in my house last night, and you know what that means," one said.

"Death be as sure as I be standing here," someone stated.

"Buzzard been swarming over Wachesaw," an old woman pointed out. "It be a sure sign."

"A dove been mourning. I heard him when I walked through the woods."

"To hear a dove mourning be a sure sign of death."

Back at the Hermitage, now, and in her own bed, Alice lay like a mummy: unseeing, unhearing, unknowing. Allard and Arthur sat by the bed. Mary One, tears trickling down her cheeks, brought coffee.

Allard felt that he was experiencing the most awesome grief he had ever known. Poor, poor Alice. Struck down so young. It wasn't fair. But the thought that pierced his heart was that he and his mother had been secretly planning to take Alice straight from Charleston to the North Carolina mountains, denying her one day, one hour, in the home she loved more than any other place on earth. How could they have been so cruel? he wondered. And they could never make it up to her.

There was no change in Alice's condition until the next day, just

243

before night descended. Her eyes opened, staring at the ceiling in a trancelike state.

"Alice," Arthur said, "can you hear me? If you know that I am here, squeeze my hand." He put his hand on hers and there was a discernible movement of her fingers. "She moved her hand," he cried. "She knows I am here."

Just then her eyes moved around the room.

"She is noticing the familiar surroundings, I believe," Allard said. "I think she knows that she is back at the Hermitage. I pray to God she knows."

Alice made an abrupt effort to sit up but was too weak and fell back. "My ring," she said. "My ring." Then her eyes glassed over, and she stared straight ahead. Within seconds all breathing ceased, and her body took on the countenance of death.

Alice Flagg died on February 2, 1849.

Allard looked completely lost, but Arthur, even in his grief, took over. "Mary, send for the nurses."

Mary One sent a message to the slave women who worked at the Sick House, a building in the slave street that served as a hospital, to come at once. They were needed to prepare the body for burial.

Later that night, Allard and Arthur sat in the drawing room. Mary One was still there, serving hot coffee, and doing anything else she could. Upstairs, nurses were selecting the clothing to put on the corpse, and there was no question but that Alice would wear the lovely white gown packed on top of the other clothing in her trunk. But an issue did arise about whether or not to put her feet into some new boots she had bought in Charleston for the social season. The nurses referred to them as being "black, spanky and shiny." Finally it was decided that Alice would not have wanted to be buried in the boots, and her feet were left bare.

Downstairs, Allard was still deep in worry. He got up with his cup of coffee and went to a window to look toward the marsh. Although he tried to push thoughts of guilt out of his mind, they invaded his meditation. For the rest of his life he would have to live with the knowledge that he had planned to take Alice from Charleston to the mountains, and deny her the summer at the Hermitage. Such an act was heartless, sheer brutality. But fate had intervened. Was it to show him how wrong he had been? Would Alice's death be a turning point in his life? He certainly hoped so, for it would be difficult enough just to live with the thoughts of what he and his mother had planned.

Suddenly one of the nurses ran into the room.

"Is the body prepared?" Allard asked as he turned from the window.

"Not yet. But Miss Alice be dressed in that fine white dress what be on the top of the pile in the trunk."

"She wore that dress to the St. Cecilia ball," Allard answered.

"You want Miss Alice to be buried with that ring 'round her neck?"

"What ring?" Allard asked, going weak in the knees.

"There be a ring on a ribbon 'round her neck."

Mary, who had come into the room with a tray of cakes, gasped. She had found the ring when she bathed and changed Alice on her arrival, and its meaning had been immediately clear to her. Since then she made sure she was the only one to attend to Alice, which everyone permitted due to her long-standing attachment to the girl. Mary wanted Alice to be buried with that ring at no one's knowledge, but she had been so distracted by her death that she had unthinkingly allowed the nurses to prepare the corpse.

Allard flew from the room and took the steps two at a time. Arthur was behind him. A nurse standing by Alice pulled back the collar so that Allard could view the ring. "That must be the ring to which Alice referred," Allard surmised. Anger twisted his stomach and his eyes filled with murderous lights. His sister had remained faithful to the lumberman until her last breath! Sending her to Charleston had not done one bit of good!

All the bitterness that Allard had just dismissed returned tenfold. He yanked the ribbon from Alice's neck and ran from the room, down the steps, out the door, off the veranda, and across the yard to the marsh, where he threw the ring as far as he could. "That ring will go out with the next tide," he said to himself.

When he returned to the house, Arthur asked, "Where did Alice get that ring?"

"Who else but a common lumberman would give a woman a ring such as that? It was nothing but rubbish."

"And you threw it into the marsh?" Arthur asked. "Oh, Allard, you didn't." Arthur's heart sank. After a moment he said, "We should wait until Mother returns before burying Alice."

"No," Allard objected. "The funeral will be held tomorrow, at

All Saints Church." Although word of Alice's illness had been sent immediately to Mrs. Flagg, Allard didn't expect her to receive the message for some time, due to the severe weather common to the North Carolina mountain winters.

"We can bury her first in the yard, under an oak tree, and when Mother returns the remains can be moved to All Saints Church cemetery to the Flagg burial plot."

Allard allowed himself to be swayed. It could be weeks before his mother's return to the plantation. The next day, Alice Belin Flagg was buried near the Hermitage, the home she dearly loved. When her mother returned from the North Carolina mountains, a funeral took place in the beautiful and graceful All Saints Church, and Alice's remains were interred in the adjoining burial ground. She was wearing the white dress she had ordered in Charleston, and in which she had planned to be married. During the brief ceremony, a man stood unnoticed in the trees at the back of the cemetery. Whit Buck had heard of Alice's death, but he still believed that she had not wished to see him again.

A flat grave marker was ordered, and it was inscribed with only one word: ALICE. The granite marker was not distinguished with a last name, or date of birth or date of death.

Alice Flagg's grave marker in All Saints Church Cemetery
(Photo by Sid Rhyne)

EPILOGUE

AFTER THE TURN of the century, Mrs. Laura Collins, a lovely lady who lived in Conway, South Carolina, visited her sister, Mrs. Willcox, of the Hermitage in Murrells Inlet. Mrs. Collins was affectionately called Aunt Lolly.

Aunt Lolly was given the room on the left at the top of the stairway, which faced the marsh and ocean. The room had once belonged to Alice Flagg, and it was where she had died, after asking, "Where is my ring?" It was a comfortable room, big and airy.

After supper the first night, Mrs. Willcox told her sister that the next morning, she would send a servant upstairs to notify her that breakfast would be served. As it happened, Aunt Lolly woke before being notified to come downstairs. She was looking into a looking glass as she combed and pinned her hair into a bun. Just at that moment, Aunt Lolly saw Alice Flagg. Alice was behind her, and it was clear she was searching for something.

When Aunt Lolly turned to see Alice with her very eyes, Alice was not there. But when she turned back to the looking glass, there was Alice, as plain as anything, and she was frantically searching for something. Why, she was looking for her ring, Aunt Lolly decided. Alice was *still* searching for the ring that she had accepted from the lumberman. Each time Aunt Lolly looked with the naked eye Alice was not visible, but when she looked into the mirror she saw Alice as plain as she could see her own reflection. And Alice was wearing the white dress that she had ordered in

Charleston. But Alice did not look like what Aunt Lolly thought a ghost would resemble; she looked like a living Alice Flagg!

Aunt Lolly flew down the steps, five on the upper level, and fifteen on the lower level. She called out to her sister that she had seen Alice Flagg, and Alice was searching for her ring.

"At first I thought that a young woman had come into the room to summon me to breakfast," Aunt Lolly said, "but when I realized that the woman was no servant, I knew instantly that she was Alice Flagg."

"Lolly, what in the world is the matter with you?" Mrs. Willcox, asked, incredulous at the story.

"I tell you I just saw Alice Flagg!" Laura Collins shouted.

"Lolly, calm down and go sit in the dining room. Breakfast will be served in twenty minutes."

"What are the measurements of that bedroom?" Aunt Lolly asked.

"Twenty by twenty."

"Then I saw Alice walk the entire room, twenty by twenty. I tell you I *saw* her. And you had better believe it!"

Laura Collins was to live to be eighty-five, and she visited the Willcoxes at the Hermitage many times, always traveling in her cart pulled by Shetland ponies. For the rest of her life she talked about seeing Alice Flagg, searching for her ring.

Sometime after the ghost's first appearance, another member of the family was rocking a baby in Alice's room and she saw Alice searching for something. Again the statement was that Alice looked just like a regular young girl, not a ghost. She was searching for her ring and she was wearing her favorite white dress. And the word spread that Alice was seen in the burial ground at All Saints Church, looking for her ring.

During those years, Mariah Heywood, born in 1855, also talked about it. "I hear tell Miss Alice wore that ring on a ribbon 'round her neck. Now she looks for that ring."

On December 12, 1915, long after the congregation had gone home on that Sunday, All Saints Church burned to the ground. The bishop's chair, the altar vases and cross, and memorials to faithful members were saved, but otherwise the loss was complete. The church had been through war and hurricane, but it had survived these. Even the vestry book had been saved, although it was with Dr. Arthur Flagg when he lost his life in the hurricane that crashed on the Low Country on Friday, October 13, 1893.

Arthur had taken the vestry book with him to his beach house so that he could work on the records, but the house was washed away and Dr. Flagg and his wife, Georgeanna, lost their lives. The vestry book, however, was found half-buried in sand. It was soaked with saltwater and torn, but in one piece.

Now the church was gone. But under the energetic leadership of Capt. St. Julian M. Lachicotte, Senior Warden, assisted by Ralph Nesbit and others, funds were collected for a new church and it was shortly rebuilt, on the same spot, and in the same style of architecture. There were some then, and some still, who would believe that Alice Flagg had something to do with the burning of the church, although most think a defective stove caused the loss. But Alice is believed to haunt that very spot as well as her room at the Hermitage.

Mr. Willcox died and left the Hermitage and adjoining property to his son, Clarke Allan Willcox, but that family continued to live in Marion. From about 1940 to 1954, his sister, Genevieve, and her family lived in the house, and that was an especially happy time in Murrells Inlet.

During these years there were many occasions when two twin girls came to the Hermitage to visit, and one of them had been born with a caul over her face and was said to have the gift of second sight. Her name was Prue. Her sister's name was Constance, and some people affectionately called them "Prue and Con."

Once when Prue was in Alice's room alone, someone grabbed her hand and squeezed it tightly. When that person released Prue's hand, her ring was gone. She flew downstairs to see if one of the resident youngsters had removed her ring for a joke, but none of them were in the house at the time, and neither was her twin sister. "I felt a hand take hold of my hand and when I jerked away, the ring fell on the floor. There was no one there," she said.

On another occasion, on a moonlit night, Prue came into the spacious hallway from the drawing room and as she walked toward the stairs a young girl in white stood by the newel-post. At first Prue believed that the girl was one of the daughters of the household, and then she thought that the girl could be her twin sister. "Is that you, Con?" she asked. There was no answer and as

Prue came closer she still believed that the girl was her sister. "Constance, it is you, isn't it?" Just at that moment the girl in white faded into the wall.

"She looked just like a girl," Prue said. "I thought she was one of the girls who lived in the house, or my sister. But it was Alice."

And then there was the day when just at dusk an electrical storm approached. Prue went to the veranda and looked toward the sea. Lightning flashed in the sky, and tree limbs were blowing frantically. Thunder shook the big, sturdy house.

"Just then I saw a young woman in white walking in the yard, and I wondered why she didn't come to the house. It didn't make sense for anyone to be out in such a storm as that." Prue went into the house and called to her twin sister and the people who actually lived in the house. They all went to the veranda and looked, but they saw no one.

"See her? There she is," Prue said, doggedly firm in her belief that a girl in a white dress was walking in the yard. But no one else admitted seeing Alice.

"I saw her as plain as anything," Prue said. "The girl in white walked to a certain point in the yard, and then she turned and walked right out over the marsh." Prue credits her ability to see ghosts when others cannot to the fact that she was born with a caul over her face, but she believed that on that stormy night, others on the porch also saw Alice but were reluctant to admit it.

By the time the present owner, the son of the Mr. Willcox who bought the plantation in 1910, moved into the Hermitage, stories of Alice had spread to many states, and visitors came every week to the home and the cemetery at All Saints Church to see if they could establish communication with Alice Flagg, the ghost of the Hermitage. There has come to be a sort of Alice mania, and there is rarely a time that someone isn't visiting the Hermitage or the churchyard to see if they can get a glimpse of her. When Alice appears, the story gets around. There are so many people who are intrigued by her that flowers are put on her grave during every month of the year.

When Julia Daniels of Greenville was a college student, she and Michael Spencer went to Alice's gravesite to see if they could see the ghost. "We got there about nine o'clock and walked around the grave. All of a sudden it got kind of light. It was like twilight.

And everything in the graveyard got real quiet. All the insect noise stopped. I'd never heard it quiet like that before.

"And then she started forming. There was a mist around the grave. She looked like a young girl, but you couldn't tell her features. She was a kind of grayish color.

"There's one curious thing about Alice's ghost. Right before you see her you smell the gardenias. We all smelled it that night. And it looked like she had something in her hand. It could have been gardenias."

According to Julia's mother, she is still affected by seeing Alice, as many others are. Although Alice's death has been attributed to hemorrhagic fever, she also died of a broken heart, and during the time of stormy weather. These elements make any ghost a stronger phantom, many parapsychologists believe.

Cy Boyd, who lived near All Saints Church during his retirement years, told of the time that some youngsters, including Margaret McClarty, wanted him to take them over to Alice's grave after dark. "That morning Margaret went over there and put a bouquet of black-eyed Susans on Alice's grave. When we got there I shined my flashlight on the grave slab and her flowers were still there. After we were there a few minutes I decided to turn the light off and give them a scare. Well, the kids all giggled. When I turned the light back on a minute later nobody was in much of a mood for giggling. There on Alice's gravestone, right beside the black-eyed Susans, was a gardenia. I'm telling you it shook me up. I don't know if the children appreciated what had happened, but me and the other adults were really afraid. You see, none of us had a gardenia when we came there and it wasn't the season for gardenias anyway."

Mr. Boyd was asked if he would go back to Alice's grave, and he said, "No, not at night."

In the gloom of dusk or the light of a full moon, the spirits of the dead begin to rise, it is said, and to those who believe, Georgetown County, South Carolina, is the most haunted place in America. Alice Flagg wanders all year, and she revealed herself one Halloween Eve to a group of young people from Columbia, including Lisa Walker, Pete Pappas, Jeff Duval, Marshall Stone, and Carrie Floyd.

Lisa told the story: "Carrie began to walk around the grave. Every time she walked around the grave a cock crowed in the background. She put her hands on the grave and then we thought we heard somebody coming. Everybody ran toward the cars. The first car took off and the car I was in stayed right there in front of the cemetery gate.

"We all looked out and there was a figure standing to the left of the grave. It was a thing that was floating—moving. I started crying. I knew it wasn't natural. It was holding its hands out. Carrie rolled the window down and yelled, 'Alice, Alice,' and the figure started moving toward us. I fell to the floor because I didn't want to see anymore.

"Carrie said as she walked around the grave she felt she was possessed by something. It was really an experience to say the least. I never want to go there again, day or night."

My first introduction to the story of Alice Flagg came in the late 1960s as I sat in the drawing room of the Hermitage. The owners, Clarke and Lillian Rose Willcox, told me the tale before a cozy gas flame. Afterwards, we went upstairs and I saw Alice's room, and from there my husband and I drove to All Saints Episcopal Church on S.C. 255, three miles west of Pawleys Island, and viewed her grave marker. (Some people, many of them members of All Saints Church, do not believe that Alice was buried there. However, the gravesite is next to the resting place of Dr. Allard Flagg.) The people I have since interviewed about seeing Alice are reputable people who described in detail each experience.

As a storyteller, I am constantly asked to tell Alice's tale. I believe I have been on nearly every television talk show in the Carolinas, and I told the story on national television on Halloween 1988. Although this book is fiction, the story is as close to the original as I found possible. During my visits to Charleston to consult old records on the planter families and certain views and aspects of a time way back when, such as the educational system in Charleston in 1849, I met scholars and others who filled in gaps. As an example: I cannot document that Alice attended Madame Rose Talvande's school at 32 Legare Street (the house where the famous sword gates are located). However, there are scholars who say that Alice absolutely attended that school, and would have been sent to no other. Ashley Hall was not in existence, the College of Charleston was not coed, and other schools were not likely choices.

I have endeavored to present the Alice Flagg story as accurately as possible and to conform to the known facts. In order to do so, I spent many hours in research, and drove many miles. The part of the research that brought the biggest surprise to me, and the portion that probably means the most, was the discovery that Alice Flagg and Alice Claypoole Gwynne Vanderbilt are both descendants of Rachel Moore Allston Flagg, who with her first husband, William Allston, built Brookgreen Plantation. Today it is a part of Brookgreen Gardens, cited as America's most beautiful sculpture garden. This William Allston was known as "William of Brookgreen," to distinguish him from William Alston of Clifton, the first of the single-*l* Alstons. Among William and Rachel Moore Allston's children was Washington Allston (1779–1843), the famous portraitist and painter of heroic and biblical tableaux.

After the death of William Allston, the wealthy widow Rachel married Dr. Henry Collins Flagg in December 1784. The Flaggs lived at Brookgreen Plantation and entertained General George Washington on his Southern tour in 1791. Their son Dr. Ebenezer Flagg married Margaret Belin in 1817. They were the parents of Dr. Arthur Belin Flagg, Dr. Allard Belin Flagg, and Alice Belin Flagg (the ghost).

Another son of Rachel and Henry was Dr. Henry Collins Flagg, Jr. His son Jared Bradley Flagg had a daughter, Rachel Moore Flagg, who married Abraham Evan Gwynne. Their daughter, Alice Claypoole Gwynne, married Cornelius Vanderbilt II, a grandson of Commodore Cornelius Vanderbilt. Alice and Cornelius Vanderbilt turned to architect Richard Morris Hunt to design their grand Newport "cottage," The Breakers.

As I stood in the Billiard Room of The Breakers, where Alice Vanderbilt's ancestors' portraits hang, and I looked deeply into the faces of Flaggs and Moores and other ancestors, Alice Flagg became even more real to me. And when I viewed the Flagg family tree at The Breakers, I believed, perhaps for the first time, that there actually had been an Alice Flagg. Up to that time she had seemed to me to be only a ghost, but there she was, right up there on the list with Alice Claypoole Gwynne Vanderbilt.

In 1990, I interviewed Robert Burgoyne, caretaker of the Hermitage. He had some interesting stories about Alice there:

> I took care of Mr. Willcox. I was his nurse for a time after he became ill. When I first went to work for Mr. Willcox, I knew nothing about the Hermitage. I didn't know anything. We had

several "experiences," I guess you would call it, the first night I was there. I heard the door open and footsteps in the room, and I thought it was Norma, Mr. Willcox's daughter. I looked around but nothing was there. I mentioned it at the table, and that is the first I had heard of Alice. They told me it was Alice. They told me I had had a visit from Alice, and Mr. Willcox was very alert, absolutely lucid. Since then we have heard noises. Lights sometimes come on for no reason, and go off the same way. The TV set clicks on and off at will. We cannot explain it.

Mr. Willcox died three months after I came to take care of him, and after he died the family asked me to stay on. The first night that I moved my family in, my daughter fell out of bed at three o'clock in the morning. She was sleeping in Alice's room, upstairs. Sometime later, my daughter Julia, nine years old, was sleeping in the piano room, downstairs. At the same time, three o'clock in the morning, she suddenly became awake, and there at the foot of her bed stood a young girl in a white dress. The apparition didn't say anything; she just looked at Julia, who was now calling out to her mother.

I got up and went to my daughter. After taking her pulse, I placed my hand over her heart, and it was beating so hard it seemed almost to come out of her chest. She had seen Alice. She would tell you the same as I have told you.

Last week a friend visited us, and he was supposed to stay with us for three nights. After spending one night at the Hermitage, he left suddenly. When I saw him later, he told me he would never again try to sleep at the Hermitage. While he was taking a shower he had a frightening experience, and he quickly left the house. He would not explain what had happened.

He is a Conway businessman, very bright and credible.

We are no longer afraid. When a chandelier begins to swing we take it in stride.

On June 12, 1989, Clarke Willcox, owner of the Hermitage, died. His stories, however, will live on. To visitors who pulled up rocking chairs on the spacious veranda overlooking the salt marsh and Garden City Beach, he enjoyed describing the corn-shuck seats of the chairs, the strong, longleaf pine of which the house was built, the English ballast brick of the front steps, and Alice. He also liked to mention the more than sixty years he spent with his wife, Lillian Rose, and how he shared the Hermitage with two women—Lillian and Alice. He also described the day in 1982 when some students from Charlotte came to the Hermitage for a chat before they went to All Saints Church to try to establish communication with Alice Flagg.

"Some girls came down here from Charlotte," Willcox began the story, "and they told me they were studying extrasensory perception. They talked to me awhile and then went to Alice's grave.

"They stood around the flat marker with the one word ALICE, and darkness set in. Just then one of the girls called out, 'Look!' A ring which she had been unable to remove from her finger for three years due to a weight gain was slipping right across the knuckles, and it flew out into the air and came to rest somewhere in the sand around the grave where no grass grows. All the students got down on their knees and searched but they couldn't find the ring. Finally the instructor said, 'We have to leave now and go to Pawleys Island for the night. Tomorrow we will come back early and find the ring.' They went to the van, climbed in, and went to Pawleys for the night.

"Early the next morning they were back at Alice's grave and sure enough they found the ring. But the student was unable to put it back on her finger, as her finger was larger than the ring. While they were discussing this, one of the girls saw a young girl in a white dress sitting on a brick wall; her feet were dangling. All of the girls but one were frightened and recoiled. A girl named Mary stood as though she were in a sort of trance.

"'Come over here, Mary,' one of her friends called, but Mary didn't move. Then the instructor said, 'Mary, come over here with us. That's Alice, the ghost.' But Mary still couldn't move. Then she swung her arm straight through the apparition.

"Just at that very moment, as everyone kept an eye on Alice, the ghost ascended into the air over her grave and became horizontal. The students were spellbound, and all eyes were on Alice as she, dreamlike, descended into her grave."

And if you visit Alice's grave, the very same thing could happen to you.